W9-BXV-933

Gopal Baratham is a leading Singapore neurosurgeon. His novel *A Candle or the Sun* is also published by Serpent's Tail.

MOONRISE, SUNSET

Gopal Baratham

Library of Congress Catalog Card Number: 95–71059

A complete catalogue record for this book can be obtained from
the British Library on request

First published in 1996 by
Serpent's Tail, 4 Blackstock Mews, London N4 and
180 Varick Street, 10th Floor, New York, NY 10014

Phototypeset in 10pt ITC Century by Intype, London
Printed in Great Britain by
Cox & Wyman Ltd, Reading, Berkshire

To Ban Kah Choon
with affection and respect

ONE

I see things different from other people. The sky talks to me, sends messages in rainstorms and lightning. The Singapore night, warm and damp like a dog's tongue, licks my face and tickles the side of my ear. People gushing out of MRT stations dance to secret harmonies and fingers working a keyboard have a choreography only I am aware of. Unconnected images string themselves into pictures and events, willy-nilly, lie one against the other till sequence is unavoidable. This is how the world has always been to me; this is how, I hope, it will always be. I keep my thoughts to myself, however. If I didn't, people would think me mad.

Not Vanita though. She listens, tries not to smile, though I sometimes sound outrageous even to myself. This is one of the many things I love about Vanita. One of the many lovely, unbelievable, heart-stopping things.

I look to the east over the tops of the ships and beyond the shadows of the islands. Look right to the edge of the world, where a gigantic red ball is emerging from the sea. A thought strikes me. An odd thought, something which normally I would have kept to myself. But I loved the woman beside me and trusted her not to laugh, or at least not to laugh too much, at the goings-on in my head. So I spoke up. "I think that moonrise looks so much like sunset that it is impossible to tell one from the other."

Vanita stopped what she was doing. "Don't be silly," she said. "Moons rise in the east, which is there." She pointed to the open sea. "Suns set in the west." She held my face and turned my head sharply round till it faced the city, "... which is there." Vanita has a lovely voice, lilting with highs and lows jumbled, like a boy's at puberty. She makes music without meaning to. I waited for its spell to subside before turning to stare at the full moon again.

For some reason it made me uneasy. Not full moons generally. This full moon. It stained the clouds which had hung about all evening a deep purplish-blue. A lovely colour, in most circumstances. Round their edges, however, were mean yellow tinges which made them look like bruises growing old. I was disturbed by this moonrise, wondered what it was trying to say to me.

I turned away from it, back to Vanita. "I have been looking at it for a long time and I can't see how I can tell without turning my head whether it is moonrise or sunset."

"My sweet, sweet boy, you are lovely to love but that doesn't stop you being a dumbo. You can't tell anything from anything unless you look around you."

"What if you don't want to? What if you can't...?"

"Never mind," she said, fishing out a piece of fried chicken and popping it into my mouth. She put another into my hand for good measure and went on with what she was doing.

Vanita treats me like a child. Perhaps, she has a right to, for she is my first girl.

When I met her a year ago, I was twenty-seven and a virgin. Vanita was surprised, though she need not have been. I am not hungry for experience, have never gone out to "grab" life in the way that is recommended these days. I tend to let things happen to me, allow myself to be buffeted this way and that by events. I must confess that I really don't pay too much attention to what goes on around me because I am confident that, when things are right and without my searching for it, a pattern will emerge and I will recognise it; and in it the time, the place, the person. And, when this happens, I would know what to do.

As soon as I set eyes on Vanita, I knew that the person I had been waiting for had arrived. I slipped into the sequence of events that followed our meeting easily; as easily as I, though totally inexperienced, slipped into her body.

I was, nevertheless, glad that she had some expertise in these matters and, to put things in her own words, "knew what went where and how things worked". I was grateful that she was knowledgeable but was never moved to find out how she had come by her knowledge or how many lovers she had had before me though she had said often enough that she would be only too happy to tell me. Vanita is not coy about such things. I discovered this very early on.

I am tall, unmuscular, and pale skinned. I have always been worried about looking effeminate. After our first night together, Vanita told me that I had nothing to be ashamed of. She assured me that I was, in the area that really mattered, better endowed than any of the men she had been with. This may have been why she handled my body with the kind of care that collectors reserve for their prize pieces; how she got it to do things I didn't think it capable of. I was flattered; pleasured beyond my wildest dreams. Now, as I watched her unpack the food she had cooked, I felt the rush of desire and was impatient to begin making love.

I tore my eyes away from her and looked around the park.

Singapore is so small that it is easy to visualise it as a diamond-shaped island lying sideways at the tip of the Malay peninsula. East Coast Park runs along its southeastern edge where the waters of the Indian Ocean merge with those of the China Sea.

We had been coming to the same spot in the park for nearly a year. Vanita had chosen it. It was some distance from the beach and away from the teenagers and their noisy Sony compos, almost far enough for the smell of barbecue sauce not to reach us. From where we were, I could see the ships riding at anchor, smell the turning of the tides and, when I listened really carefully, hear voices speaking in strange tongues.

Our tiny island is the busiest port in the world and the destination, at some time, of every craft that sails the seas. And ships bring with them the sounds of faraway places, hints of exquisite pleasures, suggestions that impossible dreams can somewhere be realised. From where we sat, I felt that I could reach out and touch the world, feel it breathe, take its pulse. It was the perfect spot for making love to the woman for whom I had waited so long.

I stretched out on the grass and looked at the rising moon. Out of the corner of my eye I could see Vanita spreading the heavy waterproof sheet on which we would spend the night. At one end of this she placed the sleeping-bag which we would pull over our naked bodies when it got cold, as it sometimes did just before dawn. Then she began unpacking the food she had cooked.

I knew what this would be and knowing made my appetite as sharp as my desire. Besides the spicy fried chicken there would be chapatis wrapped round mince and peas, fish grilled in banana leaves, dry curried vege-tables and an assortment of pickles. For dessert we always had semolina cooked in milk that had been sweet-ened with rock-sugar and spiced with cinnamon, clove and nutmeg. To this Vanita always added a generous helping of Benedictine, a liqueur which Singaporeans

believe increases desire and improves sexual performance. I do not know what it did for my lovemaking but it
certainly made me sleep soundly once this was done. And
the depth of my slumber contributed to the horror I was
soon to know.

Innocent of what was to come, we ate, fed each other
and felt one with the sea and the dancing lights of the
ships.

The food tasted better than ever. Vanita is a marvellous
cook and I was especially happy that evening. I knew,
from the moment I met her, that I wanted this woman
for my wife but I waited several months before asking
her to marry me. I was surprised when she turned me
down.

"We should spend more time together and really get to
know each other before we decide on marriage." Seeing
the look that crossed my face she winked and added, "Ask
me again next month and I'll see how I feel about it."

I did on the same day the following month and every
month after. Four days ago she agreed to marry me. I
now looked upon myself as her husband and this our first
night together as man and wife. I think Vanita saw it
that way too. I smelt her excitement as we neared the
end of our meal and my need for her became unbearable.

My mother's Chinese genes must have got the upper
hand when I was fashioned for I am odourless and almost
devoid of body hair.

Vanita, in contrast, is hairy and exudes a symphony of
aromas in the course of making love. I think of us as
Yin and Yang, two fish-like creatures coming together to
create, against all odds, the perfect circle. I turn to my
love, moved not only by lust but by a yearning to complete
the design that is a part of the nature of things.

We were both impatient and came quickly, Vanita
making the strange choking noises that signalled her

climaxes. I recalled how alarmed I had been the first time I heard them. I thought she was having an epileptic fit or a heart seizure. I feared she might die and wondered what I would do if she did. Now I waited for them because they told me we were at the rainbow's end, that I was free to reach for my own pot of gold.

Sometimes she made orgasmic noises when asleep, groping for me, grinding herself against my body when she found it. If we woke sufficiently I saw to it that what had begun as a dream climaxed in reality. Usually, however, our eating and drinking and lovemaking saw to it that once asleep we remained so till the dawn.

As soon as we finished, Vanita began working on me again. I was surprised. We usually lay around a bit, enjoying the ebbing of our pleasure, remembering the high points of its tide. Tonight, Vanita wanted things differently. I should even then have noticed the slight disturbance in the pattern, the tiny shudder of the plate-glass window before it is shattered by the earthquake. But I was too full of Vanita. Too willing to do her bidding, too happy to go with her yet again over the edge of the world.

I was quickly ready. She turned me on my back, impaled herself and rode me. Vanita liked it this way. I did too, knowing how happy she was to be able to control the rhythms of her pleasure. There was another reason why I liked Vanita on top.

I knew the Egyptian creation legend, had read of Nut and Geb and Shu. Nut, the goddess of the sky, was so in love with her twin, Geb, the god of earth, that she mounted him, impaled herself deeply and refused to be separated from him. This terribly disturbed their father, Shu, the god of wind. So terribly disturbed was Shu, that he drew an enormous breath with which he forced the lovers apart. Thus was created light and space. When night fell, however, Nut would creep up and embrace her lover, protecting him with her body till the break of dawn.

The same instinct that caused me to see us Yin and Yang made me think of us as Geb and Nut. The notion that unions such as ours had existed from the beginning of time seemed to guarantee that Vanita and I would survive for a long while if not nearly for ever. Beliefs based on arrogance are always wrong and mine proved to be so more quickly than most.

Making love a second time was a long luxurious business and we fell asleep as soon as we were done, Vanita's body lying heavily and protectively on mine. I thought I heard her choke and cry out in the middle of the night, half woke to see if she needed me, then, feeling her quiet in my arms, decided that we would wait till dawn before making love again. How was I to know that we had made love for the last time?

I woke with a start.

I realised how one could tell moonrise from sunset. It was a matter of direction. Not direction in the sense of orientation, the way one faced, but direction in the way satellite and star moved: the moon up and out of the sea, the sun down and into it. There was no need to look around. No need to compare. All one had to do was wait. Time was more important to identity than space. I had the answer to my question.

Problems prevent you sleeping; solutions don't shake you awake. Vanita is a big girl and she lay heavily across me. My left arm was numb and my left leg which was pinned down at an awkward angle ached unbearably.

I tried to shift her. As I did, I became aware of something warm and sticky seeping from her body. It smelled like the goo one encounters in a meat market, and a lot of blood seemed to be pouring out of her. I had to get her to a doctor before she bled to death.

I shook her shoulder, at first gently but with increasing violence. Her blood-covered breasts made squelching noises against my chest and her head flopped against my shoulder. Her mouth hung open and from it a warm fluid trickled on to my body. I thought it too was blood. Then I smelled cinnamon and clove; Benedictine under the heavy flavour of curry. Vanita was bringing up the meal we had shared.

I prised myself from under her. The sleeping-bag which should have been covering us lay tangled at our feet. The moon sheltered behind a cloud and a mist obscured the lights of the ships. It was pitch dark. The teenagers were asleep, their Sony compos silent. Somewhere, far away, I could hear the soft scratching of the sea as the tide changed.

I am not strong and it was with difficulty that I turned Vanita on to her back. I shouted into her ear. She did not stir. I slapped her face. Her head lolled from side to side. Her skin felt cool and tacky the way plasticine does.

I think I realised that my darling was dead but I continued to shake her. When I saw that this was having no effect, I put my ear against her heart. The silence within was complete. Blood trickled on to my cheek and a little got into my mouth. I rubbed my face against her breasts and put both my arms around her. Then I felt it: a tiny mouth just below her left shoulder blade from which a little blood still drooled.

I do not know how long I held my love for I was unaware of anything but a sense of loss. When I finally managed to let go of her, she was beginning to stiffen and there were grey streaks across the horizon.

I pulled on my T-shirt and jeans. I did not have on underwear. Vanita preferred that I wore none when I was with her. I walked a few steps in the direction of the beach then returned to rummage among our clothes for

the ten-cent coins I needed for public phones. The first
phone I came to accepted only cards. The second had been
vandalised. Finally I found one that worked. Only then
did I remember that for emergency calls neither card nor
coin was necessary. I reached the main police exchange
which transferred my call to the duty sergeant of a nearby
police station. I told him that my girlfriend had been
stabbed.

"Is the injured party male or female?"

"Not injured, dead. And it's a girl that has been killed."

"Are you sure?"

Who could be more female than Vanita, I thought, a
lump of pain rising in my throat. I forced myself to say,
"Yes, I'm sure."

"Where is the location of the corpse?"

I shuddered. Only moments ago she was bouncing on
me, talking of marriage, of children, thinking she would
live for ever. Now a stranger called her a corpse. The pain
in my throat became unbearable. I found it impossible to
breathe.

"Hello, sir. Hello, sir. You must stay on line, sir. Mustn't
hang up till you have given police all the info."

"Yes, yes," I managed to say. "We are near the three-
kilometre stone in East Coast Park."

"Near the jogging track, sir?"

"Quite near the track and not far from the beach."

"Okay, sir. You stay near corpse. We send patrol-car
round immediate. And don't touch anything, sir."

"I won't," I assured him.

My arms and face were covered with blood and my
T-shirt was stiff with it. The clots on my face began to
itch as they dried. I licked the corner of my mouth. The
crust was salty-sweet. It was the last thing of my darling's
that I would taste.

By the time I got back to Vanita the world was turning

grey. Away to the west I heard the city sigh and stretch itself as the first wheels began to roll. Soon pink cracks would appear in the east and I would begin the first day of my life without the woman for whom I had waited so long.

I knelt beside her and put my hand on her breast. The skin was cold and beginning to tighten in death. It already seemed improbable that she had ever been alive. I wanted to kiss her one last time. I was looking into her face wondering if I dared to, when the two uniformed policemen arrived.

As soon as I looked into their faces, I knew that something was terribly wrong. I couldn't quite put my finger on what it was. Nor could I understand why the cops looked at me in the way they did; staring straight ahead without speaking, hands just touching their revolvers. I looked at Vanita's body and then up at the policeman.

I wanted to burst into tears then, tell them of the cataclysm that had destroyed my world, shaken apart the pieces I had so painstakingly put together. If they waited, things would again fall into place and I would talk to them, explain things. Right now I couldn't find the will to do so.

I looked around me hoping that even this grey world, this mindless dawning would say something to me. When it didn't, I told myself that I would begin to see if I were patient, if I could force myself to wait.

The cops, however, weren't waiting. They moved forward and took up positions, one in front and one behind me. They were both Chinese though different in appearance.

The one standing behind me was fair and chubby. The man facing me was long and lean. He was darker than I and, surprisingly for a Chinese, sported a thick moustache. He was clearly in charge and on his shoulder I noticed three metal chevrons.

The moustachioed sergeant was the first to speak. "Do you have the weapon with you?"

I was bewildered by the question; more by the way he asked it: standing stiffly in front of me, not a muscle moving, eyes staring into the distance. I had read somewhere that our police force were trying out a new interrogation technique where they asked questions which had no direct relation to the crime but which told them something of the psychology of the persons affected by it. This, I thought, was what they were doing. I had become so removed from what was going on that it took me a while to realise that the sergeant stared straight ahead to avoid looking at Vanita's naked body beside which I was still kneeling.

"No," I replied. "I haven't looked for a weapon. I merely called the police." I wanted to add that finding murder weapons was police business but didn't. The sergeant's manner did not encourage chat.

He took a step closer to me and I heard the man behind me do the same. The sergeant drew his right leg back a little and even in my confused state I realised that he was getting ready to kick me in the face should this become necessary. There was a change in his voice and he snapped, "I-C? Have you got your identity card on you?"

Before I started going with Vanita, I rarely carried my I-C with me though we are required by law to do so. Vanita insisted that I should. She said that the police were peeping Toms who spied on lovers then justified their voyeurism by arresting those who did not have their I-C's on them. I didn't ask her how she got to know all this but saw to it that I had my I-C with me whenever we were together.

"In the back pocket of my jeans." I began to rise so I could fish out the laminated plastic card.

"Don't move," the man behind me commanded. I knew that his revolver was out of its holster. "Just take it out with your left hand then pass to Sergeant Wong."

The sergeant studied my I-C for a bit then handed it over to his partner. I sensed that they disbelieved the document in their hands was genuine and I understood why.

My mental processes are peculiar and in times of crisis tend to drift from the immediate. Instead of dwelling on the immediate situation, I found myself thinking about how it came about that I got my name and various other features of my life.

I am called How Kum Menon. My name, as with so many things in my life, was the result of a string of mishaps.

My father, Ma tells me, was a man called O. K. Menon. He was a Malayalee from the west coast of India. Ma spoke of him infrequently and always referred to him as that "Malayalee scoundrel". I think with good cause.

Menon had seduced her when she was fifteen and abandoned her as soon as she got pregnant. We have not heard of him since, though I am convinced that it is in the nature of things that some day we will meet. My maternal grandparents, traditional Hokkien folk, aghast at having an unmarried pregnant daughter on their hands, demanded that Ma leave home rather than bring shame into it.

Abandoned by parents and lover, Lim Li Lian, as Ma was and still is, was given sanctuary by a kindly creature called Oscar Wellington Wu, who was then thirty-two and more than twice her age. To him Ma became cook and housekeeper among other things, though she never admits to being anything other than the first two and to this day tends to call Oscar "Mr Wu" in the company of strangers. He has always been "Uncle Oscar" to me and more of a father than anyone has a right to ask for.

Oscar was born into money and lived off the family business. Much to the relief of his brothers, he took little interest in this, for Oscar was a drunk. That is not to say he was messy about his drinking. He never turned violent and was rarely incapable of looking after himself. I have, however, seldom seen Oscar without a drink in his hand and alcohol fumes seemed to follow him around like a private atmosphere. His drunkenness did not prevent him from giving my pregnant, teenage mother the support she needed and to this he added generous helpings of loving concern, which he had in abundance.

Ma recalls that, as the time for my birth drew near, Oscar became increasingly nervous and needed to drink even more than usual. On the morning when her labour pains began, he was quite drunk and had difficulty getting her to hospital. He sobered up somewhat when the crisis was over and, on seeing me for the first time, remarked that I was an uncommonly handsome fellow. Ma agreed and as she did not have a name for me thought to call me "Hao Kan", which in Mandarin means good-looking. Uncle Oscar, because he heard wrong or for some reasons which are no longer clear, wrote "How Kum" on the certificate registering my birth.

That has been my name since. I know that I can change it by deed poll but have never bothered to. I tell myself that this is because the deed poll involves a tedious legal process but this is not really the case. I have grown to like the name and, what is more, it is a name that suits me and seems to fit me better into the scheme of things.

A name like "How Kum" inspires puns even in those not given to word play. The obvious, like "How come, you're late", I look upon with resignation. Those with a semblance of originality I enjoyed. I generally tend to ask a lot of questions: inspired by my name, perhaps.

At a barbecue once, I pestered a young lady with questions, asking, several times over, how her beauty remained unaffected by the heat and smoke around. My style was, however, not to her taste and she replied, "How come doesn't turn me on." I enjoyed the rebuff more than any encouragement she may have offered. It was something that was specially designed for me: a tiny piece of the pattern falling into place.

Right now, with a man holding a gun to my back and his mate trying not to laugh at my name, it was difficult to explain the circumstances under which I came by it. All I could manage was, "Yes. My name is How Kum Menon."

"You Indian?" he asked staring at my I-C. "You look Chinese."

"I know, lah," I said, lapsing into the vernacular. I was not clear what was happening but could not fail to sense the hostility of the cops. Perhaps, using the local patois would make them more friendly. "My mother Chinese, what."

The ploy did not work.

"You stay still," snapped the sergeant. "PC Yeo has a revolver, yah. He will shoot if you try anything funny. You stay here. I go phone OC in station."

I could not understand what was happening. The woman I loved had been killed and, instead of looking for the man who had killed her, these men were being unkind to me. I looked at Vanita lying on the ground and felt more sorry for myself than ever. Her mouth was open and brownish spittle trickled from it. The puddles of her blood on the waterproof sheet were beginning to dry, their edges turning crinkly and black. My eyes were pricked by little thorns. I wiped them with the back of my hand.

It was only a slight movement but I felt the man behind me stir. I knew that he did not need too much of an excuse to shoot me. I wondered why.

Then it hit me. It should have been obvious from the outset. I was indeed an idiot. Vanita was right to call me a dumbo. Only an idiot would take so long to figure out what was happening. The question about the murder weapon, the sergeant's hard voice, the nervousness of the man behind me . . . It all made sense. These men actually suspected me of murdering Vanita.

When Sergeant Wong returned I had no doubts whatsoever.

"Up," shouted Wong, grabbing me by the hair and pulling me to my feet. "Hands on backside."

I was handcuffed and dragged unceremoniously to the police car. There we waited for the forensic team to arrive before driving off to the station.

My dreams form with my waking life a composite where contradictions no longer exist, where patterns form which are beautifully perfect: patterns that have no corners, no edges, no beginning, no end. Usually, that is. Sometimes the pieces don't fit. Images are mindless and ugly, grating against each other instead of sliding together and coalescing. Events proceed in a sequence whose logic is beyond my grasp. I know then that I am not in a dream. I am in a nightmare.

I was in one now. With one difference. I was wide awake.

"You're a piece of shit," said Inspector D'Cruz and punched me in the stomach to make his point. "A slime-covered piece of shit." He hit me again, as though the point he had just made needed emphasising.

I crashed to the ground retching. I had vomited when he had first hit me and the floor was dotted with stains. My stomach was now empty; empty of everything except a burning pain which the cold cement of the floor did nothing to relieve. I heard the door of the room open, managed to roll over slightly and saw Sergeant Wong re-enter the room.

He began talking to D'Cruz. I could not catch what they were saying. From their gestures, it seemed that the inspector was not happy with what his sergeant was telling him. I was too disturbed by the pain, too overwhelmed by the nightmare to follow what was happening.

I realised I was in trouble as soon as I set eyes on Ozzie
D'Cruz.

I had been hurried directly from the police car into the
inspector's office. This was a high-ceilinged room with
bare floors and green-enamelled walls. D'Cruz sat at a
large desk in the centre of the room. He was surrounded
by stacks of stained and tattered files and the one he was
studying looked the shabbiest of the lot. He continued
studying it for several minutes while the two policemen
stood to attention on either side of me. They said nothing.
My hands, cuffed behind me, had begun to ache. I shifted
from one foot to the other then coughed tentatively. The
inspector continued reading for a further minute, made
some notes on the margin of the page before looking up.

"Get some kind of a preliminary statement from this
mother-fucking bastard, Wong, then get him into the
special interrogation room. There, we'll really find out
what happened in the park." D'Cruz was oily-skinned and
near black. Paunchy and heavy-shouldered. We were so
different that I knew he would have no problems about
making me suffer.

I had met men like D'Cruz before. They hated my type
and found no difficulty in being cruel to the likes of me.
I understood why. I was physically so different from them
that I could be regarded as something alien, something
from another species, and therefore undeserving of
consideration.

The world, increasingly scrambled in the last few
hours, had now become a horror film with no end in sight.
I was suspected of murdering the person I most loved, a
person without whom the world was incomplete. I hadn't
killed Vanita but I was sure that, if I had not come into
her life, she would still be alive. I was guilty, in some
roundabout way, for her being murdered and would suffer
for my sin. D'Cruz was the person ordained to see to this.

As though to confirm what was going on in my head, the inspector said, "Get this fucker to make an upfront report at the desk, Wong, then take him to the Special Interrogation Room. And do an internal examination for starters. He looks the kind of pervert who needs drugs to get him going." I heard him mutter in a voice loud enough to me to hear, "God knows what the world is coming to these days. Fucking murder-rapists look like fairies and the blokes who like it up the bum prance around flexing their biceps and showing off the hairs on their chest."

I was escorted to the front desk. Neither Wong nor the duty officer seemed interested in what I had to say. Wong inserted several pieces of carbon paper into a thick pad then wrote down in longhand my account of what had happened at East Coast Park.

I asked him how far back I should go and he said, "As far as you like. This is only the prelim. No value in court or in making out the charge. We'll make a full report after Inspector D'Cruz has interrogated you."

The paperwork was over quickly and I was led to the Special Interrogation Room. This was a tiny windowless box. The door which was its entrance and exit had SIR marked on it in ornate capitals. It could have been the entrance to the gents in a high-class restaurant except that there was no accompanying door marked MADAM.

The fear which had been building up in me became unbearable as soon as I entered the room. It numbed my senses and overcame the little will I had left. My actions became automatic. I looked to Sergeant Wong to tell me what to do. Animals became this way in slaughterhouses, I have heard, as did men on their way to the gallows.

Yet, there was nothing particularly frightening about the room: no bloodstains on the floor, no instruments of torture on its walls. The single neon tube on the ceiling illuminated it shadowlessly. At its exact centre was a small wooden table. On this was a box of Kleenex, a tube of KY jelly and several outsize plastic gloves, the kind used by handlers of food in supermarkets. Under the table were several pairs of boxing-gloves, an assortment of jogging shoes, and a skipping rope with knots in the strangest places. I wondered what the sporting paraphernalia was doing here. The room did not seem to be the kind of place to which policemen came for their workouts.

"We uncuff now but don't try anything funny," Wong warned.

My hands should have been cramped and painful from being held behind me for such a long time. They weren't. I knew why. With terror comes a sense of disembodiment; a disaffiliation from one's body and its purposes. I examined my fingers. Their tips were a little blue. They seemed otherwise okay.

"Take off your clothes," Wong ordered.

In my present state of mind, the request did not seem unusual. I kicked off my joggers and peeled off my shirt then my jeans. As I stood naked before them I noticed a look of envy pass between the policemen.

When we made love for the first time, Vanita confirmed what I had long suspected from the hostile glances of men in showers and changing-rooms: I have an exceptionally large penis. I had inherited my skin, my eyes, my shape and just about everything else from my slender Chinese mother; everything except my high nose and, perhaps, the size of my cock. The genes for both these must have come from my father for the Chinese have flat noses and oriental men are said to be somewhat under-endowed in the cock department. I had examined myself in the mirror often enough. I did not think I was particularly big but accepted in this, as in most things, the judgement of others.

As soon as he got over his surprise, Wong said, "Kneel on the floor and bend over."

I did, but not before I saw the sergeant put on one of the outsize gloves and smear his index finger with KY jelly. I felt hands, presumably those of PC Yeo, spread open my buttocks and a finger enter my rectum.

"Clean," said Wong withdrawing his finger. "No drugs hidden." I was relieved. I don't use drugs. I certainly didn't have any stuck up my arse. I had heard of the police framing the innocent when it suited them. I knew that anyone found to be carrying more than 15 grams of heroin was deemed a pusher, and in Singapore the penalty for drug-peddling was death.

I was still kneeling on the floor, bum stuck in the air, when Ozzie D'Cruz entered the room.

"Clean, yah, Wong," he said, not bothering to hide his disappointment. Then he brightened. "But not to worry, my friend. If we can't get this mother-fucker to swing for pushing, we'll have him dangling for murder-rape." He casually put a boot against the side of my chest and kicked me as I lay on my back. "I just can't wait . . ." I knew what had stopped him in mid-sentence. "Sweet mother of God, you mean he shoved that monster into the girl before stabbing her?"

Trembling with rage he kicked off his boots and slipped on a pair of joggers. Then, making sure that I saw what he was doing, he put a boxing-glove on his right hand and got Sergeant Wong to tie up the laces. With his left hand he yanked me up by the hair.

"On your feet you shit-bag," he shouted, his voice high pitched and unnatural like that of the masked actors in a Japanese Noh play. "You combination of scum and slime." His voice rose to a scream and he punched me in the solar plexus.

I stopped breathing. Everything dimmed as I hit the

floor. I was aware of jogging shoes kicking me, boxing-gloves thumping me. My mind, disconnected from my body, registered and recorded instead of feeling, scream-ing, working out means of avoiding punishment. Thump. My kidneys were wrenched from their moorings and shoved into my chest. Thump. An electric shock shot from the base of my spine to my head. Thump. A heel landed, ground itself into my testicles and a balloon of pain exploded in my abdomen.

"Stand up you big-donged freak," said D'Cruz. He pulled me to my feet and held me up by my hair.

His face was strangely impassive. The furrows and acne tracks could well have been putty; the trickles of sweat made from grease-paint.

"You hear this and you hear good." A blow under the heart and another across the kidneys to ensure that I did. "I don't know exactly what happened in the park but I'm sure gonna find out." He slapped my face with an open glove to make sure I was following his line of thought. "Now you're going to do something for Uncle Ozzie here. You're going to open that sow-arse of a mouth and let the truth come out of it."

His voice dropped and became almost gentle. "You tell us the truth, son, the whole goddamned truth including every nitty-gritty detail and I'll tell you what I'm gonna do for you. I'll get you the best lawyer in town." He let go of my hair and let his hands fall to his sides. "Who's to know what can happen then." He shrugged. "A few deliberate mistakes by our forensic boys, a couple of well-planned lies from so-called psychiatric experts and you'll get off with a DR plea. Diminished responsibility, you understand. Means you're bad because you're crazy."

I should have begged the man not to hurt me more, agreed to the option he was offering me. Instead I stared at him and said nothing. Something perverse prevented me from speaking. I knew that my silence would enrage D'Cruz further and cause him to make me suffer even more.

Was it just the difference in our physiognomies that made him want to hurt me or was there something more behind his cruelty? I did not think the inspector was an evil man or one who enjoyed causing pain. There was something about Vanita's death that fuelled his cruelty and made him a sadist. That was why his face was a mask, his voice theatrical.

The respite was brief. Insufficient time to rearrange things, rotate the kaleidoscope to form a new picture.

"But don't think, you big-donged pervert, that you can claim your confession was beaten out of you. The shoes and gloves won't leave marks on your body so, whatever you say, you said of your own free will." He hit me in the gut and I crashed to the floor. I saw him pick up the peculiarly knotted skipping rope. He placed this round my ankle so the knots lay on the bony prominences. Then he began twisting the rope. The pain was unbelievable. From a great distance I heard myself scream.

He took the rope off my leg and placed it around my cock.

"You listen very carefully, my friend. If I twist this rope, you won't have a great big salami hanging between your legs, you'll have a hamburger." A thought struck him and he laughed. "May not be a bad idea. After all, our liberal, soft-hearted American friends cut the balls off rapists."

He smiled. "I tell you what. You get up and jog round this room ten times. Slowly, mind, so you can think of what really happened in the park, not the crap you put down in your statement." He paused and stared into my face. "You tell us what you hoped to gain by calling the cops yourself. Whether you thought it would actually throw us off the scent. Run slowly round ten times then sit on the floor in front of me and tell me the whole goddamned truth."

I got to my feet and began to run slowly round the room. My ankle hurt when it hit the ground, the pain in my side made breathing difficult. I don't remember counting but, after going round ten times, I sat on the floor. The cement was cool on my bum. Rough but pleasant.

For a moment D'Cruz dropped the Noh mask. In a near-pleasant voice he asked, "Now tell us if you forced the girl to go to the park with you or if you found her there?"

"We have been friends for nearly a year. We were going to be married. We went there often. . ."

I didn't feel the kick but the next thing I knew was that I was face-down on the floor. There was a buzzing in my right ear and the right side of my head throbbed.

"The truth, you turd." The voice was again metallic, artificial. "Tell us how you met the victim."

"We work in the same offi. . ."

The jogging shoe that hit the side of my throat stopped me talking. The kick was strong enough to knock me on to my back, my arms and legs flopping to my sides. D'Cruz raised his foot high in the air, like he was goose stepping, then began to bring it down. Faster and faster it neared my cock, my balls. I drew in a breath. I would need to scream. A corner of my mind wondered if eunuchs didn't feel sexual desire or simply couldn't do anything about it even if they did. The shoe touched my pubic hair and stopped.

The inspector's voice, soft, cajoling, real, once more suggested, "Okay, okay. So you know the girl, you take her to the park, you fool around but she won't let you go all the way." The voice got even softer, cooing. "I know what some of these bitches are. Cockteasers who fool around and give a fella ideas. But when it gets so hard the poor guy feels its gonna burst, they act like nuns who have never uncrossed their legs." He laughed. A friendly we're-all-boys-together laugh. His face became understanding and he nodded his head several times.

I shook my own, began to say; "No. . ."

His foot moved from my crotch to my throat. His face was once more grease-paint and putty. "You mother-fucking, sonofabitch. I know exactly what happened. You don't get what you want so you pull out the knife, then she lets you, but when it's all done she cries, threatens to go to the police. You panic and stab her. Then you get really worried. You wipe the knife clean and get rid of it. Your best shot will be to call the police, make out you're innocent. Honest John citizen doing his duty. The good Singaporean full of respect for the law."

The eyes were little more than pockmarks, the voice rose to a shriek. "Maybe it's the other way. She won't let you so you kill her first. Then you can stick that thing of yours wherever you want to. In her mouth, up her arse, anywhere. Maybe in the hole you made with the knife." He turned to Sergeant Wong. "Get on to forensics and ask them where they found semen. Ask them if there was any in the stab wound."

The sergeant left the room.

D'Cruz seemed to have run out of steam. I used the interval to enjoy the feel of the stone floor on my back. Breathing was difficult with the shoe against my throat but manageable with an effort.

A sequence began to form. I knew it was monstrous. But I had to have things fit, couldn't have pieces of the jigsaw lying about. A picture had to exist in my head even if it was the wrong one. There was only one person who could have killed Vanita. Me. After killing her I had become amnesiac. It is easy to forget what one cannot bear. I began to invent reasons for the murder.

I used to think that psychoanalysis was bullshit. I could have been wrong. Maybe we are driven by strong currents working in our subconscious. Consciously I loved Vanita. Loved her desperately. I never felt so complete as when I was in her body. But deep down, did I not resent the power she had over me?

I thought about my mother. I did not like admitting this, even to myself. But I am very attached to Ma. I owed much to her. She had been a child when she had me. Suffered so I could be born. This affair with Vanita must be affecting her even if I chose not to notice how disturbed she was by it. Things between us had certainly changed after Vanita had come into my life. There was one sure way of returning things to normal. I had taken it.

The picture wasn't convincing. I decided to try one even more bizarre.

I was a pervert for whom fucking was only a substitute for what I really wanted to do: stick knives into women. Was that not really why I had remained a virgin for so long?

I looked back into my childhood and remembered how I loved standing beside Ma in the kitchen, watching as she sliced meat. I remembered enjoying the hiss as blade moved through muscle, remembered enjoying the sight of blood squeezed from dead flesh. How much more would I have enjoyed it if the flesh had been alive, shuddering, capable of feeling pain?

I was so involved with what I was putting together in my head that I was barely aware of what was happening. D'Cruz had pulled me to my feet and was slapping my face rapidly, the way one does an unconscious person. It was almost friendly. I turned, attempted a smile. He hit me in the stomach. I crashed to the floor and strained to vomit.

Out of the corner of my eye I saw Sergeant Wong re-enter the room. He held a whispered conversation with my tormentor. D'Cruz shook his head several times, his eyes widening with disbelief. I sat on the floor and put my hand on the part of me that seemed responsible for the trouble I was in. Feeling slightly more secure, I began to listen to what they were saying.

"Are you sure?" the inspector asked.

"Yes, sir. Report just in from PC Marcus and Sergeant Ali Mohamed."

"How far from the scene of the first crime?"

"Four kilometres to the east, sir."

"And modus? The same?"

"Yes, sir. But this time both killed, sir. Boyfriend and girlfriend." He stopped though there was clearly something more he wished to say.

"Yes," D'Cruz prompted.

"Very good Singaporean this one, sir. Very law-abiding." Wong smiled before adding, "We can't even fine him one thousand bucks for littering, sir. He dropped the knife in a garbage-bin after the murders."

His joking reference to Singapore's harsh anti-littering laws did not amuse his superior.

D'Cruz shot him a dirty look before pulling off the boxing-glove. A change had come over the inspector. His podgy cheeks had crumpled. His tiny eyes flicked from side to side. He was a boxer on the ropes. Worried. Human again.

He said to Wong, "Give him back his things, then bring him round to my office." He pushed the door open and walked out of the room.

Something happened to me too. The piece of my mind which had been detached merged with the rest. I began to feel my body, first piecemeal, then all together. My scalp felt raw and tingled. My ankle throbbed. My side hurt when I breathed deeply. But all in all, I felt good. My will had returned. I didn't have to look to Wong or D'Cruz to tell me what to do. I got to my feet and stretched. Pulled on my jeans and shirt. Smiled at Wong and PC Yeo, ran my fingers through my hair.

When I faced him in his green-walled office, D'Cruz seemed harassed. There were more files than ever on his desk. They seemed to be closing in on him.

He stared at my identity card balefully. "Menon," he said. "That's a Malayalee name. You look like a Chink." No smile or look of apology. "You look Chinese."

"My mother's Chinese. My father was an Indian, from the west coast of India."

"Was? Is he dead?"

"No," I said. "He ran away. Left me and my Ma."

"I'm Malayalee too. But from Singapore and a Catholic. We are not allowed to run away from our wives." The eyes were tired, looked into mine for sympathy.

I was in no mood to offer any. "I don't know. I don't have a wife." I paused and added, not without self-pity, "Maybe I'll never have a wife."

The voice was gentle, pleading. "That was a mistake, Menon." His eyes scanned my face. "What happened back there was a mistake."

"I know. I knew all along. I tried to tell you but you didn't give me a chance to." I looked hard into his face and drove down his piggy eyes. "How did you detective geniuses find out you were beating up the wrong guy?"

"The bastard did it again in a different part of the park. Killed both the man and the girl."

"Good. So you've got somebody to beat up all over again. Cheer up. There may be many suspects. You and your boys could have a ball."

The eyes stayed down. "I said it was a mistake. I'm sorry."

"So that's it. You're sorry and How Kum Menon, the Chinky-looking guy with an Indian surname, runs off like a good boy and says nothing more about it."

He looked up. The voice rose, the eyes were glinting. "What do you expect me to do? Fall down and kiss your arse? Go down on my knees and give you a blow-job?"

"You keep clear of my cock, whatever you do."

The eyes fell. The voice too. He said, "I can't stand murder-rapes. I know too much about them. One happened close to me." He looked at me hopefully.

My head ached and the side of my chest throbbed. I felt humiliated and dirty. I wasn't in the mood for confidences. "Sure, I understand," I said. "You have good reasons for picking up innocent citizens and beating the shit out of them." He shifted about in his seat. "What happens now?"

"You got somewhere to go?" The face remained blank but the eyes were concerned. "Some place you can tidy up before seeing your mother?"

"I'll go to my lawyer." The inspector's head snapped back in alarm. I took my time about adding, "My very good friend Jafri al-Misris."

He seemed surprised. "You know al-Misris?" I nodded and he pushed the phone towards me. "You have his number?"

Jafri was home. He didn't ask what I was doing in a police station so early on a Sunday morning. Perhaps lawyers expect ordinary citizens to spend a portion of their time in such places.

"I'll be there in fifteen minutes," he said, his voice, as always, confident and reassuring.

Sergeant Wong brought in a cup of sweet tea. There was a knot in my throat and I drank it with difficulty, but I felt better when I had.

Jafri was always punctual. Thirteen minutes after the phone call I stood up.

D'Cruz said, "She was your girlfriend, was she? The girl who was rap . . . stabbed?"

"Yes. Four nights ago she agreed to become my wife."

"I'll get the bastard who did it. I promise you that. I'll get him whatever happens."

I thought of saying "But don't beat up too many innocent guys while you're about it."

I didn't.

THREE

I am not really good at anything and am, therefore, unhappy with people who are. If a man has a single outstanding talent I hold it against him. If he has more than one, I hate him. My relationship with Jafri al-Misris is the more surprising for this. The exception is, I guess, proof of the rule. Jafri is good at everything but is my dearest friend.

At school Jafri was the sportsman, the leader, the outstanding scholar. What was worse, and something I wouldn't have forgiven in anybody else, was that he was well-liked: a nice guy that came first. After law school, he became Deputy Public Prosecutor. Then he went into private practice. To better serve what he saw as the cause of Justice, though Jafri never took the moral high-ground or spoke of Justice with a capital "J". He quite quickly became the town's leading criminal lawyer.

I like to think that his confidence and success stemmed from the fact that Jafri's family go back a long way. If you know where you're from, it's easier to be sure where you are going. The al-Misris family originated in Egypt from where they moved to Saudi Arabia. They came to Singapore at the turn of the century by way of India and had a thriving business selling the spices essential for Malay and Indian cooking. In the course of this, they have somehow provided Jafri with all the ingredients necessary for success.

A voice within, which speaks to me as much as does

the world outside, reminds me of Jafri's success, of the headstart he had in life. It often incites me to feel animosity for the man who has always shown me kindness and concern. Sitting beside him now, I am too relieved by Jafri's presence, too comforted by his voice, to listen to the murmurings inside my head.

"Don't talk," Jafri advised, "unless you feel you must. It might be better if we got you home and settled you down. Then you can tell me how you got into the state you're in."

We were driving through Katong. This part of Singapore has always been in less of a hurry to develop steel and plastic high-rises than the rest of the island. Katong had originally been the enclave of the Eurasians, half-breed fisher-folk from Portuguese Malacca. Over the years they had all but disappeared as a community. But they had left their spirit in Katong where the people were easy-going and there were more Catholic churches than anywhere else in Singapore. I contained myself as Jafri avoided several citizens who, Mass over, were blindly drifting across the street demonstrating their absolute confidence in the Almighty.

When we reached the expressway I said, "I really need to talk, Jafri."

Before he could say anything, I told him all that had happened. Jafri had liked Vanita. When I came to tell him how my shirt was covered with her blood, he sighed, squeezed my shoulder and let his hand stay there. I was touched. It took a lot to make Jafri al-Misris drive with one hand, especially on an expressway.

"You must come home, have a bath, eat something, then maybe lie down for a while." He smiled. "You've been through so much that I'll let Zainah spoil you for a bit."

Zainah was his wife. "A simple girl from a kampong" was how she described herself. When Jafri married her that was exactly what she was: a girl fresh from a Malay village. She was pretty in the soft way of Southeast Asian women and talked in the singsong voice of a little girl. I was strongly attracted to Zainah and Jafri, quick to notice such things, accused me of coveting his woman. He did this jokingly. But only half so.

Right now I was so sore and weary that even the prospect of being spoiled by Zainah failed to excite me. Nevertheless, I said, "I need a long, hot shower. Then we'll see what your lady can do for me."

He was silent for a while then said, "I'm sorry D'Cruz gave you a bad time."

"Not more than I am. Is there anything I can do about it?"

"Like what?"

"Like getting someone to literally chew his balls off. Like allowing me to shove his head in a pail full of shit till he drowns."

He shrugged. "I guess you can make a complaint about ill-treatment while in police custody but these things are difficult to prove in court." He hesitated for a moment before continuing. "D'Cruz is a very good investigator and some of us . . . , his superiors included, realise why he acts the way he does when he thinks he's on to a murder-rape."

"There are reasons to justify beating up an innocent bloke whose girlfriend has just been murdered?"

"I'm not trying to justify D'Cruz's behaviour. In fact justify would be quite the wrong word. Perhaps, explain or offer extenuating circumstances would be a better way of putting it.

"When I first joined the Deputy Public Prosecutor's office I was warned about the inspector and his handling of suspects of murder-rape cases. Some fifteen years ago Ozzie's sister was raped and murdered. The killer was never found. Though it had happened years ago, there was still much talk about it, and every investigator was only too keen to give me his theories about the case.

"You know how I feel about the ill-treatment of suspects and I was determined to find an instance of D'Cruz assaulting an accused person. If I did I would have him charged and sent to prison."

He steered the car down the ramp to the basement garage before continuing.

"Then, as luck would have it, I had to work with the inspector on a number of cases. True, we did not have to deal with a murder-rape but, apart from foul language, he worked by the book. What is more, I found him to be an excellent investigator, who knew his job was to unearth the truth and to apprehend the culprit. He never sucked up to his superiors nor, even when pressured from above, made the slightest attempt to protect those in power. He is an honest-to-goodness, old-fashioned policeman."

He parked the car and guided me to the lift.

My shirt was bloodstained and my face bruised and swollen. I must have been a sight. Instead of asking questions, Zainah produced a clean towel, a set of Jafri's clothes, and directed me towards the large bathroom adjoining their bedroom.

I spent a long time under the shower, letting the hot water soothe my bruises, enjoying the thought that the fragrant soap I rubbed on my body had but recently been used by Zainah. I was definitely recovering. I dried myself and slipped into Jafri's trousers before presenting myself for Zainah's ministrations. Jafri watched as his wife applied disinfectant to my abrasions and rubbed fragrant, medicinal oil into my bruises. These were still sore enough for me to be soothed rather than aroused by her efforts.

When she was done, we sat down to a breakfast of

French toast and sweet, black coffee. As we ate I realised how much the shower had done for me. My appetite was good and I was beginning to regard Zainah, dressed in a sarong and a thin blouse, with something more than gratitude.

When we finished breakfast Jafri asked, "Do you want to go home or would you rather stay with us for a while?"

I was tempted to stay, and not simply because of Zainah. My father O.K. Menon made a habit of getting into trouble and Ma always felt that it was my fate to do the same. That I was involved in a murder investigation would justify her worst fears. As soon as I was home I was sure to be subjected to an interrogation, less painful, but more rigorous than the one I had just been through. But if I stayed away and she read of Vanita's murder in Monday morning's papers, she would be distraught.

"Thanks, Jafri. I think I'd better get home and tell Ma and Uncle Oscar what's been going on."

"Good." He picked up his car-keys. "I'll run you home." Zainah, who had spoken little the whole morning, came over to my side of the table. "I'm so, so sorry," she said, putting her hands on my chest.

I held her by the waist and looked down at her. Suddenly I missed Vanita terribly. She would be lying on a cold slab now. A stranger in a white coat would be sticking test-tubes and other scientific things into her secret places. Then they would cut her open and tear out her organs in the same way as was done to chickens being prepared for a table.

I tightened my hold on Zainah.

"So sorry, How Kum, but I don't know how to say, lah."

Zainah, in spite of the fancy condo in which she lived, was at heart a simple girl. Folk from Malay villages often end sentences with "lah", which is a contraction of Allah. Unlike the western expletive "God!", "lah" was not a curse nor a condemnation but an acceptance of the way things were and a thankfulness that God had made them so.

There was a warmth within me that Zainah felt. Standing on tiptoe, she pressed her lips to my face. Her mouth was hot, the way one's mouth gets when one is about to cry. My throat was cracked and I didn't try to speak. I was aware of Zainah's body pressed against me. It was soft and pliable, so different from Vanita's, which was full and firm. Yet it reminded me of Vanita, told me that the woman I loved was dead. I knew then that, however many women I had, it would always be Vanita that I held in my arms.

Oscar was asleep when I got home. I was glad. For all his generosity of spirit, Oscar was not good in a crisis. I told Ma what had happened and answered her questions as best I could. These were probing and did not avoid intimate details. For all the veneer of reticence that my mother usually affected, she seemed not to mind getting into the nitty-gritty now.

Just when I thought we had got over the worst she began to weep, not violently but in a niggling way which meant she was dissatisfied with something.

"What now, Ma?" I asked, taking her hand.

"Oh, my son, my little boy, did I not tell you everything? Did I not warn you enough?"

"What are you going on about, Ma?" I asked, more sharply than I intended.

"Your father was a hot-tempered man. He beat me so many times. Sometimes I thought I would die and sometimes the pain was so bad I wished I would die."

"But I'm not hot-tempered, Ma."

"Maybe not always. Maybe not on the outside." She stopped to wipe her nose on her sleeve. "I don't know how this Vanita angered you. I don't know if she made you jealous. Who's to know what goes on inside us."

"Come to the point, Ma."

"You say that the girl was stabbed, yes?"

"Yes, Ma. What about it?"

"One of my kitchen knives is missing. The stainless steel one I just bought from Robinson's. I don't know who took it. Maybe it's you."

For a moment I felt like I did when D'Cruz was interrogating me. I had killed Vanita because I was jealous of her past, because I knew that death was the only way to secure her entirely and permanently for myself. Ma stopped snivelling and buried her face in my chest. I looked over her head and out of the window.

Like most Singaporeans, we live in a Housing Board flat. Our living-dining room looks out on to a square surrounded by shops. It was a Sunday morning and there were lots of people about: shopping for things they had forgotten to get during the week or looking for the bargains that always came up on weekends. On one side of the square a group of teenagers chatted in loud happy voices, touching each other frequently, giggling as they did. Two old men smoking pipes watched them, their faces impassive, their bodies as still as the outline of trees at dusk. On the far side of the square, overweight housewives haggled with a man selling fresh fruit.

No, said the voice inside me. It wasn't the dark unknowable forces of psychoanalysis but the obvious, everyday things that made the world turn. It was unthinkable that I killed Vanita. I loved her. She gave me joy; made the world complete. I was going to see her in every woman I touched. . .

"Look at me, Ma," I said, holding my mother at arms' length. "Do I look like a murderer to you?"

She stopped snivelling and rubbed tears and snot on

Jafri's beautifully laundered shirt. "I'm sorry, son, but sometimes I think bad things. It's like your father is still around, or has left behind something in you that will always cause me trouble. Something that will never go away." She touched my cheek. "You tell me I'm a silly old woman for thinking these things."

"You're a silly old woman, Ma, and I hate you." I took her face in my hands and kissed her. "Now go wake Uncle Oscar, Ma. I'll make coffee this morning."

Oscar always went to bed drunk and waking him was quite a business. It took longer than usual this morning, and there were several minutes of whispering before the pair appeared.

Oscar had with him the bottle of brandy that always accompanied him to bed. He poured some of this into his coffee and pushed the bottle across to me. "Café royale," he said. "Good at all times but indispensable in moments like this." He took a good swallow of his drink. "God gave us trouble so we have reason to need brandy. And from what your mother has been telling me, you have reason enough."

He indicated the bottle again. I shook my head and he continued, "I am acquainted with this D'Cruz character. Said to be a good policeman but a ruffian of the first order. Unfortunate that you should fall into his hands after your lady. . ." he hesitated.

"Vanita," I prompted.

". . . after your Vanita was stabbed."

He poured brandy into his cup and topped it up with coffee. "I understand that two other people in the park were stabbed."

"Yes, Uncle Oscar. They were killed about four kilometres from where Vanita and I spent the night."

"Oh me, oh my," he hummed, shaking his head. "We have yet again the age-old riddle of the mass murderer."

"Why riddle, Uncle Oscar. Aren't they all just lunatics?"

"There are, dear boy, as many theories as there are killings." He sipped his coffee. "You know, of course, about Jack the Ripper, the grandaddy of them all?"

"Not a thing," I lied. I knew that Oscar was dying to tell me, so I added, "Who was this Jack the Ripper, Uncle Oscar?"

He smiled, happy. I was again the child to whom he could tell stories. He cleared his throat. "Between 1888 and 1891, five prostitutes were murdered in the East End of London. They were stabbed and had their organs ripped out of their bodies. There were suspects in abundance, ranging from a mad midwife to the brother of the Prince of Wales."

"And the man responsible was never caught?"

"Why man? Why not men? Woman? Several persons? One person commits a murder and gets away with it. Others think it is a good time to settle old scores and make out it's all the work of a mass murderer. Perhaps there's only one person at work but he realises that the best way of concealing his motive and, with it, his identity is to commit several murders. Conceal a poisoned apple in a barrel of apples."

"So you think Vanita was killed because her murderer wanted to hide his motive for the other killings?"

"Or vice versa." He hesitated. "The other couple may have been killed to confuse the police as to the motive for Vanita's murder."

Oscar toyed with the brandy bottle but made no attempt to add more liquor to his coffee. Ma picked up her spoon and began stirring the contents of her cup. This was odd because Ma took her coffee without sugar or milk. I realised that the two subsequent killings did not automatically absolve me of the first.

The doubts that the scene outside our window had put

to rest began to return. Was it possible that, for some unfathomable reason, I had killed Vanita, run four kilometres across the park, killed an innocent pair of lovers and returned to the side of the woman I had slain. Stranger things had happened.

Oscar read where my thoughts were leading me and said, "You must understand, dear boy, that whatever it is you have done, or think you have done, your mother and I will not let you down. Our support will be unquestioning and absolute." He held Ma's gaze for a moment before going on. "I know Phillip Caplan, a damn good QC, with an unbelievable record of acquittals in what looked like the most open and shut of murder cases. . ."

"Uncle Oscar, . . . Ma." I reached across, gripped my mother's shoulder and shook it violently. "Are you accusing me of murdering Vanita?"

"Steady on, old chap. No one is pointing fingers. All we are saying is that we will stand firmly behind you, however rough the going gets."

Ma shook my hand off and began to ostentatiously massage her shoulder. "You are just like your father, How Kum. You get violent when you are angry."

"My God, Ma, there you go again . . ." I began. Then a thought struck me. "OK. Assume I killed Vanita, for whatever reason. There would be two options before me. I could either stay in Singapore and stand trial, hoping that with the help of your QC friend, I would be found innocent. My second option would be to get out of the country while I still had the chance. I have very little money of my own and either way I would need your help. If I did kill Vanita, I would eventually be forced to admit it to you, so what is the point of my lying now?"

The argument convinced Oscar. He smiled and nodded in Ma's direction. She turned and reached out for my hand.

"That's all we wanted to know, old chap," said Oscar, reaching for his drink. "That's all we wanted to know."

They were relieved and happy. I tried to be too. I told myself again and again that I could not in any way be responsible for the death of the woman I had loved so much. But she was lying on me when she bled to death. It seemed impossible that someone could have sneaked up and stabbed her without my being aware of it. But how could I have stabbed her while pinned down under her sleeping body? Unless, of course, she had rolled away in the night, I had stabbed her, then dragged her dying body on to mine. Then there was the business of the missing kitchen knife. I know little about stab wounds but I knew what Ma's missing knife looked like. It seemed to me to be just the sort of weapon responsible for the wound that I found below Vanita's left shoulder blade.

My doubts pursued me into my dreams. We were making love again in the park. As we did blood began to pour from all Vanita's orifices. I could taste it in her mouth, feel it trickle out of her ears, hear it squelch in her vagina. She took my hand and put it on her back. I found it easily enough, the little orifice below the shoulder blade. I recognised as pleasurable the sensation of slipping my finger in and out of it rhythmically. Blood welled around my finger as it neared orgasm. I awoke with a painful erection, masturbated and fell asleep again.

Vanita was again in my dreams. It was the time before we started going together. She was teasing me about being a stay-at-home mama's boy and I promised to take her out that very evening. Even in my dream I remember thinking that we would soon be making love, that this was the woman especially designed for me. I had more dreams of her but the details of these were hazy.

I was woken, as always, by sounds in the flats around us. Half asleep, I felt Vanita in the room with me. So strong was her presence that I thought I could smell her in the stale air stirred ceaselessly by the ceiling-fan. I knew that I couldn't live the rest of my life accompanied by this ghost. I knew also that there was something I would have to do before my darling could truly die. Time would tell me what this was.

FOUR

Like most Singaporeans, I have ceased to wonder at the phenomenon of Singapore. Our diamond-shaped island, forty-two kilometres wide and twenty-three kilometres long, is not only the busiest port in the world, what is more, its airport rates among the best. Some eighteen million passengers, more than six times our population, pass through it every year. We have made a fine art of servicing aircraft and our National Airline Terminal Services, which with our fondness for acronyms we call Nats, is something of which we can be justly proud. I am what is called an environment inspector, and look after the hygiene of the food we supply to aircraft.

It is an undemanding job, suited to my temperament. As soon as I had done my O-levels, I began looking around for what Uncle Oscar would call "gainful employment". Jafri, who had won a scholarship to study law at the university, was upset at my reluctance to acquire any kind of higher qualification. Ma, I think, agreed with him but said nothing. Oscar, however, applauded my decision.

"That's right, dear boy. Do something that doesn't fill your day and occupy your mind so you will have time and energy for the things that matter." He ignored Ma's pointed silence and continued, "The family business provides enough for the three of us to be getting along with, and I'll make sure that you and your mother are well taken care of when I am gone."

I had a go at several jobs before settling into my present

employment. At school I had found biology easy, and did a short course in environmental health and hygiene which led to my getting a diploma in the subject. This qualified me to apply for the position at Nats.

I remember the job interview well. I was nineteen, naive and flattered at the obvious interest that Symons, the manager of Nats was taking in me. I did not realise that the pleasant-faced Eurasian who leaned across several times to touch my hand and squeeze my shoulder was homosexual, still less that he thought that I was too.

I had been at work for a week when Symons phoned and asked me up to his office. Nats were building new kitchens then and the manager said he would like to discuss these with me before approving the plans that the designers had put up. I was flattered to be involved in so important an assignment and hurried upstairs. He invited me to come round to his side of the desk so that we could better study the drawings. All innocence, I did, suspecting nothing, even when he insisted I sit on the arm of his chair.

Architect's drawings are unwieldy things and shuffling them about involved a lot of physical contact. I paid no great attention to the fact that my manager was breathing heavily, failed to notice the state of excitement he was getting into. Only when the arm, which had somehow found its way around my waist, tightened and he began nuzzling my armpit did I think that something was wrong. I tried to draw away but Symons put his other arm round me and tried to pull me on to his lap.

"Don't worry," he said. "No one will disturb us here."

Before I could protest, he unzipped his fly and exposed a hugely erect penis.

"Play with it," he said, reaching towards my crotch. I struggled and shook my head. "Just hold it, once," he begged.

I do not, till today, understand why I did. As soon as I touched him, he jerked several times and ejaculated over the drawings on his desk.

It took me several weeks to get over the episode. I have not told anyone about it, not even Vanita. It is something that does not fit into my scheme of things, something that disturbs the way I view my sexuality.

I was disgusted with myself and with Symons. Felt that the memory of this encounter soiled all the memories that I carried in my head. Finally, I came to terms with it. I did so by viewing the whole incident as something terribly funny. It was a joke episode and had about it all the elements of farce. I entered into a playful relationship with the manager rejecting, in a light-hearted manner, the advances he continued to make, in much the way a young girl does those of a man too old for her. I have, over the years, even come to think kindly of the man for, whatever his sexual preference, he was, on the whole, a good manager.

On returning to work on Monday, I went straight to his office. The morning's *Straits Times* carried details of the gruesome murders that had taken place in East Coast Park. The photographs of Vanita and the murdered couple, a man called Tay Lip Bin and his fiancée Esther Wong, contained in their identity cards, had been blown up and adorned the front page. The report included the fact that the girl Vanita Sundram had a male companion who had been detained for questioning but had been subsequently released. Everyone at Nats would guess who this was and I would face a barrage of questions, condolences, warnings and large doses of advice I did not need. I felt that Symons, being the good manager he was, would tell me how to deal with the situation.

He was studying the *Straits Times* when I entered his office. He folded this neatly and placed it under a paperweight before looking up at me. His face was expressionless.

"I knew something like this would happen. I had a feeling. As you people say these days, I had bad vibes about that girl."

"I don't understand. You felt that Vanita would be murdered?"

"Oh, I didn't know she would be murdered. I simply had an uneasy feeling about her. There was an aura of violence about that girl. I did my best to tell you that but you simply didn't want to know." He smiled, reached across the table and put his hand over mine. "I supposed it would take you time to realise what you really are. I can assure you that, the world being as it is, it takes the likes of us a while to know our true natures. There is nothing wrong with experimenting a bit, I suppose, and I'm sure you've now come to your senses."

I was genuinely puzzled. "I don't get what you're talking about?"

"About you, and what you really are, HK." However much I protested, I couldn't stop Symons from calling me by my initials.

"Me?"

"Yes, HK, you. You're one of us, no matter how hard you try to deny it, no matter how much you try to make it on the other side. I knew this as soon as I set eyes on you years ago, just as I knew that you would take time accepting your real self." He smiled beatifically and squeezed my hand. "The girl's death was a blessing, an undisguised blessing. You are free, HK, and your eyes have been opened."

"You pitiable old pervert," I shouted. "What makes you imagine that, even if I was as bent as a hairpin, I would think of going with an old fart like you?" I pulled my chair back so I was out of his reach. I was revolted at the thought of being touched by the man, even in friendliness. What had happened nine years ago came to mind and the memory was so fresh that I could smell semen on draughtsman's paper. "I came to tell you, Symons, that the girl I love, that I was about to marry, has been murdered. I wanted your sympathy, your advice on what I should do to make things easier at the office, and you grab the opportunity to make a pass at me." I stood up. "I'd better get out before I throw up."

"Think carefully on what I have said then. . ."

I stomped out of the room and slammed the door behind me.

Just outside Symons' room was the staff toilet. I locked myself in one of the cubicles and sat on a seat. My face was hot and my heart pounded uncomfortably. I felt strangely guilty, wondered why I had been so accommodating to Symons at our first meeting, why I had not responded to his advances with anger the way a normal man would. I couldn't understand why I had been playful, almost coquettish, toward the ghastly man these past nine years. Then, in the silence of the staff toilet, I thought I began to see what Symons had been getting at.

I had read in one of Ma's women's magazines of homosexuals who denied their true nature. "Closet gays", the writer had called them. These unfortunates had, in their need to prove their maleness, even married and had children only to discover tragically and too late what they really were.

I had been disgusted by the episode with Symons, but initial revulsion was, the writer of the article maintained, a common feature of the closet gay syndrome. Even my attraction to Vanita pointed towards it. Closet gays were occasionally attracted to women. These women tended to be large, hairy and smelled like men. Vanita was all of this while I was hairless and delicate, attractive to my own sex. Could our relationship have been more than the simple attraction of opposites?

I had just about persuaded myself that I was homosexual when someone entered the cubicle beside mine. The bottom half of the wall separating us was cut away and I could see the man's feet pointing towards the bowl. I waited but there was no splash of urine. Then I heard the rhythmic whispering of flesh rubbing on flesh. The man was masturbating. To my horror I found that I was terribly excited, waiting, all attention, for the slapping noises that would precede his climax. I was indeed gay, for who but a homosexual would be turned on by the thought of a man masturbating. I might as well admit this to myself and, for that matter, to Symons.

Something stopped me from doing so. Something that gave me great relief. My being homosexual did not somehow fit into the way that the world was shaped for me. What was an even greater relief was that, with my excitement running high, it was Vanita that I thought of, not the man masturbating on the other side of the wall. I needed to sink my face into her breasts, find release in her body.

I closed my eyes. Suddenly I felt her in the cubicle. I kept my eyes closed and breathed in deeply. Over the deodorants and disinfectants I could smell her smell. She was alive and well and with me. It had all been part of a nightmare. The blood, the policemen, D'Cruz, the room marked SIR.

I stood up and reached out for her. My arms passed through empty air. I opened my eyes. I was alone, foolishly waving my arms about in a toilet cubicle. Then, and I think really for the first time, a deep sense of loss struck me. I began to cry, at first tentatively then in uncontrollable sobs. Finally I gave up all restraint and howled. When I calmed down, I washed my face and ran a comb through my hair. I was ready to face the rest of the staff at Nats.

Like many modern offices, mine is a small glass box. To secure some kind of privacy, I had plastered the walls with large calendars and posters. As soon as I got in, I took off my joggers and slipped on light rubber boots. I was buttoning the white doctor's coat that I use at work when Loong entered.

Loong's full name is Loong Wan Suay but I have never heard anyone call him anything but Loong. Even his wife, a spindly creature with pimples and hairy legs, calls him by his surname. I guess this is because they are a traditional Chinese couple. Traditional Chinese couples are allowed to ignore or insult each other in public, but any display of intimacy or demonstration of affection is proscribed. Adhering to such a tradition makes it possible for them to see the red and dark skinned devils who publicly kiss and cuddle as separate from themselves. It also serves to keep them distant from each other which Oscar said was *the* essential requirement for preserving racial unity.

Loong, an energetic man with brisk movements, spoke in clipped sentences which resembled the spiky hair that stood to attention on his head. His short arms were muscular and, from rough skin, strong black hairs sprouted. Some people considered him handsome. I didn't. I hated the man. He was my immediate boss and, what was worse, had been Vanita's lover immediately before me.

"Very sad, Miss Sundram's death," he said. "But must not be allowed to affect smooth running of office."

"I'll do my best," I replied, picking up the schedule on my desk.

He held up a hand. "Routine jobs later," he snapped.

"Problem has risen in meat preparation area. One sluice blocked and whole zone in danger of contamination."

Contamination is a word that galvanised the normally lackadaisical staff at Nats. If airline passengers complained of upset stomachs, and if this could be in any way attributed to the food originating in our kitchens, Nats would lose a contract. A lost contract would automatically lead to a decrease in our annual bonus.

I finished buttoning my white overall and said, "I'll look into it right away."

"Wait," he said, touching my sleeve. "Were you the man papers say was with Miss . . . , with Vanita when she was killed?"

"Yes," I replied, brushing away his hand.

"What you say to police? What did police do after girl die?"

Loong wasn't the kind of person to be particularly concerned about police brutality. But he wasn't the kind of man who indulged in idle curiosity either. He was threatened in some way by Vanita's death and afraid as to what I had revealed to the police. I decided to play on his fear.

"I told the police whatever I knew about Vanita."

"You knew about me . . . and the Sundram girl, yes?"

I had for something like a year tried to get used to the idea of Loong and Vanita being lovers but the thought still caused me pain. "Yes . . . Vanita told me."

"And you told police, no?"

I hesitated. I did not think that the affair had anything to do with the murder. It had, after all, been over for a year. But I disliked the man sufficiently to want to keep him on tenterhooks. "I talked a lot. I don't remember exactly what I told the police." I paused. "Anyway, you have nothing to be worried about. Whatever went on between you and Vanita was over a year ago, wasn't it?"

He hung his head then looked at me over the side of his shoulder. "No action going on for a long time but my wife, Mrs Loong, know nothing about happenings in office." A prim smile touched his face. "I am traditional Chinese, Menon. I don't bring dirt from outside into family home."

I had an enormous urge to hit the man. I didn't. Loong was expert in various martial arts and was forever holding forth on the merits of taekwando over karate or vice versa. Remembering this made my impulse to violence easier to control. I swallowed a few times then asked, "Did your wife not guess what was going on?"

"Mrs Loong no waste time guessing. I, head of household, make sure that wife no lose face. Harmony of home is preserved. Face and harmony are most important factors in Chinese family life." He allowed himself a little smile. "You English-educated say, what? 'Ignorance is bliss', yes?"

"So you are quite happy to deceive her?"

"You look like Chinese, Menon, but you not Chinese, so you not understand."

"What don't I understand, Loong?"

"Concept of face, Menon. Need for maintaining appearances and propriety." He smiled. Nostrils flared, eyes half-closed in disdain. "You just like Sundram girl. Talk too much. She open mouth wide like she open everything. Sometime I worry Mrs Loong finding out, sometime . . ."

A thought struck me. "What would happen if Mrs Loong did find out about you and Vanita?"

"Oh, disgrace. Loss of family honour. Sure divorce. Maybe suicide even. Future prospects of children all lost."

I remembered Loong's two sons. Ugly like their mother and, judging by their behaviour at staff parties, horrors in every sense of the word. Like most such children, they had the unconditional affection of their parents.

"So Mrs Loong didn't know anything about the affair?"

He shook his head. "No. Nor about other matters connected with Sundram girl."

"Other matters?"

He looked at me suspiciously. "You not listen to office chitchat?"

I shrugged. "Sometimes. Sometimes I let it go in one ear . . ."

"I arrange for Miss Sundram to do continuous night shift two years ago. This give her night allowance and two days off per week."

"Why on earth should Vanita want to work . . . ?" I knew the answer before I completed my question. Working nights meant that she was free to spend her afternoons with Loong who, I was sure, would be hard pressed to find reasons to leave honourable family home after dark.

I bit my lip and swallowed hard. At some time I would have to find a way of coming to terms with these ugly memories: memories of Vanita with Loong, of her with lovers before him. I would have to be able to look at them without balking. To rid them of their sting, I would have to incorporate them into the way I saw the world.

This, however, was not the time for that kind of an exercise.

There was something that Loong had said, a word he had used which didn't seem quite right. It took me several moments to realise what this was.

Loong had mentioned "other matters" connected with the "Sundram girl" but had only mentioned one.

"So getting Vanita to work a continuous night shift was not the only thing you arranged for her?"

The supervisor's manner changed abruptly. "No time for wasting any more," he snapped. "Problem has arisen in meat preparation area. Health inspector must inspect urgently and take necessary action to rectify situation." He bustled out of the room.

Nothing seemed to have changed in the packaging hall where meals were put together. The women, called "preset girls" irrespective of their age, sat close together in neat rows and placed items of food into preset compartments of the plastic trays that moved on belts in front of them. Vanita had been a preset girl. Like them she had worn a long-sleeved, white coat over her dress and enclosed her hair in a paper cap to protect the food from contamination. I shuddered when I noticed the outsize plastic gloves the girls had on.

I rushed through the packaging hall and into the smaller room where meat was prepared. I hoped to God that Mary would not be on duty that morning.

She was.

Mary Magdalene Lourdes was a tall girl with poppy eyes and pimples. She managed to be ill-proportioned without being fat or thin. This was obvious even though she had on her standard white coat. The fact that she was unattractive did not stop Mary from behaving as though she was forever in a beauty contest. She preened herself whenever she passed a reflecting surface, pirouetted rather than walked across a room and was constantly shooting glances at men who, in her eyes, were the judges of the contest in which she was unendingly engaged.

Mary was ostentatiously religious, attending mass every day and twice on certain saints' days. There is no contradiction between religiosity and vanity. They may, in fact, be part of the same phenomenon.

I once heard Mary telling one of the preset girls, "God wants us to look after our appearance just as He wants us to stay pure down below for as long as possible."

None of us guessed how serious she was about the last part of her statement till she married Dominic Jeyaraj, a timid-looking boy whom Loong put in the meat preparation section the day he joined Nats. He was, by virtue of the fact that he was Tamil and a Catholic, regarded by Mary as a suitable husband. That he looked innocent and seemed of an undemanding disposition increased his desirability.

Within a week she had announced their engagement. They were married in a grand church ceremony two months later. Office gossip had it that the marriage was unconsummated. The chaste way in which they held hands at work, called each other "dearest" in public, and the look of increasing tension on Dom's face, suggested that the gossip was correct.

All doubt was removed when Dom ran away with a pretty preset girl called Mee Li.

Mary Magdalene Lourdes announced, as soon as her husband's defection became known, that she had kept herself pure till she was sure of the sort of man Dom really was. She did not see that this was exactly what had caused him to leave her. Quite the contrary. She maintained that Dom's behaviour vindicated her unwillingness to consummate the marriage.

"He was only interested in one thing, and thank God I didn't give it to him. I can still give my purity to a better man."

Unfortunately, I was the better man she had in mind and she repeatedly informed me that ". . . nothing has been touched in my body and you will find me exactly as God made me."

When Vanita came into the picture, Mary's advances became less obvious but only slightly less so.

When I entered the meat preparation room that morning, Mary was sticking a skewer into a chunk of partly cooked meat. She withdrew the metal after a few seconds, smelled it and placed it against her tongue.

"Not quite fresh though the cooking temperature seems right." She put down the skewer, brushed her hair with the back of her hand and looked at me, her head at an angle.

"Loong tells me that you have a problem here, Mary."

She nodded and indicated the corner of the room where water was beginning to pool.

"A blocked sluice. Have you called plumbing?"

She laughed and said, "Look more closely, How Kum."

I did and saw that the grilled outlet of the sluice had been stuffed with toilet paper.

"You did that, Mary?"

"Yes."

"Why?"

"To get you over here. We can see more of each other now that the Jezebel is out of the way."

She stuck the skewer into the chunk of meat and began twisting it around. "I read the papers this morning and was glad." She looked heavenwards. "Forgive me, oh Lord." Then she smiled to herself. "I wonder who the man was. The man the papers said she was with when she was struck down in the act of fornication?" She shot me a cunning look. "How Kum, it was you?"

In my better moments I would have appreciated the pun, unintentional though it was, but now it hardly registered. "I know, I know. She took you to East Coast Park? To the grassy patch by the tree beside the jogging track?"

"How do you know where Vanita went with me? How do you know the exact spot?"

"Detective work." She touched her nose. "I followed her a few times. She went there with everybody, you know. Not just you." Her mouth twisted bitterly.

I felt a stab of pain at the thought of Vanita spending

nights in East Coast Park with others; spending nights in the place from which we listened to the sea, heard songs from a distant world and watched the moon rise.

I asked, "She went there with the supervisor, with Loong?"

Mary grinned. "No, not with Loong. With him she went to the Meridien. The one in Changi, just ten minutes away from Nats. That's where she and the Chinaman spent their afternoons." She picked up a knife and began cutting the piece of meat before her into tiny squares.

"How do you know all this?"

"I know because I followed the bitch once or twice . . . when she was on the path of sinfulness. Followed her to find out what she was up to."

"Why?"

Mary began fragmenting the squares of meat with her hands. "I followed her because I could see that she was after my Dom. I wanted to know where she went so I would know where to find her if she disappeared with him."

"But Dom wasn't interested in Vanita. He ran away with Mee Li."

"But it was the Jezebel who put impure thoughts into his head. It was she who made him so difficult to control when I told him that he would have to wait till I was sure that God wanted us to do it before I'd let him." She dusted crumbs of meat from her palms. "Oh, yes. I'm not blind. I saw everything that she was up to. The bitch used to look at him in that funny way. Up and down she would look at him. Up and down so he knew what was going through her head." She nodded. "Yes. I'm sure that it was she who started him thinking bad thoughts. Once a man starts thinking dirty thoughts, there is nothing to stop him looking for ways to make them come true. It is in man's nature." She uplifted her eyes. "From the time he ate the apple. And once he starts thinking that way, he will find the girl who will give him what he wants. Girls like that Mee Li who ran away with Dom and is giving it to him even though they are not married."

She brushed the scraps of meat on to the floor. "Yes. If not for that bitch, my Dom would have been happy to wait till God told me I was ready." Her manner brightened. "But I'm not worried. I tell myself that God takes care of things for me. I think it was His way of getting you and me together. Dom running away and the Jezebel getting killed. How Kum, He has kept me pure for you."

I ignored the pun like I did her outstretched hand and said, "I must get on with my work, Mary, and report to Loong that the sluice has been fixed."

My main function in Nats was to make sure that the food we supplied to aircraft was germ-free. A good part of my day was spent walking between the rows of preset girls, making sure that they followed exactly the rules prescribed for putting together the food trays, seeing that the air-vents were functioning and that the temperature in the room was right for the packaging of food. As I walked around, Vanita's voice talked to me. It complained of how unfairly her memory was being treated. Told me why each of the people I had spoken to had reason to dislike her.

". . . that fairy Symons wanted you to be in his pants instead of mine."

". . . and Loong. The last of the Ching-Chong Chinamen, with their upside down values. Liked to stick it here and there but 'wife's face must be preserved'. Sure I'd tell that dried-up prune what went on in the Meridien Hotel in the afternoons. Tell her how her man liked it and what she had to do to keep him in 'honourable family home'. I could tell her but it wouldn't do any good. She couldn't do it any other way than on her back with her legs slightly

parted and her head turned to one side. And as for exposing Loong . . . , what fun would I get out of that?"

". . . and the Virgin Mary Lourdes. Oh-ho, that one
really wanted you. She looked at your thin, clean body
and thought that you wouldn't make dirty sexual
demands. If only she knew what you could get up to once
you were under way."

Vanita continued to talk to me as I sat at my desk and
sifted through the various items on it. I found the desire
to talk back almost uncontrollable and struggled to prevent myself from speaking aloud.

I was about to go on a further round of inspecting
the food preparation area when the phone rang. It was
Inspector D'Cruz.

"I'd like to meet you to discuss a few things."

"Is this a request or is this something that I have to
do?"

"We have no evidence against you, nor do I think you
are withholding information from the police. I am asking
a favour . . ."

"Forget it, D'Cruz. I don't want to see you ever again
or to be reminded of what you have done to me. Goodbye."

Before I could hang up he shouted, "Menon. There's
things I know about this business that you should know."

I put the receiver back to my ear. "What things, and
why are they so important to me?"

I wanted to hear him say that the person who had
killed Vanita had been found. I wanted that more than
anything in the world. It wasn't that I wished to see the
killer hang. I was not out for revenge. I needed to know
the killer's identity for a different reason.

Vanita had been someone I had searched for. When I
finally found her, she had not simply become a part of
my life. She was an integral part of the scheme of things.

It would be impossible to reconstitute my life if I didn't know who killed her . . . and why.

I altered the tone of my voice and asked, "Have you discovered who the killer is?"

"Not yet, Menon, but I will." He paused. "What I wanted to talk about is something a little different," he said before asking, "do you feel that the dead girl is still with you, talking to you, following you around?"

Vanita's presence became stronger than ever. Her ghost was sitting on my desk and jumped off it to get closer to the phone. I felt the air move as it did.

"Well, sometimes," I admitted. The ghost nodded vigorously. "I must say I find it difficult to think of her as dead."

"She won't die, Menon. Not till we catch her murderer and hang the bastard. I know about these things, Menon. Believe you me, I know about them."

I remembered Jafri telling me about D'Cruz's sister who had been raped and murdered. I asked, "What exactly do you want to chat about, D'Cruz?"

"I need to talk with someone who knows the whole cast: the dead girl, her friends, enemies, family. Someone who was in touch with the whole goddamned shooting match."

"What makes you so sure that I didn't kill Vanita as well as Esther Wong and her boyfriend?"

He laughed. Knew I had taken the bait. "I know that you have doubts about this whole affair, Menon. Doubts so great that you sometimes aren't sure if your arse is following behind you. You see me today and maybe I'll be able to sort some of them out for you."

There are times in my life when I see things coming together, when the picture begins to make sense. Usually it is when the last few pieces begin to fall into place, only rarely when the first two pieces of the jigsaw fit. I knew, however, that I was now on the edge of a design.

D'Cruz and I were so different. Opposites, natural enemies. It was impossible to make sense of us being friends, working together, unless at some point we could be of service to each other, some point at which the circumstances of Vanita's death would lead to the resolution of problems the inspector faced.

It was clear from what Jafri had said that the inspector was the person who was most qualified to solve Vanita's murder. But, for the pattern to be complete, I would, in turn, have to do something for him. I couldn't, for the life of me, imagine what this could be. I was not unduly bothered about it, however. I only had to wait and I would tell moonrise from sunset.

"Where shall we meet?"

"In the big coffee-shop in Katong near the Eastshore Hospital. You know the place?"

It was funny that he should choose a rendezvous so close to where the murder had taken place, so near to where Vanita was going to live when we were married. I paused to listen to the goings-on in my head. I was aware that somewhere ahead of me fragments were falling into place. I didn't as yet know what these were or how they would affect my life. But I would.

"I know the coffee-shop," I said. "At what time?"

"About five-thirty," he said, and added as an afterthought, "There are things I will tell you which I want you to be tight-arsed about, Menon."

"Meaning you're going to reveal high-tech police investigation techniques? I already know a lot about them, Inspector."

"Meaning I want it to be just you and me at this meeting."

I remembered the inspector's piggy eyes, the oily skin, the room marked SIR. My confidence that the policeman and I were both part of a design disappeared. "I never

want to be alone with you, D'Cruz. If we are to meet at
all, I'll come with a friend. My lawyer."

"Who? al-Misris?"

I uh-ed into the mouthpiece and he said, "Good. I like
old Jafri. We worked together for a bit when he was in
the DPP's office. He's a good guy. Not like some of the
other blokes there whose eyes are so fixed on promotion
that they wouldn't recognise the truth if it jumped up
and licked their arseholes."

I called Jafri as soon as he hung up. He seemed only
too happy to help, thought it was a good idea for me
to be involved in the investigation. Vanita's ghost, too,
approved.

FIVE

I got to the coffee-shop well before five-thirty. I was glad I was early.

I had been in the office all day. A stroll, I felt, would do me good. It would let me brood about Vanita's murder and think about my relationship with D'Cruz. It was just yesterday that the man was beating the shit out of me. The memory of that had to be removed, ugly pictures washed clean away. It needed something as big as the swing of the sea to do this: something that would rise, wash away the debris, smooth the sand. I would have to feel the tide, float naked in it, be washed in the current of events, as yet unknown, that was to carry the inspector and me towards a common destination. That was the only way I had of getting reconciled to what D'Cruz had done to me. That was the only way I had of capitalising on the unlikely conjunction of events that had brought us together.

It would be easy enough to persuade myself of this. I believed that contrariness is what design and purpose are about. If this were not the case, what would be so wonderful about a tree that opposed gravity to reach for the sun, a salmon swimming upstream to spawn in its birthplace, people smiling at each other instead of snarling, making love when it would be more rewarding to make war?

I began walking around. But, instead of dwelling on the connection between the policeman and myself, I looked around me and began thinking of other things.

Joo Chiat is older than the rest of Katong. Here roads are narrow and winding. Houses are still made of wood and have swing-doors and verandahs. In Joo Chiat one could still find grandparents minding babies, women gossiping behind fences, children playing games of their invention in lanes in which it was still safe to do so.

Vanita's ghost joined me, its presence strong. So strong that once I reached out for her hand. I felt silly grabbing empty air and looked around me. No one noticed. On the verandahs overlooking the lane, the old dandled babies, housewives continued to gossip behind fences. I was glad. There were, perhaps, things which would never change. They would be my signposts, the marker-buoys around which a new course could be charted after the storm. I made my way back to the coffee-shop and D'Cruz.

The inspector had a glass of beer in front of him. The bottle from which it had come was empty. He too had been early. D'Cruz was relaxed. Even likeable now. Perhaps it was the atmosphere of the coffee-shop. Downmarket and friendly: humanised by the smell of food, sweat and cigarette-smoke. Perhaps it was the mood into which I had worked myself.

Jafri arrived the moment I did. We both ordered Cokes.

D'Cruz lit a cigarette, looked at Jafri over a cloud of smoke, and said, "Will I be doing the talking or will you?"

"You start, Ozzie. Begin, perhaps, by telling us how far you have got with the investigation." His voice was firm as always. And comforting.

"I'll do my best," the inspector replied. "For starters I'll tell you about the other couple who, at the moment, are just a thorn up my arse."

"Are you telling us that the two crimes are not connected?"

"Except that the same fucking weapon was used in both."

The hair on my neck began to bristle. Bits and pieces were coming together in my head. But the pattern was unacceptable, ugly in the extreme. I asked, "And what was this weapon?"

"A common kitchen knife. The kind housewives use. In this case it was Prestige brand, stainless steel, made in Sheffield, England. The kind that my mother, God rest her soul, used to swear by."

And mine still does, I thought, rubbing my neck against my collar to reduce the tickle of hairs standing on end.

"And I understand from How Kum that the murder weapon has been found. You confirm this, Ozzie?"

"I sure can. In a garbage-bin near the spot where Tay Lip Bin and his fiancée, Esther Wong, found the Everlasting together. Believe you me, this Esther was sure one overheated lady."

Jafri smiled. "I am certain you can justify that statement, Ozzie."

"Sure as hell, I can," the policeman retorted, drawing on his cigarette. "On the surface, our Miss Wong was a fire-breathing Christian Evangelist. But only on the surface." He paused.

"Go on, Ozzie," said Jafri, the slightest impatience detectable in his voice.

"I'll start with the good lady's blood group." He nodded, pleased by the surprise on our faces. "Her blood type was B, rhesus positive. This is the commonest blood group found in Singapore. Her fiancé, the unfortunate Tay Lip Bin, also belonged to this blood group. The semen found in her vagina, however, came from a man who had type A rhesus positive blood."

"So it wasn't the fiancé's semen," I said, my voice rising.

"Good sir," said the inspector turning on me, "one is humbled by your deductive genius." He applauded silently. "The semen certainly didn't come from the fiancé, but where the cum came from we may never know. And there is more." He sipped his beer. "The good revivalist lady was four months pregnant. . . ."

"Well, she was engaged. . ." I began.

"Too true. And, pregnancy is hunky-dory if not mandatory in the about-to-be-married in the mind-boggling horseshit that passes for morality today. Yes, all would be fine except for one thing. The baby Esther was carrying was blood type O. So it couldn't have belonged either to the fiancé or to the bloke who had just screwed her. Our pathologist tells me that there were more blood groups floating around in our Esther than you would find in a middle-sized blood-bank."

I wanted to throw back my head and clap my hands. Laugh, not with amusement but with relief. There would be no need to rearrange my life. No need to start piecing together a fresh design. I was not obliged to find Vanita's murderer, not obliged to understand how her killing fitted into the scheme of things. She had been a victim in a shootout, a casualty in a blood-bath brought about by the promiscuous Esther. If one is hit by a meteorite, there is no compulsion to believe that God threw it.

"So you think the killings came about as a result of this Esther Wong's complex sex life," I said.

"Not for a moment. In fact, I wouldn't bet a prawn's headshit on it."

I was silent, relief wiped out.

Jafri spoke. "Let me get this straight, Ozzie. You tell us that this Esther person spread her favours around a bit. That she was engaged to be married, was pregnant by someone other than her fiancé and that she had had sexual relations with some third person not long before she was killed. Despite this complex and, might I say, unsavoury sexual scenario you have painted, you do not believe that Esther was the murderer's prime target.

What, may I ask, makes you so sure that this woman, with her devious sexual arrangements, was not the murderer's prime object? And why are you so confident that How Kum's Vanita was not killed simply to confuse us as to what the motive for these murders truly was?"

Thank God for Jafri, I thought.

D'Cruz said, "I don't think Esther or Lip Bin were the object of the exercise. They were killed *after* Vanita Sundram." Our faces must have told him that this emphasis on something that was so obvious impressed neither Jafri nor me and he explained. "No murderer, however dimwitted, kills the decoy first then the person he is really after. That would be putting the fart before the arse." He laughed.

Neither Jafri nor I joined him and he went on. "Let us start by assuming that there is a motive for the killings. In ninety-nine out of a hundred cases, murder is not a mindless business but has a definite purpose.

"We have been able to establish no connection between Miss Sundram and the engaged couple. It is therefore safe to conclude that the bloke was either after the Sundram girl or the couple. He could have been just after either Esther or Lip Bin but, when it came to it, had to kill both. In that case, as I have said, Esther and boyfriend would have been killed first.

"Most murders are purposeful acts and murderers tend to be economical in their killing. They might, if they have to kill again and again, become indiscriminate. That's usually because they have panicked. When this happens, we have the phenomenon of the mad dog, who kills for the slightest of reasons: fear of discovery, the belief that another murder would throw the police off his trail and, sometimes, just to prove to himself how powerful he is. When he reaches this point, I think, a murderer has some inner need to kill and finds all sorts of reasons for doing so."

I knew nothing about the minds of murderers. But what D'Cruz said made sense. Yet I found myself saying, "It still seems to me that, with a person like this Esther, things like jealousy, revenge. . ."

"Listen – you," snapped D'Cruz. "I know that, more than you want God doling justice from on high, you wish your girlie's death to be some kind of accident. Then you can let it go. No need for looking into the killer's motive, no need to try to understand how someone could hate her enough to want to kill her, no need to make big changes in your life."

I was impressed by his intuition; even more by the fact that our minds seemed to be following the same path.

D'Cruz looked at my face and his voice softened. "There is one other thing which you had better get used to from the start. We uncover worms as fat as turds whenever we investigate the life of a murder victim. They need not have to be people like the evangelist with the flying twat. It would happen if the Pope got snuffed.

"We may be a bunch of ruffians, we policemen, but if we understand one thing it's this: the dead are defenceless and we are careful with what we find out, and we go out of our way to protect the memories of murder victims." His voice became hard again. "But we are not so considerate that we don't dig for the facts nor do we operate any kind of cover-up if the evidence we uncover offends this or that person." His eyes locked on to mine.

Jafri intervened. "Let us assume that you are right. That Vanita was the killer's primary target. . ." A thought struck him. "Why could How Kum not have been the one he was after? The girl was lying over him so he kills her, and . . ."

". . . with her out of the way, he gets bored with the

whole business and pushes off to kill two people in another part of the park."

Jafri laughed. I did too, but a thought bothered me. "What makes you so sure that I am not the killer?"

D'Cruz looked deliberately mysterious. "My nose, twenty-five years experience on the Force, knowing that half-breeds like you don't kill on the nights of the full moon... You can't get out of what you have to do that way, my friend. But, if you want facts, I'll tell you the facts. The kind of facts policemen are supposed to dish out all the time.

"Forensics are, for once, prepared to put their money where their mouth is and give us, to a matter of minutes, the times at which your lady and the loving couple were killed. We also know the time at which your call came in and the exact location of the box from which it was made. It would have been impossible for you to have killed your girlfriend, run four kilometres across the park, killed Esther and fiancé and then, in the time available, got back to the box from which you made your phone-call.

"As we say in criminological jargon, 'no washee, no wipee'. So you can cut out all this self-doubt horseshit." His voice had become nasty and shrill. It changed slightly when he added, "I understand quite well, big fella. You're lost without this girl and all these bloody self-doubts that you keep coming back to are ways to hide from yourself what you are missing terribly. You are fooling yourself if you think that, if you pretend hard enough you won't have to do something positive: like helping find out who killed the lady." Then his manner became confidential, almost gentle. "I know young people today think that it's not cool to be inexperienced but I suspect, my friend, that the dead girl was your first woman. Right?" He looked at me, got his answer from my face and continued. "First for you, but I guess you know that she's been around a bit?"

I nodded. "How did you find out all this?"

"My nose and from the autopsy, fella. Forensics tell me that she's been pregnant but never had a baby. Ditto she's had an abortion. And you, my friend, seem, especially on second inspection, to be the kind of bloke who'd marry a girl rather than put her through the horrors of getting a pregnancy terminated."

Jafri laughed. "I'll say this for you, Oswald D'Cruz. You've got the facts and the psychoanalysis is dead right. But where is all this taking us in terms of solving these crimes?"

"As I see it Jaf, we have two scenarios. Both bad. Scenario one: we are dealing with a nut case. A crazy killer like Son of Sam or the Boston Strangler. With that kind of situation there's no way of knowing where to start. I have no great experience with this sort of thing, but I am told that this kind of killer can kill just once or again and again.

"The trouble is, as with most of these psycho things, no one knows why he kills. Often we don't even know if we are dealing with one person or a casebook of crazies. Even worse than the killers are the so-called psycho-detectives who claim to understand their minds. They're the kind of con-men who would make you rush to consult the nearest calendar if they told you what day of the week it was."

He drew on his cigarette. "Scenario two: we have a really clever killer. One who has thought the whole thing through, knows what he's after and is trying to bury his real objective under a mountain of murders. This man . . . , person, realises that, as far as the police are concerned, all murders are of equal importance. That is to say, we are obliged to investigate each and every one down to the last detail. This not only means a helluva lot of work, it also means that we could get snowed under with information that public-spirited people send us. We could get a pile of shit so high we don't know where the stink is coming from."

Jafri interrupted the inspector's musings. "How do you plan to go about things, Ozzie?"

"First, we follow my policeman's nose." He put a finger on the organ in question. "This tells me that Vanita Sundram was the one the murderer was after. Then we ask ourselves who wants the girl dead and why. To answer these questions we need to have someone on the inside. We need someone who not only knows the girl but also knew the people around her. We need someone like our friend here." He poked me in the chest.

"I think," said Jafri, his voice even more controlled than ever, "that you two didn't," he raised his eyebrows, "hit it off the first time round." D'Cruz choked on his cigarette and coughed violently. I shot Jafri a hurt look. "I am happy to help sort things out between you two and I am in an ideal position to do so. I have worked with you, Ozzie, for several years, and I know How Kum as well as I know anybody. What happened is over and done with and I am sure that How Kum is quite happy, now that the situation has been clarified, to . . . ," he stopped to smile at what he had called the most preposterous expression in the world, "to help the police with their inquiries."

"OK big guy," said the inspector, his fit of coughing over, "you tell me if you heard or saw anything that you think might have any bearing on the murders."

The noisy teenagers said nothing to me. Neither did the swinging of the ships at anchor, or the sounds that came to me from across the ocean. Apart from the moonrise, there was nothing that was alarming or terribly different. I recalled being surprised at Vanita's hurry to make love a second time, being more sleepy than usual when we were done. Much more sleepy. I remembered being awakened by Vanita making noises in the night and thinking that she needed me again.

"I thought I heard Vanita cry out in her sleep. I was more sleepy than usual. I didn't wake up to investigate. I thought they were just. . ."

"Dream comes I call them, but I am sure that sex manuals have discovered some highly technical explanation for what has been known from time immemorial." He grinned and punched me in the chest. "Not surprising that she should dream about you having seen the kind of equipment you pack. Not surprising at all."

I knew what the sounds were; the sounds I had heard and ignored on the night of the full moon. "I know what I heard, D'Cruz. I heard a cry of pain and was too sleepy . . . , didn't bother to investigate. The woman I loved was bleeding to death beside me and I did nothing."

The inspector's manner changed, became serious, bordered on the fatherly. He said, "I don't know how often you and your girlfriend actually spent nights together. I have been sleeping with my Philomena for nearly twenty-five years. Without thinking about it, I listen to her breathing and know she is there beside me. If for any reason this changes, if she stops breathing even for a moment, I am instantly awake."

How could I have forgotten the comfort of feeling her breathe as she slept beside me? I often woke a little before Vanita did and put my hand on her breast to enjoy the feel of it moving. Up down, up down, up down. I would catch a long nipple in my thumb and forefinger and watch it thin and lengthen as she breathed out, grow tight and squat as she inhaled. Sometimes I leaned my head against her nose to feel her breath whistling past my ear telling me that she was alive. Telling me that I was alive. How could I have been unaware of it stopping?

"I don't know what I'm going to do," I said. "I think of Vanita dying beside me in terrible pain and my sleeping on. I have horrible visions in my head. I can't see things clearly nor can I get rid of them."

"I guess I'd best tell everything," said D'Cruz. "You're smart enough to see through any lies I make up and, if I leave you guessing, you'll only imagine worse than actually happened."

Jafri nodded. "Tell How Kum all you know, Ozzie, and don't spare him the details forensics gave you."

"I won't," he said. "The autopsy report says the girl was stabbed just below the left shoulder blade. The knife passed into the left atrium . . ."

Jafri interrupted. "I am sure How Kum has forgotten the little biology he learnt at school, so it might be a good idea for you to explain the forensics as we go along."

"The atrium is the collecting chamber, where all the blood in the body winds up before it is pumped out again. It has no muscle in its wall to seal off any hole that is made in it. Bleeding from a wound in the atrium is massive and uncontrollable, so death is rapid. As near as one can get to immediate. I would say that your girlfriend cried out when the blow was struck, then she must have become unconscious very quickly from loss of blood." I thought of the blood-red moon, of clouds that looked like old bruises. Remembered feeling the wound on Vanita's back, realised that I had not looked at it, wondered if there was a bruise around it. I said, "Oh God. I really cannot forgive myself. I'm sure I could. . ."

"There was nothing you could have done, big fella. Nothing anybody could have done. Only a cardiac surgeon equipped with a portable heart-lung machine and surgical equipment could have saved her life and these are

difficult to find in East Coast Park at four in the morning."
His voice softened. "Listen, son. Die we all must and,
when we do, haemorrhaging from the heart is as nice a
way of going about it as any. There's no great pain and
you're unconscious before you know what's happening."

He stopped, poured himself more beer and lit another
cigarette.

Jafri wriggled around in his chair and fiddled with his
glass of Coke. We were silent: trapped in the moment of
Vanita's death, wondering about our own.

Jafri broke the spell. "Let me try and understand the
sequence of events you are postulating, Ozzie. Someone,
for reasons as yet unknown, wants the girl dead. This
person either follows How Kum and Vanita to the park
or knows exactly where they will spend the night. He
watches them make love and waits till they fall asleep.
It is dark, but somehow our murderer is able to confirm
that it is the girl who is on top and, though she is covered
by a sleeping-bag, stabs her accurately through the left
atrium so she bleeds quickly to death without disturbing
her lover." He drew a breath. "Surely we can do better
than that, Inspector D'Cruz."

"You're a defence lawyer, Jaf, and it is your job to make
policemen look like arseholes." He added bitterly, "Don't
have to work up a sweat to do that with the types coming
out of the Police Academy these days.

"But, I'll tell you why I think things happened the way
I say they did, and big guy here can tell us how right or
wrong my reconstruction is." He waved for more beer.

"First, it was the night of the full moon, and though
the moon was low when the girl was killed, visibility
wasn't bad, especially if one kept one's head at ground
level." He extended a finger. "Two. My policeman's nose
tells me that this is a carefully planned murder, not the
work of some loony driven wild by the full moon. True, it

looks like the work of a madman but that's because whoever's done it wants it to look that way. For my money,
our murderer has overplayed his hand a bit. There's too
much drama. It's too much like the work of a nutcase to
actually be the work of a nutcase.

"Let us accept, for a moment, that this murder was
committed by a rational person. This would mean that
the killer has probably been watching these two for some
time. He knew that they did things in just about the
same way whenever they spent an evening in the park."
He looked at me and raised an eyebrow.

I nodded. "We did things the way we enjoyed them.
Didn't change our routine much. . ."

He held up a hand. "That's all I was asking, son. Three.
Our killer didn't have to guess where the girl's back was.
She wasn't stabbed through the sleeping-bag at all. It
had slipped off her body and she had a naked back. . ."

"How on earth could you know that?" I remembered
the bag tangled at Vanita's feet as I tried to get out from
under her.

"As with most things in detection, it was obvious."
D'Cruz filled his glass. "There were no holes in the
sleeping-bag."

"Since How Kum has not raised any objections," Jafri
said, "I guess that's the way things could have happened."
He paused.

"But what about the other couple. Were they killed in
the way that Vanita was?"

"Give or take a few minor details. They were both fully
clothed. Perhaps they had no need to be otherwise for, as
I said, our Esther had had her pussy fed elsewhere. Also,
and for the aforesaid reason, they were not lying in each
other's arms. Both Esther and Lip Bin were stabbed in
the chest. I think the boyfriend may have tried to fight

or make a run for it for his body was found some distance from the girl's."

I knew what his answer would be, but still I asked, "And the same weapon was used in all three murders?"

The inspector's head snapped round. "I thought I told you earlier that it was a stainless steel kitchen knife and that this was recovered from a garbage-bin."

I should have told him, at that point, that a knife such as this was missing from Ma's kitchen. I didn't. Kitchen knives go missing often enough and Ma could not possibly have anything to do with the murders. "Yes, you did, but it slipped my mind." I picked up my Coke.

"If there is one thing I know about murders it is this: the first victim is the one the killer was really after. Subsequent murders are usually committed because the killer has reason to fear discovery, has panicked, or wants to throw up a smokescreen. Sometimes murderers go on a killing binge. We don't know why, but it serves to confuse the police." He laughed. "I know I said all this before, but our friend here," – he shot me a quizzical look – "seems to have developed some kind of a memory problem."

Jafri, who had been following the inspector closely, said, "Let us assume that you are correct, that these killings were not the work of a madman." He paused. "I am, mind you, not agreeing with you, but will, for the moment, view things the way you want us to. What do we do now?"

"We find out from big fella here who would want her dead." He looked at me expectantly.

This was a point in my relationship with the inspector that I had foreseen, feared. It was one of the myriad of binary branchings which can determine the course of events.

What he was asking was simple enough. It was a request for information: the kind of thing the police routinely required. My agreeing to provide it was a different matter. What I said could supply that tiny shaft that altered the balance of things, the shake of the kaleidoscope that changed the pattern forever.

In agreeing to investigate Vanita's death, I would find out more about her than I had known in life. I could uncover unspeakable details of her life, come upon questions that could hurt me terribly but could not be resolved with her dead. And I would have to share all that turned up with a man I had every reason to hate. I hesitated.

"I can't think of anyone who would really want to kill her," I said. "Vanita had, in many ways, a pretty unconventional lifestyle and she did rub it into the faces of those who hated the way she behaved." I thought of Mary Magdalene Lourdes, dismissed the notion that her disapproval was strong enough to lead to murder, wondered about Mrs Loong, who may have wanted revenge for her husband's infidelity. "Also, she may have hurt one or two people sufficiently for them to want revenge."

D'Cruz noticed me hesitate. "Balls," he said. "Revenge, disapproval and that kind of thing are only motives for murder in TV soaps. In the real world people kill for money. Especially in Singapore where they do everything for money. Tell me who stood to gain by her death or, better still, who stood to lose by her being alive.

"But tell it the way you see it. I want to see this case through your eyes." His face hardened. "Spare me the bull about you yourself being the killer. Things are complicated enough without that kind of horseshit." I looked doubtful as to where to begin and the inspector said, "Start with the folk in the office."

I began with Mary Lourdes, the least likely of my suspects. I told him of her religiosity, her disapproval of Vanita, of the advances she made to me. He pursed his lips, rocked his head about but said nothing.

Then I told him about Symons and the passes he had
made at me. I did not describe what had happened when
I first joined Nats but did admit that my manager's insist-
ence that I was homosexual made me have doubts about
my own inclinations.

What D'Cruz said wasn't reassuring. "Sometimes you
smile and toss your head in a way that makes you look
as gay as an arsehole with wings. Even I thought you
might be a fairy when we first met." He shrugged apologetically. "Anyway, tell me more about this faggot,
Symons."

"He must be about fifty, Eurasian, good-looking . . ."

"Is he a fem-type or is he a macho bum jumper?"

"I don't really know what you mean."

"Aw, come on, fella. Is he all mass, muscle and moustache or is he a pansy like you?"

I ignored the insinuation and said, "He's not thin but
he's not musclebound either. I don't see him as a physically strong person."

Jafri said, "I can't help noticing that you were not
interested in the girl Mary Lourdes, nor can I ignore the
fact that you seem suddenly fascinated by the muscular
development of potential suspects."

"You are indeed perceptive, my learned friend," said
D'Cruz bowing slightly. "Muscular development may be
of enormous relevance when we come to consider the
identity of our murderer. In the case of the Sundram girl,
the knife was slipped between the ribs. No great strength
was needed for this. Esther and Lip Bin, however, were
stabbed through the front of their chests, the blade cutting through ribs before it reached the heart. This
required the kind of strength that your Mary Lourdes
didn't have. Neither, from your description, does the fairy,
Symons, though I will look at him myself before I definitely make up my mind. What other offers do we have?"

I had kept him to the last. I hated him most. Wanted him to be guilty. The shapes moving around in my head told me I was wrong. I defied them, forced myself to think of him as the killer.

"There's a bloke in the office who is strong enough to have done the kind of killing you describe."

The inspector did not miss the change in my voice. "And you think or want to think that he is guilty."

"He's a shortish, muscular fellow who's a great one for his martial arts."

D'Cruz put down his cigarette, grasped my chin with his fingers and turned my face towards his. "Tell me, tell me eyeball to eyeball, why you so much want this man to be the killer?"

I told him about Loong's affair with Vanita, about the afternoons spent at the Changi Meridien, of how painful the knowledge had been to me. I told him of how the duty roster had been fixed so Vanita worked nights and was free in the afternoons. I described Mrs Loong, prudish and unattractive, and their obnoxious children. As methodically as I could, I built up a case against the supervisor. The more I forced the pieces together, the less convincing did the picture become. I had to wind up saying, "All in all, I don't think that he would murder to keep his affair from coming to light."

For a while the policeman was intent on his cigarette. Then he said, "I am never quite sure with the traditional Chinkos, big fella. They put a great premium on keeping up appearances, 'face', as they call it. They do the darndest things on the quiet but nothing is out in the open. I know a towkay who has a yen for fucking children. But this tycoon, as is not uncommon with such types, also donates vast sums to orphanages.

"You may see this as hypocritical. But not John China-man. He honestly sees it as having a private face and a public face. They are quite separate things to him and public face does not know about private face. But God help anyone who shits on his public face. And that is what your girlie may have been threatening go do."

I was not convinced. Vanita didn't die to protect some bigot's sense of respectability. The way I looked at the world would be meaningless if this was so. I could accept her being murdered by a madman. That would make it an accident. Part of the mindlessness that goes to make up so much of the universe. If her death was premeditated, if it was something that would in time become part of a pattern, there had to be better reasons for it than the ones I was offered.

So much did I want the supervisor to be guilty that I chose to ignore the voices in my head. I asked, "What are you going to do about Loong?" The inspector looked sharply at me and I rephrased my question. "What are you going to do about the two men, I mean?"

"Find out what our heroes were doing on the night of the murders." He laughed. "I don't go in much for alibis, though. In my experience a cast-iron alibi is almost proof of guilt. Who but a guilty person would go to the trouble of having one?" He shrugged. "My own feeling is that these two, with or without alibis, don't seem to have enough motive for the murders."

Jafri asked, "What happens when they turn out to be innocent, as I am certain they will be?"

"We look elsewhere," the policeman replied.

"Like where?" Jafri persisted.

D'Cruz looked at me. "Like who gains moneywise by the girl's death."

"I don't really know . . ." I began, not understanding till his next question the direction his interest was taking.

"What do you know about this Sundram family, big fella? I met the father and brother when they I-D'd the girl's body. I made the usual sympathetic noises and asked routine questions. Didn't get much out of them. Certainly didn't get a feel of things and they didn't do anything to offer me a backstage seat at the play."

I told him as much as I knew about the Sundrams.

Vanita's grandfather was a small time businessman who had migrated to Singapore from Sri Lanka before the second world war. He had in the fifties invested wisely in real estate. No one knew where his capital had come from. Gossip had it that he had been a spy for the *kempei-tai*, the Japanese secret police, and that he had been responsible for the torture and death of several Chinese businessmen whose fortunes had been confiscated and given him. Nothing, however, was proven and he was not involved in the War Crimes Tribunals held immediately after the war. I added that, even if the rumour was true, it could not have no bearing on his granddaughter's murder half a century later.

"I'm not sure about that," said D'Cruz.

I was puzzled. "I thought you said that revenge was not a good motive for murder."

"It is when money's been lost," he retorted. "But move on and tell me about the girl's father."

Vanita's father, K.S. Sundram, had been a minor official in the Ministry of Labour. Sundram was a man of the utmost respectability and was highly regarded in the Hindu community in Singapore. He was a prudent soul who saw to it that his inheritance grew in the sixties and seventies. He had retired from the Civil Service in the mid-eighties a wealthy man.

"What about his wife?" the inspector asked.

"She died when Vanita was five."

"And where's the old geezer been sticking it all this while?"

"Nowhere I know of. Sundram is very much into

religion and doesn't have mind for that sort of thing. He does a lot of work for the temple and various charity organisations."

"I'm not at all sure that stops a man from waving the wick. On the contrary. . ."

"If there had been anything like that, Vanita would not have hesitated to tell me about it. As I said, she was not a girl to hide things."

D'Cruz shrugged. "OK, tell me about this brother then."

Vanita's brother Mohan was a bit of a mystery. He was twelve years older than she and, though into his thirties, remained unmarried. He taught A-level physics at a government school but his driving passion was yoga. His speciality was hatha yoga which taught mastery over the body and its processes. He had, from time to time, tried to engage me in a discussion of what he called "true Hinduism" but I had never been sufficiently interested to find out what he meant by the term. Whatever else, his interest seemed to distance him from his family and Vanita did not look on him as close.

"What's the relationship between father and son?" D'Cruz snapped.

"Cool, at best," I replied. "The old man thinks of himself as being quite religious but Mohan feels that all the observances that Sundram puts himself through have nothing to do with the kernel of the religion. He once told me that his father 'lives on a diet of spiritual chaff, having thrown away the wheat'. The old man, for his part, has made it clear that all he wants from Mohan is for him to marry and settle down."

The inspector snorted and examined his cigarette. "What happens to the dough, when the old man unites with the Godhead or whatever Hindus do when they snuff it?"

"I'm not sure. Sundram loved Vanita above anything

else. If he was allowed his way, I think he would leave the money to her. I understand though that it is a custom, virtually unbreakable in the Hindu community, for the eldest son to inherit." I considered brother and sister as dispassionately as I could and added, "Vanita took life as it was. Mohan was happy to contemplate the Infinite and practise yoga. Neither seemed to have a great use for their father's money."

D'Cruz looked as though he very much doubted this but said nothing. A change had come over the policeman and he seemed to be in two minds about speaking. "There's something I gotta say, Menon. It'll tear me apart to get it out but get it out I will."

Jafri interrupted. "I called Ozzie after you phoned me. It seemed appropriate that you and he should straighten out the personal problems you had at the start of this investigation. I told Ozzie that you were an accommodating person with a forgiving disposition." He raised a hand before I could interrupt. "I also stressed that no one, however good-natured, could remain unaffected by the kind of treatment that you had been subjected to."

D'Cruz had screwed his eyes up tightly and bit his lip before speaking. "Jafri says that he told you something about Tessie. . ." His voice was strained, his face that of a child about to cry. I should have felt sorry for him. I didn't.

I remembered the knotted rope around my penis, the same rope crushing my ankle. My face still burned at the thought of bending over and letting a man shove a finger up my arse. "I don't care what the fuck made you do it, D'Cruz. You assaulted me, you humiliated me. I was innocent and you treated me like. . ."

Jafri cut in, holding together forces that tended to pull apart. "All you say is true, How Kum, and the inspector here is not going to deny it. It looks to me, however, that you two will have to see this thing through together and it might be a good idea for you to hear him out."

"Why?"

"Because I have worked with Ozzie for several years. I have no doubt that he is the best investigator we have on the force."

"I must solve this crime, Menon," said D'Cruz, in a voice that shook slightly. "I kicked off wrong, fucked up before I got properly started. Which is all the more reason why you must give me a chance to get things right and hang the bastard who did it."

"What does it matter to me whether or not Vanita's murderer is caught? Will hanging her killer bring her back to life? Will his dangling from a rope make it possible for me to make love to her one more time?"

I asked the questions but I knew I had to find out who her murderer was. I had waited all my life for Vanita. When she came I recognised in her the missing piece to a picture. Now she had been snatched away, there was again the incompleteness. I needed more images, more facts, more fancies, if I was to put together a new picture.

My face must have betrayed what was going on in my head for D'Cruz's voice had become a little more confident. "No, Menon. Nothing can bring her back. But unless we find out who and why, the girlie's ghost will never rest. I am sure you get the feeling that she is still with you. Talking to you, seeming to get into the action as though she were still alive."

He continued without acknowledging my nod. "It's that way with my Tessie, though fifteen years have passed since she was raped and murdered." He took a big sip of his beer and drew deeply on his cigarette. "She was my baby sister. Came to live with us when the old folks died. We can't have kids, me and the wife. We thought that God had sent us the child we couldn't have.

"Tessie was a happy little soul and popular with everybody. She sang, played the piano, made people laugh. Then, when she was sixteen, some animal raped and strangled her. The killer was never found. The Commissioner says that the case is closed. Thirty per cent of murder-rapes are unsolved, he tells me, so let the case rest. But the case stays open in my head. I think of the child's terror as the brute ripped his way into her. I think of her screams choked off as he strangled her, strangled her with her panties.

"That is not all. Sometimes I come home and find the old piano open and a note hanging in the air. You see, my friend, the poor child can't even die properly, because the bastard that killed her is still walking around."

He finished the beer in his glass and lit a cigarette from the stub of the old one. I looked into his face. Beer and cigarette smoke make the eyes water terribly.

The next two days were uneventful. In the office I worked at routine jobs with the zeal of a novice in a nunnery. As soon as I got home, I locked myself in my bedroom and stayed there for as long as possible. Ma controlled her urge to interfere. Even she guessed I needed time: to come to terms, to shuffle things about and make some kind of sense of what was happening.

Oscar understood and, I suspect, had much to do with Ma's restraint.

As though to confirm what D'Cruz had said, Vanita was always with me. Her presence was, at certain times, stronger than others, but she never quite went away. She followed me about and watched what I was doing. Like all ghosts she could read my thoughts, smiled when she did, but always silently. Only in the quiet of my room did she speak. That too only when the lights were out and darkness drew us together.

She told me things I didn't know or only half remembered. She spoke of her loneliness when her mother died, of the bond between her and the maid Leela who had become like a mother to her. She told me of her father and how he had come to dote on her. Confessed how much she feared this love that wanted to control everything she did, that wished to possess her completely and make her what she could never be: a traditional Indian daughter. She talked of Mohan too. This brother from whom she was separated by more than the differences in their ages.

Of the protectiveness he had offered, which she had at first accepted but later rejected. She told me of how Mohan had become more aloof and enigmatic over the years.

We talked in long silences. Had, usually, no need for words. Sometimes, when her presence became overpowering, I felt her weight on the bed, smelled her body. At such times I heard her voice, lilting, two-toned. Then it seemed right that I too should speak out. And when she made jokes, said outrageous things about people we knew, I laughed out loud.

I don't know if Vanita was influenced by what D'Cruz had said about his sister Tessie's singing but she often sang to me. Alive, she had done so. She sang in the afterglow of lovemaking or as we nursed desire and watched it grow till it could not be contained. They were strange songs, my Vanita sang. Long chants. Sequences that had no words but seemed to yearn for something beyond words.

Long, long ago I had asked her what these love-songs were about.

"They're not love-songs, dumbo. They're bajans, Hindu hymns."

"How come you know these bajans?"

"My father taught me them when I was a little girl."

"I hear sounds but I can't make out words. What do their words say?"

"How would I know what the words say, dumbo? They're in Sanskrit."

And so Monday passed.

Tuesday too went the same way.

I was content being with my dead love and, try as I might, I couldn't persuade myself that I needed more than a ghost for company. I realised that I hadn't yet talked to Vanita's father and Mohan. It was unforgivable not to have done so. Vanita had been killed early on Sunday morning. It was already Wednesday.

Nevertheless, as soon as I got home from work, I locked myself in my room and began communing, as I had come to think of it, with my dead love. I spent two hours in my room after getting home on Wednesday, then came out to join Ma and Oscar at dinner. Vanita had been pretty boisterous that day and had made many jokes.

Ma looked worried as I took my place at the table. "You feel all right, son?" she asked.

"I'm fine, Ma. Fine." Anxiety was her customary prelude to inquisition.

Oscar toyed with his glass, his face expressionless. "Sometimes the dead don't seem to want to go away. They don't even seem to be actually dead. Sometimes our minds seem to need more than proof to understand that they are really gone."

"What are you trying to tell me, Uncle Oscar?"

"That perhaps you should see someone who misses the girl as much as you do. . ."

"I'm OK. Actually. . ."

"Then why do you talk to yourself?" Ma asked. "And laugh like a madman when you are all alone?"

"Sorry, old chap." Oscar shook his head over his glass. "You were carrying on so loudly that we couldn't help overhearing. No intention of eavesdropping, mind you."

"To be honest, Uncle Oscar, I do feel Vanita's presence quite strongly and have been allowing myself to do so for the past few days. I don't want the situation I'm in to last forever so I have been toying with the idea of visiting her father and brother."

"A capital idea," said Oscar, finishing his brandy. "Propriety demands no less and it will get you out of yourself." He replenished his drink. "Cliché has it that a sorrow shared is a sorrow halved. I'm not at all sure that is the

case but grief does bring us a little closer to each other."
He laughed and looked at me for encouragement. "Perhaps that's really what's meant by 'absence makes the
heart grow fonder'. We grow fonder of each other, not of
the person that is missing."

Oscar was playing his favourite game of finding new
ways of interpreting hackneyed sayings. I ate my dinner
without saying anything. If I spoke, he would expect me
to join the game and I wanted to be on my way to the
Sundrams.

In less than an hour I was on Orchard Road, where
people rushed in and out of cinemas, fast food joints,
department stores; crowds bustled everywhere. Orchard
Road is a bustling place. But to me it is more than this.

My own memory of the street does not go back very far
but I have access to Oscar's, which merges with that of
his grandfather and goes back to the turn of the century.
The MRT now runs under the road, but I knew steam
trains once ran on a bridge over it. Traffic stopped when
they did, for people were afraid to pass beneath the char-
iot of steel and fire. I still think I see cars hesitate when
they come to a bridge that is no more. But the traffic was
different then: pedestrians were pigtailed or turbaned,
carriages drawn by horses or, in the case of the humble,
by men between the shafts of a jinriksha.

I used to tell Vanita how I could see the street as it
used to be, hear the babble of tongues as street-hawkers
called out their wares, pause at the honk of an air-horn
as a de Dion or Daimler glided past. There were moments
when I moved further back in time; when I could smell
the nutmeg from the orchards at the north end of the
street. I told Vanita this too. Told her because she listened
and did not laugh or think me mad. I told her because I
loved her and wanted her to see Orchard Road as I could
see it. Now there was no one to tell.

I paused at a pedestrian crossing. There were people all around me, jostling me; noisy people chattering to each other. I felt miserable and alone.

The Sundrams live in Cairnhill Circle, once the heart-land of the English-educated. There was a time when this had been a place of terraces with front gardens, bungalows with lawns. A place where children played on quiet streets. Now it was a cleft between high-rises, occupied by a dual-carriageway and lit by the eerie glow of sodium lights.

One corner of a terrace, however, remained standing. In front of it was a postage-stamp of a garden, and a short path leading to the door. This was number 39 Cairnhill Circle, which had been Vanita's home. All the other houses on the street had gone, their owners having sold out and moved into condos or into housing estates on the outskirts of town. Sundram had stayed on, living in the house in which his children had been born, comfort-able in the knowledge that its value increased by the day if not by the hour.

As I stood outside the door, I remembered my first visit to the house.

Vanita and I had been lovers for a month but we had never properly been in bed together. She didn't under-stand why I found this necessary.

"We make love under the stars. Why do you want to do it in a stuffy old bed?"

"I just want to," I said, petulantly. It was all very well for you to talk, I thought. You've tried it. But I haven't. I added, in a more friendly voice, "Sometimes my bum gets cold."

"OK, then. I'll come to your home and we can fuck there till your bum burns."

Ma knew that I was going with someone; guessed that the relationship was serious and that we were having sex. Knowing this was one thing. My bringing the lady in question home and making love to her in our thin-walled flat was another.

"My home is no fun," I said. "Why don't we go to a hotel?"

I didn't at the time know about the afternoons she spent at the Changi Meridien with Loong. Vanita, however, may have been thinking of them when she said, "Naw. Hotels are sordid places. The looks we get on check-ing in and checking out would make even you, my darling, droop." She thought for a bit then said, "If you are so keen on this fucking-in-bed business, why don't you come round to my place? Father and Mohan are out most of the day and we'll have the place to ourselves."

Three days later I found myself in an old-fashioned house with high ceilings, swing doors and hanging fans. Vanita showed me around.

In a room behind the kitchen, we found an elderly woman ironing and humming to herself. "This is Leela," she explained. "She's been with us from the time I was a little girl."

I had expected the house to have been completely empty and was disturbed that this was not so.

"Won't she be upset at your bringing . . .?"

Vanita shot me a smile. "Leela loves me. She is happy with what makes me happy and I have told her how happy you make me."

My fears about Leela somewhat allayed, I was anxious to get into bed but Vanita insisted that I first saw her brother's and her father's rooms.

"You're better when you're a little impatient," she said taking my hand.

Mohan's room was in the back of the house. It was spartan. In its centre was a wooden bed that had no mattress. There were book-shelves on the walls, mats on the floors but no chairs or cushions anywhere.

"Mohan fancies himself as a Hindu ascetic. Likes to keep his room as bare as possible. He keeps telling me that this way his mind is freed for meditation but," she laughed, "I think he just likes having a mind that is undistracted and empty."

Sundram's room was located immediately above the main living-room. In contrast to his son's, it was cluttered with religious books, idols and pictures of Hindu gods. It smelled strongly of incense. In one corner of the room was a tiny altar in which a lamp burned.

I got increasingly uneasy as we moved around. The house was dark, musty smelling and seemed full of secrets. I felt ghosts around me, some of whom I feared might be those of Vanita's previous lovers.

This did not interfere with our lovemaking, but as I lay on Vanita clutching her close and moving my haunches as fast as I could, I felt a tingle in the back of my neck: the feeling one gets when stared at by a stranger. We were near the height of our pleasure and I couldn't stop to look but I was sure I heard a footfall and the sound of a door being quietly closed.

Later, as we drank tea in the living-room, I heard some-one pacing the floor in Sundram's bedroom and turned my eyes upwards in surprise. "I thought you said no one would return till . . .?"

Vanita wasn't bothered. "Father must have returned while we were in my room," she said.

"Won't he mind about us . . .?"

She shrugged. "I have told him the way things are. Why should he mind?"

It is one thing, I thought, of suspecting what your daughter and her boyfriends get up to, quite another to actually find her in bed with one of them.

All this came back to me as I pressed the doorbell of the last terrace house in Cairnhill Circle.

Mohan opened the door and said, "How Kum," in a voice halfway between a question and an exclamation.

I resisted the urge to make a witty rejoinder. "I should have come earlier, I know, but I too had a lot to get over."

"I understand. Father understands too." He led me into the living-room. "The newspapers were not explicit but we understand from the police inspector that you were with Vani when she died."

"Yes," I said. "We were together. In East Coast Park."

"Yes, yes," he said, indicating a chair. "Where you often go."

"You knew?" I exclaimed, my voice rising.

For a moment he seemed confused. Then his face cleared. He laughed. "There is no need for embarrassment. Vani told me everything. We were close you know." His voice dropped. "Very close."

I had got quite the opposite impression from Vanita, who rarely got things wrong. I wondered how the discrepancy had come about. Perhaps death did bring people together and Mohan had, after her death, imagined himself to be much closer to his sister than he had been. Oscar had, perhaps, been right. Mohan started speaking before I could give the matter thought.

"Father has been anxiously awaiting your arrival. I was going to telephone to request you to drop in, but he counselled patience and said you would come in your own time." He rocked his head noncommittally. "It was a matter of some urgency for he wants you to be with us when we cast sister's ashes into the sea tomorrow. This casting of the ashes on the fifth day is, as you know, an important part of the religious ritual he follows." He leaned towards me confidentially. "I don't believe in all this superstitious nonsense. They are not really a part of

Hinduism but, the older father gets, the more he seems to depend on rituals and ceremonies." His voice dropped further. "I tell him that the vedas talk to the spirit in abstractions. Time and again I have had to remind him that Hinduism is not concerned with forms and observances but with the very substance of things, but he is not happy with my views. Not at all happy."

There was the sound of footsteps somewhere in the house and Mohan looked anxiously over his shoulder. "I try, as much as possible, to go along with father's wishes. He had a heart attack last year and seemed to have another when we got the news on Sunday. I tell him to go to the General Hospital for X-rays and a full check-up, but what's the use. He doesn't even take the tablets prescribed for his high blood-pressure. Just swallows some homeopathic rubbish and talks nonsense about the wisdom of age-old systems of healing."

As he spoke he moved to the swing-door at the end of the room and reached for it. Before he could touch it, it opened and Sundram walked in.

Unlike his son who was soft and podgy, Sundram was a tall muscular man, turning gaunt with age. He had Vanita's eyes: large and heavily lashed. He was wearing a dhoti and his torso was bare. The grey hairs and loose skin on his chest made him old and especially vulnerable. His forehead was streaked with holy ash which emphasised the greyness of his complexion and the furrows of his face. He smelled of incense and had obviously been praying at the altar in his room.

He embraced me and touched my forehead with ash. I was astonished by the greeting and, even more, by the benediction for Sundram had never liked me. He had good reason not to.

His voice was soft, even at close range, barely audible. "My daughter, Vani, is dead. But I look upon you as her husband and, therefore, as my son." There was a catch in his voice.

My own snagged in my throat. "I truly loved your daughter, sir, but we weren't even formally engaged."

"That matters not in my eyes nor in the eyes of God."

"Oh, father," Mohan exclaimed irritably. "Get to the point and tell How Kum what you want him to do."

Sundram turned wet eyes toward me and said, "You will not deny a request an old man makes from the abyss of his grief?"

"I will do whatever I can, sir."

"Yesterday the police returned her to us. After the necessary prayers and ablutions, the cremation was conducted. Her ashes are now in an urn in my room where hourly I say the appropriate prayers for the tranquillity of her soul as it unites with the Infinite. Tomorrow at dawn we cast her ashes into the sea so that all that remains of her physical presence becomes one with the universe. The religious ceremony will be brief and I will perform the main part of this."

"I will come with you and Mohan, sir."

"That is not all I ask. As Vani's husband, as my son, I am asking you to cast her ashes." He ignored the look on my face and continued. "I should, as her father, do this myself but I am weakened by a heart attack and fear that my emotions might overcome me at the crucial time. Also my strength may not be sufficient for me to wade out into the sea if it is rough. So I ask of you, with heaviness in my heart, to do for my daughter what her father cannot do for her."

"I'm not quite sure . . ."

He looked at me steadily. His tears had dried and the flame burned in his eyes with a greater intensity than ever. "Can you deny the request of an old man sick of heart and heavy with grief?"

"What exactly will I have to do, sir?"

"Good." The flame in his eyes died down a little. "At the appropriate time I will put the urn into your hands. You will walk into the sea holding it above your head. When the water is up to your chest you will immerse yourself and the urn three times saying as you do 'gunga arppanam'. Loosely translated the words mean 'Mother Ganges, accept this offering'. The invocation over, you turn round for all to see, throw the urn over your left shoulder and walk ashore." He paused, satisfied himself that I had understood, then continued, "Whatever you do, you must not look back once the urn has been cast."

I dislike ceremonies of any kind but what was required of me was simple enough, and Thursday morning found me again at the house on Cairnhill Circle. Sundram, Mohan and a strange man met me on the porch. All three were wearing dhotis. Sundram had in his hands a full-bodied clay urn.

I wanted to ask Sundram if I could hold it for a moment, perhaps just touch it. The little that remained of my beloved had become unbelievably precious. I didn't dare ask. I noticed that the old man was clutching the urn to his bosom and, when he thought no one was looking, he stroked it lovingly.

I tore my eyes away and looked at the stranger in the group. He was fairer than either of the Sundrams and was clearly from the north of India. He had prominent hazel eyes and a few strands of well-oiled hair were slicked across his bald head. He carried a transparent plastic bag which contained a censer, chunks of incense, numerous oil-lamps and an assortment of coloured powders. Sundram introduced him to me as Kishore. I assumed that he was the Hindu priest who was to preside over the ceremony.

Just before we left, the two older men huddled together

in prayer. Mohan pulled me to one side and whispered, "That scoundrel Kishore claims to be an Ayurvedic physician." He noticed the question on my face and explained. "It's some kind of Indian mumbo-jumbo in which herbs are combined with prayer and ritual to cure disease. I wouldn't bother with his nonsense except that he is intent on cheating father."

"I thought he was a priest."

Mohan laughed. "He does a bit of priesting too. Anything as long as it's dishonest."

As soon as the prayers were done Sundram announced, "We will be travelling in two vehicles."

"Where are we going to dispose . . ." I began and stopped.

"We will cast my daughter's ashes in the lagoon off East Coast Park," Sundram informed me.

I was stunned that Vanita's remains were to be dispersed so near to the place where she had been murdered. But I guessed there were practical reasons for this. Singapore is a small island with few spots from which one can wade out and drop things into the sea.

It was early and the traffic was light. Mohan drove at a leisurely pace. As he did he complained, "Father is a fool and he has fallen into the hands of a crook. I have been aware for a long time how involved he has been with all the absurdities that are conducted in our temples. You will see, as an intelligent man, How Kum, that this has nothing to do with Hinduism."

"I don't know anything about religion, Mohan."

"Hinduism cannot be considered to be a religion. Not in the way that people usually regard religion. It must be seen more as a philosophical analysis of the forces that make things happen the way they do. Simply an analysis of forces."

"And what are these?"

"The laws of nature and the laws of man." He slowed down to enter a slip road leading to the expressway. "The laws of nature are governed by what you and I call causality which we Hindus try to grasp in its entirety and call karma."

"I thought that karma was fate. Something unavoidable and determined by one's previous existence."

"That is a distortion of the original concept. And Hinduism, because it is free from dogmatism, is especially prone to distortions of one kind or another.

"Karma is unavoidable simply because what results from setting in motion a chain of causality is unavoidable. It is different from dharma which is what men consider proper actions. We can choose or flout dharma but karma cannot be avoided as as long as natural laws operate."

Mohan had a high-pitched voice, not unpleasant in its own way. I found myself listening not just to what it was saying but to its cadences, its melody. Around me a symphony was organising itself. A voice with an Indian accent was the theme. The throb of cylinders in the heart of the motor-car formed a background which provided rhythms and harmonies: second violins.

I followed what the voice was saying. I was beguiled, hypnotised, anticipated what was to come. I was happy about this, felt that I was again part of a sequence. I believed that if I stayed close to the purpose of the voice, I would be led out of the confusion that had begun with Vanita's death. The voice prompted questions. I asked them. It answered. I asked again.

"If Hinduism is not a religion, how come it's got Gods?"

"Ah," he laughed. "Gods are all-embracing creatures. They mean different things to different people. Our Gods, our primary Gods, are not people, like the Christian deities. They are the primary forces of the universe.

"There is energy which causes change. This is both

creative and destructive. We embody this in the God Siva. Then there is inertia which resists change. This is Vishnu, the preserver. Then there is Brahma, the undefined spirit of the universe, in whose consciousness everything that happens, happens."

"Even if you have no Gods, you must have some moral laws?"

"Ah, yes. But these are man-made. Dharma is our code of propriety. It's not fixed or final like the rules of Christianity and the other Semitic religions. No ten commandments for us. No thou shalt not this or that.

"Dharma is an elastic stocking. It stretches to allow room for individual variation. You discover your dharma in yourself, for it is not difficult to see that good and evil are different for persons."

We stopped at a traffic light. Mohan's voice which, till now, had lilt and variation, became monotonous, a chant requiring no responses, allowing no interruption.

"Everything that happens, happens in the Divine Awareness and as such is a part of God: the child that is beaten, the man that beats it, the cane that breaks the skin, the reason for the punishment, the cry that escapes from the infant's lips. We are but cogs in a machine whose purpose we are not designed to understand. We act as events prompt us, recognising the insignificance of our action, taking neither credit nor blame. All that dharma requires is that we recognise a purpose beyond our own." The voice changed, became almost jocular.

"Well, that's what Hinduism is about, not the foolish lighting of lamps and walking around in circles that you are going to be involved in shortly."

We pulled into a carpark near an area designated "safe for swimming". It was the morning of a working day and the beach was deserted. I was glad and wondered if the casting of remains infringed our anti-litter laws. It was a frivolous thought for one participating in the last rites of the woman he loved. I shrugged it off and concentrated on what was going on.

Kishore was lighting lamps and censers. The smells of oil and incense mingled with those of the incoming tide. Sundram offered me a dhoti. The material was thin; so thin that it would offer little protection from nakedness once it got wet. I accepted it without protest. Since Vanita's death I routinely wore underwear. Kishore smeared red powder on my head, throat and chest and followed this with liberal applications of holy ash to my torso. This done, he took the urn which Sundram still clutched, removed its gauze cover, and poured into it milk mixed with rose water. Then he drew a circle in the sand and made various designs in it with a stick.

"Yantras," Mohan informed me. "Mantras are protective spirits realised in sound. Yantras are the same spirits realised in shapes. Or so these benighted people claim."

In the centre of the circle he had drawn, Kishore placed the urn and all that remained of my Vanita. She was now entirely on her own and I was glad that she was protected by yantras. Then the two older men began to chant and walk round the circle. I could not exactly catch what they said, still less understand, but recognised the aums and shantis that littered their prayers. Mohan caught my eye, wobbled his head and grinned. I glared at him and shook my head.

After about five minutes they stopped chanting. Kishore turned to me. "Take the urn and walk into the water holding it high above your head. When you have got as deep as you can, turn round and face the shore. Then immerse yourself and the urn completely three times, each time saying the words you were taught. When you emerge for the third time, throw the urn over your left shoulder and walk directly back to us. Under no circumstances, no circumstances whatever, must you look at the urn after it has been cast."

My eyebrows must have gone up involuntarily for Kishore, speaking in a stern voice, added, "If you do, her atman, her soul, will be impeded on its journey towards the Absolute." He put the urn into my hands.

Vanita had been a good-sized girl and I had had, on the few occasions that I had attempted it, difficulty in lifting her. What remained of her was surprisingly light. Yet I needed both hands to hold on to the urn. I clutched it to my heart and walked into the sea.

The water was cold and I shivered. I had not appreciated how salty sea-water was or how much it stung the eyes. Blind with grief, I walked on. When I was waist-deep I realised that there was a strong current beneath an apparently calm surface. I am not a strong swimmer and the undertow seemed to clutch at my dhoti, wanting to pull me out to sea. I reduced the length of my stride and held the urn high above my head.

In the distance I thought I heard Vanita singing, crooning the way she used to after we had made love. I was glad of my imagination. It provided me with the sounds that could still my fear. I wanted Vanita's singing to get louder but her voice seemed to fade the further out I got from shore. Then I realised that the sounds were real and came from the beach. Sundram was singing the very same bajans he had taught his daughter. They were, as Vanita had claimed, holy songs, and funerals are a good place for hymns.

When the water reached my shoulders, I stopped. Kishore had joined Sundram and the intensity of the chanting had increased. I found myself clutching the urn more tightly than ever. I turned and faced the shore, determined to do as I had been ordered. Then I stopped. I was afraid to submerge myself completely, afraid of the current that might pull me out to sea. What was more, I had forgotten the words I was supposed to say.

Then my ghost began to speak and Vanita's voice whispered in my ear. "Don't be afraid, my darling. Just allow yourself to slip in slowly."

My heart ached as I remembered when she had first spoken these words to me. Then as now, I did as my beloved instructed. I allowed the sea to close over my shoulders, my neck, my head. Even as it did, I remembered the invocation I had forgotten.

"Gunga arppanam" I whispered. "Mother Ganges accept this offering. Gunga arppanam." The words were lovely and, so being, became sacred. The water was warmer now and pleasantly salty. I stayed down for as long as I could, then emerged. I did this again and yet once more, each time staying below till my breath ran out. I surfaced for the third time and hugged the urn tightly to my chest. It was with difficulty that I released it and shoved it over my left shoulder.

Then I began walking back to the shore. I walked very slowly. The urge not just to look at the urn but to retrieve it, clutch it to my body once more, was very strong. The course of our lives may be determined by an immutable causality, our behaviour controlled by a code that must persist over our feelings, but what remained of the things that we loved had a power more than these combined. I wanted to go back to the urn, retrieve it, and keep it with me forever. I resisted and continued walking toward the three figures on the beach.

I felt cold and my dhoti clung uncomfortably to my legs, dragging me back into the sea. Vanita's voice was not singing now. She was desperate, calling me, pleading to be saved from the depths of the ocean, wanting to be rescued from the infinity of the universe. I ignored it and strode towards her father.

Sundram offered me a towel and I dried myself. We shook hands. Both of us realised how meaningless the gesture was. We had just thrown away all that remained of a person we had dearly loved. Her presence remained with us but, instead of bringing us together, it made us uncomfortable with each other. We were happy to part and I took the bus to work.

On Mondays and Thursdays, fresh supplies of meat are delivered to our cold room. Supplying meat to Nats is a million-dollar business, and selecting our suppliers involves an elaborate system of tendering about which I know nothing. Nor am I usually curious as to whether or not the meat supplies conform to the specifications of the tender, and the ratios of the edible portion to bone and fat are, I don't think, my business. My job is to check the freshness of the meat and to ensure that it has been sufficiently chilled to remain fresh and germ-free.

The first thing that I did when I got to Nats was to go to the "cold" room. I turned on the red light on the door as I entered to ensure that no one accidentally locked me inside.

Vanita's presence, which had been with me from the moment I had relinquished her ashes, became stronger as soon as the cold hit me. I realised why.

Once, early in our relationship, we had made love in the cold room. It had been Vanita's idea. In her usual style, she told me that she had made love in just about every place in which it was possible except in freezing conditions. She would, she said, liked to have done it in the Arctic but, since that was not possible, the cold room at Nats would have to do.

I did not ask why we should. She wanted to do something with me that she had not done with anyone else.

Nevertheless, I was nervous about the idea. We had to leave the red light on or risk getting locked in and the light often provoked people to look inside. Vanita insisted that anxiety would increase our pleasure and, as with most such things, she was right.

All this came back to me as I entered the room.

It had been freezing but the cold only made our bodies feel warmer, our points of contact sweeter. I remembered, too, how the fear of discovery made my heart race even faster than when we made love in the park.

The room was soundproof. This caused the noises we made to seem louder and our pleasure more intense. I remembered how cold the back of my body was when compared to the front, could taste the ice dust in Vanita's hair as I buried my face in it. I heard her moan, begin to gasp. I began to lose control and go over the edge myself, my hips taken over by irresistible rhythms.

Then I felt my beloved's arm around my waist. I had, in the past, felt Vanita's ghost with me, heard her voice, smelled her body. Never had I made physical contact with her. Faint with desire I began to push her hand down.

"I thought you'd come round in the end, HK," said Symons in a hoarse voice.

"You fucking pervert," I shouted, flinging his hand away.

"But HK," he remonstrated. "I saw the red light and thought it must be you in the cold room. I come in to find you breathing as though you were about to have a wank. I touch you. You say nothing but push my hand downwards. I speak and you scream blue murder."

"You go to the bloody top end of Orchard Road to find perverts like yourself but you fucking well leave me alone, Symons."

His manner changed. "Actually it's good I came upon you. I wanted to tell you about what your wonderful

policeman friend's been up to." He moved to the far corner
of the room to reassure me of his intentions.

My curiosity was aroused. "You've met D'Cruz?"

He shrugged. "For several hours and much against my
will."

"He's been talking to you?"

"Interrogating would be a better word."

"Did he assault you?" I asked hopefully.

"Only with his foul language."

"What did he actually say?"

"He seemed to think that I might have had something
to do with the wretched girl's murder. Went so far as to
imply that I may have wanted the girl dead myself. I
asked him why this might be as I had no interest whatsoever in the depraved creature . . ."

"And he said?"

"He started to harangue me about an unnatural . . ." he
sniffed, "unnatural relationship that I may be having
with you. I assured him that the only unnatural thing
for people like you and me was the one you seemed to be
having with the girl." I could see it. Symons all prissy,
D'Cruz sweaty and foul-mouthed. Imagining what had
gone on cheered me up. "I hope he set you straight about
my being gay."

"Yes." He paused dramatically. "On the whole he
seemed to agree with me that you were homosexual." He
grinned at my discomfiture and wiggled his bottom. "The
inspector seemed to think that we were two of a kind.
But I could see that that was not what he was really
interested in."

"And what was the inspector interested in?"

"The whole point of his inquiry was to find out what I
was doing on Saturday night."

"As a matter of interest, what were you doing on Saturday night?"

He folded his arms and rocked back and forth. "What I always do on Saturday nights. I was watching TV with Mummy."

"Did D'Cruz buy that?"

"I guess he'll check it out with Mummy. But she'll say I was at home, even if I wasn't."

"Are you trying to tell me you were somewhere else on Saturday night? Like East Coast Park, perhaps?"

"Listen, HK," he said, serious again. "You know how I feel about you. Thought I had a dream come true when I found you in the cold room in the state you were in. But you'd better get this straight here and now. I wouldn't stick my knife or my anything else into that bitch for all the tea in China."

I tended to agree with him. I could not see Symons as a murderer. Perhaps this was because a tiny bit of me still wanted to believe that the killer's real target was Lip Bin or Esther, that Vanita's murder was part of the cover-up of a clever killer.

Despite my wishful thinking, I understood what the inspector was doing. He was shaking things up, throwing pieces into the air. I hoped I could make sense of the shapes they formed when they fell to earth.

SEVEN

Late on Thursday night I heard Oscar and Ma arguing. Oscar's voice was louder than usual and had a determined ring to it. He hadn't sounded like this for a long time. I remember that, when they were young, Oscar and Ma quarrelled a good deal. Ma, I think, was the one to blame. She would, without any provocation that I could think of, begin to nag Oscar about his drinking. At the same time she would badger him about taking over the family business. Ma's hassling only caused Oscar to drink more. At the height of one of his binges, it would have been impossible to reach Oscar. When he was relatively sober, however, he argued that there was no reason why he should not get drunk as often as he wanted to. He also maintained that we were more than comfortable with what we had and that, if we got involved in his family business, they would interfere with our lives.

I agreed with Oscar and, often enough, told Ma to stop pestering the poor chap. When Oscar could no longer stand her griping, he would disappear from the house. He called it going "walkabout". This he explained was a term used by Australian aboriginals when they interrupted their lives and wandered into the bush without apparent purpose. These excursions of Oscar's usually lasted three or four days. When he returned he would be smelly and unshaven, shaking the way the very old do, his clothes a mess from being slept in.

Ma never asked Oscar where he went or what he did

on his "walkabouts". She missed her man so much that she was just happy to have him back. She would bathe him and cook him his favourite food. She even provided him with an expensive cognac, a bottle of which she kept hidden away especially for these reconciliations. Their reunions were happy times, better than Christmas or the Chinese New Year. The warmth about them was unrehearsed and went on for several days.

Though Oscar never spoke to Ma about them, he did give me some idea as to what happened on his "walkabouts".

"I get back to the old places to see what the world's been up to in my absence. Who knows, dear boy, it may have changed for the better."

He told me about whores, pimps, touts and small-time drug peddlers who had been his friends and to whom he returned from time to time. What amazed me most about these people was the kind of information they seemed to possess. They knew of scandals in the government long before they broke, offered stock market tips and had details of world events before these reached the newspapers. This was not why Oscar went back to them. He went to keep in touch with old friends, to hear the gossip that was circulating in the world he had inhabited before Lim Li Lian had come into his life.

In time Ma found it less and less necessary to change Oscar, and the "walkabouts" became less frequent. I was surprised, therefore, at the way in which they were now carrying on. It had been years since they had shouted at each other like this. I wondered what it was that Ma wanted to change at this stage of their relationship. After eavesdropping for a bit from my bedroom, I joined them in the dining-room.

I glared at Ma and she said, "It's not me that wants him to change anything, son. It's him that wants to go."

She looked her man straight in the face. 'You tell How Kum, Os, what you want to do and why."

Oscar seemed more sober than he usually was at this time of the evening, though his brandy bottle was two-thirds empty.

"It's like this, dear chap. This girlie of yours gets murdered and two people with her. If I understand the papers," he laughed, "and it's not always easy to understand what the *Straits Times* is getting at, the police seem to have nothing to offer us in the way of suspects.

"I was worried they might be hiding things so I called Jafri. He apparently is in touch with that rogue elephant D'Cruz who heads the investigation." He looked longingly at his bottle and, despite Ma's disapproving look, splashed brandy into his glass. "According to Jafri, the police have drawn a complete blank. Nothing seems to lead anywhere." He sniffed. "A fine situation indeed. Three people murdered and all suspects innocent."

I sat down beside him. "What were you thinking of doing about it, Uncle Oscar?"

"No concrete plan, dear boy." He sipped brandy. "Thought I'd drift by the old places and meet some of the friends. They often have a good notion of what's what. Like to get a feel as to what they think this whole business is about."

Ma interrupted. "His restlessness didn't start with the murder, son. He's been wandering off here and there for some months now. Sometimes he's out till very late into the night." She sniffed to remind us that tears were on standby. "Tell him, Os. You tell How Kum how worried I've been and why. Also tell him how you've been feeling."

"To speak the truth I've been a touch restive, of late. Slope into the coffee-shop downstairs and chat. Sometimes I sit by myself so as not to be a nuisance. Lili doesn't like me at home by myself when I'm a little overwhelmed by the grape." He paused, touched his glass then changed his mind. "And you, dear chap, have been away quite a bit with your lady."

"Yes," Ma added. "Most of the times you've been out, I've been on my own." She nodded several times.

"I've told Lili that we can't expect, delightful though they've been, for things to always be the same with the three of us." He seemed relieved at being able to get this off his chest and sipped his drink again. "You must have a life of your own, I've told your mother often enough, but, I must confess, I've had problems getting used to the idea myself."

There was a tough look in Ma's eyes. "He has been lonely, How Kum. Very, very lonely. You've been spending so much time with that Vanita of yours, it's no wonder you've so little left for your mother, let alone your Uncle Oscar."

"That's not fair, Lili. I miss the dear chap right enough but not enough to want to get in the way of his courtship of a lady." He drank more brandy. "But there's more than a grain of truth in what your mother says. I am finding it a mite difficult to cope with the notion that you are no longer the little lad that your mother and I have been looking after all these years."

"There," said Ma, the argument concluded in her favour.

Both of them smiled and looked a little away from me: embarrassed, guilty at the resentment they felt for a dead girl.

I was surprised. I had guessed that Oscar and Ma were a little jealous of the effect that Vanita was having on our lives. I had even used it, when the picture got really distorted, to see them involved in killing her. But these, I knew, were glitches on the screen, sub-plots, unrealities.

Ma, I knew, had a strong maternal instinct. I was her little boy and she would resent me being in arms other than her own. Nevertheless, she was also an Asian mother and, from time to time, badgered me about finding a girl and settling down. Vanita, however, would not have been her first choice. Oscar, I was convinced, would welcome any woman into my life. All that was required of her was to produce the grandchildren he so yearned for. Children he could tell stories to and spoil just as he did me.

But Oscar was more than an indulgent uncle. He saw himself as a knight, duelling for his Lili, her kerchief flying from his lance. His main role in life was protecting Lili: caring for the maiden in distress who had turned to him when everyone had abandoned her. I watched as his hand crept across the table and covered Ma's. I knew that her free hand squeezed his thigh under the table. I saw them exchange looks, their faces carrying on a conversation they had had many times before. They were immersed in each other, unaware of the world around them. Complete.

Normally I was warmed by such moments, rejoiced at being a spectator at this tableau of romance. Today, I felt differently. I was suspicious, frightened. The way they smiled at each other, the way they avoided my eye, told me that nothing really mattered to these two except each other. The hand that comforted could become a fist, wield a lance . . . or a kitchen knife. I did not know the suffering that Ma and Oscar had gone through or the extent to which they would go to protect what they put together over the years. I was very much a part of their happiness, was, possibly, responsible for holding them together; perhaps more than I would have been if Oscar was my real father. Vanita threatened to disrupt this.

I raised my voice, forced myself to intrude. "But you didn't say . . . either of you, that you minded . . . had any objections to my going with Vanita."

"Object is too strong a word, old chap. But we will not deny that we, your mother and I, had reservations about how hopelessly involved you were with a person that neither of us knew at all and, we suspected, you yourself not very well." He stopped to busy himself with his drink.

Ma butted in, "I never thought it my duty to tell you who you should marry. I have always said to your uncle here, it's How Kum that's going to sleep with the girl not me, so let him choose." She looked down at the table and allowed her shoulders to slump forward on it. It was an attitude Ma assumed when she wanted sympathy. One didn't need a psychic to guess what she was going to say. "Who am I to give advice about marriage anyway, after what the Malayalee rascal did to me."

"Now, now, Lili," said Oscar taking her head in his hands and turning her face toward his, "you mustn't distress yourself by talking like that. The past's over and done with. You always have me," – it was almost an afterthought – "and How Kum at your side."

At the coffee-shop in Joo Chiat, D'Cruz had told us what the murder weapon had been. I began to see a tiny corner of a picture then and what I saw was so ugly that I quickly put it out of my mind. Now I was being shown more of the canvas and what I saw was monstrous. It was true that I did not stick a knife into Vanita. I might as well have, for she was killed not because of anything she had done but because of her connection with me: the peculiar relationship that existed between Ma, Oscar and me, a relationship that was so tight and tangled that it would not permit another person entering it. Had my life not been what it was, hers would have been spared.

The possibility that Ma and Oscar were involved in Vanita's death was not something that I could come to terms with. It was not one of the composites that I could put together to give a semblance of meaning to my life.

I stared at the picture, the unacceptable jigsaw that I had fashioned. I stared at it for a long while. Then suddenly I realised that there was something wrong with it: two wayward pieces that wouldn't fall into place: pieces that refused to make the ugliness correct.

It was impossible for Oscar to have actually killed Vanita, Lip Bin and Esther. It was just imaginable that he could have hired someone to do the job for him. If he was using a hired killer, why on earth should he give him Ma's kitchen knife with which to do the job?

Secondly, if Oscar arranged Vanita's death, he would have done so as a testimony of his love for Ma and would certainly have told her about it so she could understand how far he was prepared to go on her account. Oscar was a knight, a flamboyant one. He was not the kind of knight who'd keep his lady unaware of the things he would do for her.

When I came in on Sunday morning, Ma was convinced that I had killed Vanita. She feared that, like my father, I had an uncontrollable temper and was given to violence. I was convinced that her reaction was genuine. Ma did not have the cunning for it to have been otherwise.

I relaxed and began to notice what was going on around me.

Oscar, who was spending an inordinately long time getting the proportions of his drink right, was finally satisfied with what he had in his glass, took a tiny sip of this and began speaking, "If there's one thing that must be put properly in its place, dear boy, it is this. Whatever our misgivings about the suitability of the girl, Lili and I are awfully sorry that she is dead." He took a large gulp of brandy and swirled this appreciatively round in his mouth before swallowing it. "And since the girlie was so dear to you, it behoves me to find out all I can about her death. I thought I'd sniff around the old places and see if the team have any idea what's going on."

"Do you really think, Uncle Oscar, that your friends would know anything about these killings?"

"Of course, dear fellow." He leaned back in his chair and proceeded to tell us of the times his friends had been in possession of knowledge no one else had. Ma stared, or rather gazed at him, eyes shining, mouth open.

Oscar told us of murders which, but for the intercession of his cronies, the police would have written off as accidents. He told of drug-plants and treachery in high places. I knew most of his stories and did not interrupt him. I was again a little boy, safe in the heart of my family, cocooned from the world by the voice of my uncle Oscar.

More than an hour passed before Oscar said, "It's like this, dear boy. You don't see the world if you are too close to it. And its processes become invisible if you are actually a part of them. Now my friends, they like to remain distinct from things, keep their hands clear of the machinery. That's why I look to them whenever I need perspective."

The next morning Oscar had gone. Ma was subdued the way she always became when her man went "walkabout".

"Don't worry about me," she said. She poured out my coffee as always. "I'll look after myself. You go ahead and do whatever you have to do."

There was not much to do at Nats and Vanita's ghost wouldn't leave me alone. It is nice to have at your side someone that you love, but it is irritating beyond belief not to have some time to yourself. I could have screamed as she followed me down the rows of preset girls, leaned against the stacks of paper on my desk, bowed and let me pass ahead of her when I left my room. I knew why she was being persistent: I was not doing enough about finding her killer.

I was in my office apologising to her, mouthing words, my voice almost about to become audible, when Jafri phoned.

"Would you like to come round to the flat today? There's something I want to talk to you about?"

"To do with Vanita?"

"Yes."

"I'll come straight from work . . ."

"Come for a cup of tea."

Zainah was alone when I got to the apartment. I was not sure what Zainah did with her time but she seemed to spend a good deal of it on her own. Normally she was bubbly, flirtatious, finding excuses to make body contact. Today she was subdued, distant. She poured tea in silence, said nothing as she walked across the room to fiddle with an ornament on a book-shelf.

"What's the matter, Zainah?" She put down the figurine she was holding and stared at the wall. I walked across, touched her hand. "Tell me, Zainah."

"It's Jafri, How Kum."

She took my hands and put them on her shoulders; leaned on me, not heavily but enough. Zainah smelled of soap and talcum: an infant after a bath. Her body felt boneless, like a baby's. Cuddly too, I thought. I became conscious of my breathing.

"What's Jafri been up to?"

"He's not been up to anything with me. He works late and I'm alone every night . . ."

"He's got a new law practice, Zainah." Her body was soft. Vanita was dead. I was only half-joking when I said, "If Jafri's too busy with the practice, I'll take care of you."

"Maybe he's busy with the practice. Maybe with other things." She gave a tiny sob and shuddered. Then her body seemed to collapse, needed me to hold it against mine lest it fall.

"Come on Zainah," I said. The thought of Jafri womanising was absurd. Which man could want something else when he could come home to this. "Jafri's not that kind of man."

"You say that, How Kum, but you don't know Jafri nowadays. He's not the same like the man you know. Not the same like the man I married.

"The Jafri I married was a brave man. So confident also. First he works in Deputy Prosecutor's office. He wants to use the law to bring criminals to justice. Then he becomes defence lawyer. He works from other side of law: finds justice for accused persons. But he is still the same Jafri. Still thinking of good and bad, still believing in justice."

I let my arms drop to the small of her back so I could hold her more easily and asked, "But that hasn't changed, has it?"

"Yes. That has changed also." She sniffed slightly. "Now Jafri says there is no good or bad, no guilty or innocent. He says he don't know why people commit crimes. Maybe they cannot help it. Jafri don't need justice any more. Also, he don't need his wife."

"But that's unbelievable. Jafri has always had definite views of what was right and what was wrong. It's impossible for him . . ."

"Not nowadays, How Kum. He says that maybe there's no innocent and no guilty. After your girlfriend's murder and the two other murders he is more sure of this . . ."

"What has Vanita's death got to do with Jafri's state of mind?"

"He tells me that nobody is going to catch the killer because we are all looking for the wrong sort of person."

I suspect I had tightened my grip on Zainah. The messages reaching me became confused. The softness of her body produced a familiar ache in a familiar place.

But the voice inside me was saying something different. Something more important. I responded to the voice. "I don't understand this, Zainah. Jafri seemed to approve of what the inspector was doing and encouraged me to cooperate with him."

She leaned back slightly and looked into my face. "Yah," she said. "Jafri talks this way sometimes and that way sometimes. But I know what he thinks. He says that D'Cruz is too. . ." she searched for the unfamiliar word her husband had used, ". . . too crusading, too angry in his approach. Jafri says that the inspector will never find the killer as long as he uses this kind of method."

I moved away so our bodies no longer touched. "If the inspector can't find the killer, who can?"

"Jafri doesn't know but he says that newer criminological techniques will have to be used."

We heard a key in the lock. My arm was still round his wife's waist when Jafri entered. Zainah and I were at one end of the room and our tea at the other. Jafri didn't seem to notice anything untoward about this. He walked across, touched his wife's cheek, then my shoulder. As he did I smelled aftershave. Being collected at all times is an infuriating trait in most people. Now, more than ever, was I grateful that Jafri possessed such a quality.

"Tea for my tired husband?" Zainah asked, leaning her cheek against his arm.

He buried his nose in her hair and inhaled deeply. I missed Vanita more than ever as I made my way back to the sofa.

Zainah produced brightly coloured cakes, fragrant with lemon-grass and tacky with glutinous rice. I found it difficult to talk as I ate.

Jafri had no such problem. "I have spent a good deal of time talking things over with the inspector and we have come to certain conclusions." He smiled. "Some held mutually, others individually.

"There are essentially two ways of looking at these crimes. They could be the work of a psychopath, a mass murderer. D'Cruz has rejected that possibility. . ."

"Why?" I still harboured the tiniest of hopes that we had been included in somebody else's tragedy.

"Because the man has gone through some forty years of police records and claims that, outside of race riots, there have been no mass murders in Singapore. Our killers he told me are rational men, men with motives. Their motives may be crazy, but they are not."

"You agree with the inspector, Jafri?"

"I'm not sure what I agree with." Zainah looked at him anxiously and he chose his words carefully. "I was brought up to believe in good and evil, crime and punishment. All these years I saw things as black or white separated by the narrowest band of grey. Now the band of grey seems to have expanded so much that everything seems to be one or other shade of grey. So much so that I am having to revise my views on innocence and guilt."

"Meaning?"

"There may be persons with certain genes which determine their attitudes. . ."

It was Zainah who spoke, her voice shrill with disbelief. "Are you saying that there are people born to be killers?"

"It's not quite like that. I am saying that given a certain inborn disposition, external circumstances may trigger off a chain of responses over which the individual has no control. It would be wrong to punish such people for doing things they cannot help themselves doing."

I was not unfamiliar with that kind of thinking. The sharpness in my voice reflected only my surprise at Jafri's choosing to give it credence. "How come we've no record of such killers till now, Jafri?"

"The genes for this type of person must have been present in our community as they have been in all human communities. However, we have not seen this form of killing in Singapore because the conditions didn't exist to activate this kind of killer."

"What's happened to bring him out of the woodwork now?" I tried to control it but my voice was still shriller than I wished. "What's changed?"

I recognised the look on Jafri's face. I had seen it in debates at school, while he was prosecuting in the courts. Sometimes even in the course of trivial argument. It was a look of triumph, only slightly concealed. "Everything, How Kum. Everything." He smiled. "Aren't you always telling me that there is nothing left of the old Singapore, the island that Oscar tells you stories about. Houses are different, streets are different, ways have changed. People nowadays simply have no connection with the past. They have lost their sense of community, they no longer share common values. They cannot connect reward with a good deed or punishment with a bad one. They are angry, frustrated and confused."

Zainah interrupted, "When I'm angry and frustrated I don't go out and kill just anybody. I know who's to blame and I want to kill him."

She shot her husband a sidelong look, accusing but deeply affectionate.

I wished some woman would look at me like that. Jafri didn't seem to notice it or to take his wife's point. He continued. "We live in a pressure-cooker world. We are offered all sorts of technological goodies but we have to fight each other for them. Under these conditions those with inappropriate gene-complexions will find difficulty expressing themselves. Their pent-up desires, their aggressions, have one outlet: murder." He paused. "I feel that we are seeing only the tip of the iceberg. There will be more murders like this. Mark my words. This is the price we pay for development."

"Assuming you are right," I asked, "how do we go about finding this killer?"

Jafri looked miserable and his face tended to collapse. "I don't know. The phenomenon is new to Singapore and I don't think anyone in the country really knows what to do. We just have to play along with the routine stuff and hope for the best." He shrugged and shook his head. "And thus far routine investigations have not led us anywhere. As things stand the situation looks pretty hopeless. Unless the killer does it again we will have no way of finding out who he is. And even if he kills again our chances of catching him don't seem all that bright."

"What does D'Cruz say about your theories?"

"Ozzie, as you have seen, is an old-fashioned policeman. He sees all crimes as having motives. He sees the investigator as the person who builds a bridge between the motive and the crime. He cannot understand or accept motiveless crimes."

"But you have made your views clear to him?"

Jafri was embarrassed. "Ozzie is an obstinate man. Not the kind of person who will alter his views without very good reason. . ."

"Are you saying, Jafri, that you have not told D'Cruz what you feel about things?"

"I have intimated to him that this may not be the kind of crime he is used to investigating but he seems only to be capable of following his own line of thought."

"What does he suggest we do to find the killer?"

"He wants you to get more involved with the investigation."

"Me?"

"You remember what he told you about Vanita not being able to die properly till her killer was found and your being the one who would benefit most from finding the killer. Well he now believes that you not only have the motivation but also the ability to do so."

"Who on earth gave him that impression?"

"I did," said Jafri, forcing a grin on to his face.

Once again I felt I was being used to shape a design which I could not as yet visualise: I was a needle moving in and out of a fabric which did not, as yet, have even the outline of a tapestry on it.

This didn't stop me asking, "You told him I could help with the investigation, Jafri? Why?"

"Because I believe he's right." The grin had faded. "I told Ozzie about your mystical abilities. How you feel visions and taste the words on other people's tongues . . ."

"How do you know that?"

He smiled slightly. "I've known you from school, How Kum. I don't exactly know what's going on in your head but I know when something is. And you have an ability that I envy terribly."

"What's that?"

"You seem to be able to see things before they happen, seem to know how the pieces are going to fall." He was quick to add, "I don't mean that you possess any supernatural power." He looked at Zainah, "God knows I don't believe in that sort of rubbish. But I think you have a way of looking at the world differently from the rest of us. You latch on to tiny signs and from them deduce what's going to happen. I suspect that you don't do this consciously."

"D'Cruz agrees with this?"

"Ozzie says he knows what I mean. He believes that you will, more likely than not, see things opposite to the way he does and because of this wants very much for you to be with him in this case."

I understood. Too well, I understood. There is a con-

trariness about design. There are not many people who
from dabs of paint on a canvas, steel wires sticking out
of concrete blocks, blobs and flourishes confined between
five ruled lines can see a painting, look up at a skyscraper,
hear a symphony. The inspector and I had quite different
natures, even looked as though we did not belong to the
same species. Yet we were drawn together, found need for
each other. I saw purpose in this alliance of contradiction.

I asked Jafri, "What exactly does the inspector want
me to do?"

"He wants you to get the feel of things, find out how
the land lies."

"He is aware that I know nothing of police methods
and I may muck things up for him?" I had visions of
walking over tracks murderers are supposed to leave on
flower-beds.

"Our Ozzie is not very keen on science in detection. He
says that science is great for proving your case in court
once you have got the killer in your hands. He does not
think it helps very much in actually recognising and
apprehending the guilty party." Jafri smiled at me imp-
ishly. "D'Cruz suggests that you shuffle around and get
the feel of things."

"All right, I get the feel of things; then what?"

Zainah poured him more tea and Jafri drank some of
this before answering. "Then you stir them up. I didn't
quite understand what Ozzie meant by this but he said
that you would know."

I remember watching Ma make marble cake. Into the
vanilla mix she would pour blobs of chocolate and straw-
berry mixes. These she would encourage to flow into the
vanilla. Even as she did I could see the slices of cake
with intricate brown, pink and yellow designs on their
surfaces. It is sometimes possible to see the end-point
even as one sets forces in motion.

"Yes. I think I know what he means."

"He said to cause as much disturbance as you can. Feel free to ask any questions you want and even suggest that you are working with the police and know who they suspect."

"I understand what D'Cruz is getting at but what happens if I do uncover anything?"

Jafri smiled. "You speak to me or to him. As Ozzie said 'We must not expect mummy's boy to get shit on his hands.'" Jafri continued, "He said to tell you that you have motive and method to solve this crime. Now we are providing you with opportunity."

"Aren't motive, method and opportunity the things murderers are supposed to have?"

"Yes," he replied. "You may not realise this yet, How Kum, but hunters and prey have a good deal in common."

Later as the al-Misris drove me home I asked, "You don't quite approve of the way in which D'Cruz is conducting his investigations, do you, Jafri?"

He shrugged. "No. I think good old Ozzie is barking up the wrong tree. The killer we are looking for is not the kind that he is accustomed to dealing with." He stopped talking as he overtook a car. "The poor tormented soul who has committed these crimes is, I think, more a candidate for psychotherapy than the hangman's noose."

I was upset by what he said: by the fact my best friend Jafri could view the person who had stuck a knife into Vanita's heart with anything like sympathy. The smell of soap and talcum powder wafted across from Zainah in the back seat. I inhaled deeply and didn't bother to hide from myself the kind of longing it roused in me.

EIGHT

On Fridays I go through our stocks of meat at Nats. I do
this with Loong. Checking the meat supply is a relaxed
affair and gives us plenty of time for chat. Normally
Loong used this time to fill me in on the variety of ways
in which Chinese culture was superior to all other cul-
tures and so enumerate the spiritual rewards that come
with a mastery of taekwondo.

Today he was quiet. It would have been a good time to
stir things up and provoke the supervisor along the lines
suggested by D'Cruz. Several openings presented themselves but I hesitated. I knew why. Loong had been Vanita's lover for over a year and was in a position to make
revelations that could be painful, raise doubts that, with
Vanita dead, could never be resolved.

I knew that, to come to terms with Vanita's murder,
I should have the courage to see the world I had
fashioned around her destroyed, and the ingenuity to put
together another. Right now I possessed neither. I was
overcome by a lethargy that made even walking between
the rows of frozen carcasses an effort. Instead of talking
about Vanita, I prodded a piece of meat and remarked
that it looked like it had been thawed and refrozen.
Loong examined it, humphed and said that he would
bring it to the attention of our suppliers. We passed on
to some egg-mix. I remarked how susceptible this was to
infection by salmonella. It had a slight curdle on the top
which suggested that it might already be harbouring the

germs. I didn't go on to take a specimen to find out if it
was.

My lassitude stayed with me while I sat alone in my
office. It kept Vanita's ghost at arm's length. I understood
why I felt the way I did. I was waiting. Waiting for something to happen. Waiting for something to tell me how
things were making out, the way in which I should stir
the cake-mix. Something that would tell me if I was looking at a moonrise or a sunset.

I picked up the phone. Almost before it rang.

Mohan's high-pitched, amiable voice said, "Father is
wanting to know if you could dine with us this evening?
There is something he needs to say but he has not
revealed the nature of this communication to me.
Nevertheless . . ."

I agreed before he could go any further. Things had
begun moving again.

It was dark when I arrived at Cairnhill Circle. Number
39 seemed more forlorn than ever, the amber glow of
its antiquated lights almost invisible in the aggressive
fluorescence of the surrounding high-rise apartments.

The past was gone but there must be ghosts. I stooped
and touched what little there remained of the past, an
old-fashioned kerb-stone. Ghosts gathered around me.

I see children playing in the narrow gardens of terraces
and on the manicured lawns of bungalows; hear the voices
of mothers calling them in to dinner. In the shadows I
can make out lovers, young, impatient, fumbling in their
caresses. In them, I see myself and Vanita, realise that
the pain of her loss will extend into the past and continue
into the future. Escape was impossible. Resolution had
to be found.

I stood up and dusted my hands. Walked the last few
steps and rang the door-bell.

Leela let me in. I noticed how tiny and wizened she

was. She reached up and touched my face. Her hand was rough as a root. She smiled at me in the way of the very old, bringing to life the wrinkles around her mouth and eyes. Her smile was a beacon. It told me that that my life was again on course. It also told me that I had found an ally.

The front rooms of the house were empty of everything except the smell of incense, and Leela indicated that I go to the room at the back. Here I found Mohan doing his yoga exercises.

He had explained these to me before. I found him in what I knew was the padangustansana posture. This was supposed to strengthen the spine and reduce the demands the genital organs made on the body so that the energy one put into sexual activity could be directed toward higher things. I don't know what it did for the libido but there was no doubt that holding it required great strength and muscular control.

Mohan squatted on the toes of his left foot while his right leg was rigidly extended in front of him. His arms were crossed over his chest and his eyes looked straight ahead. I knew better than to disturb him.

After a measured number of breaths he moved out of the padangustansana and into the myurasana position with which he always concluded his exercises. To get into this he knelt forward and placed first his head then his hands on the floor. Then very slowly he began lifting his knees off the ground, supporting the entire weight of his body first on both hands then, unbelievably on one. His body was soft, effeminate. His belly, with a deep navel at its centre, hung close to the floor. Yet he held the position with ease and the face he turned to me when he was done had no trace of sweat on it.

"You are displaying the kind of patience that all students of yoga aspire to." He slipped on a shirt. "Father should have completed the lengthy prayers he engages in these days and I can only hope that the smell of incense has not demolished your appetite." We moved out of his room, "It will have to be an all-vegetarian meal that we are eating today as it is a Friday. I heartily enjoy vegetarian food myself and often eat it in preference to meat. My only objection is being compelled to eat it on certain days. Why Friday and not Thursday? Why not every day if we subscribe to the ecological arguments our vegetarian friends are every day advancing? It is not this or that practice that I am objecting to. It is irrationality and superstition that I cannot. . . will not subject myself to."

We were now in the dining-room where Leela was setting up the meal. In the manner of old servants she ignored us and went about the business of putting pickles and various condiments on to brass trays on the table. In the centre of each tray was a large depression intended for the rice. Into this Leela sprinkled a few drops of water.

"We wipe these off before the rice is served," Mohan explained, "symbolically washing our plates." He giggled. "Notice how we adhere painstakingly to all the nonsensical rituals of our religion but ignore its essence." He jerked his head upwards.

I listened and heard the sounds of bajans from the room upstairs. I felt an emptiness in the middle of my chest as I listened to the songs my beloved used to sing and I wondered if it would ever be possible to fill the vacuum that seemed to have replaced my heart. I listened more carefully and detected two voices singing. Then I looked at the table and noticed that Leela had set four places.

"Yes," said Mohan with a snigger. "We are having His Lordship, the high-priest of mumbo-jumbo with us tonight as we do more and more these days."

"Kishore?" I asked.

"Who else but that scoundrel. He sticks to father as a leech to a man's life-giving veins. The rogue realises that father is weakened and made foolish by the loss of sister. He also knows how rich we are and that father is in sole charge of the family's moneys and ownings."

I had told D'Cruz that Sundram owned a fair bit of property. I had not actually worked out how much this was. The house in Cairnhill alone would be worth several million dollars. In addition to this Vanita had mentioned several small shopping complexes and a few houses in choice locations around the island. Sundram was a millionaire several times over.

Mohan seemed to have tracked my thoughts. "Yes," he said, "this house alone is worth a million or two and we have four residential properties besides. We also own sizeable commercial properties. Kishore has knowledge of them all. He has told father that he needed to see them to understand more fully the conflict between father's soul and his material circumstances. He was, as will be clear to any one with a fragment of common sense, making an assessment of the real estate we owned."

I asked, "Who will inherit all this when your father dies?"

Mohan looked at me sideways. "It is customary among us Tamils that the family fortune passes to the first-born male child. This has been our tradition for thousands of years. It is also the dharma that is strictly adhered to. And because dharma is generally accepted by us, wills have never been necessary in our community." His mouth drooped. "But recently some doubts have been entering my mind. Father has seen a lawyer and a document has been drawn up. It is not clear how the property will be divided but I have reason to suspect I may not be the main beneficiary."

"Are you trying to tell me that your sister may have been your father's heir?"

"Father loved Vani. Perhaps more than a man should love his daughter. He has hinted that this gives him the right to contravene the dictates of dharma. Only a man who does not comprehend Hinduism can talk like that but I think there is some sickness that has entered his mind and is destroying it. Also he is guided by a man who is as cunning as he is dishon. . ."

The door opened and Kishore led Sundram into the room. Tears streaked the older man's face and his lips still trembled. I was not the only one who was moved by the singing of bajans. I reached out to him and he embraced me.

"You are all I have for comfort," he said. He ignored the dirty look Mohan shot him and continued, "You must understand this for there are plans that Kishore-ji has drawn up in which you are to be included."

"Plans? What plans?" Mohan shouted, not bothering to hide the suspicion in his voice.

"Kishore-ji wishes to invoke the spirit of my dead child. He will do this tomorrow. What he intends to do is to halt her atman as it flies toward blissful union with the Infinite."

"And how," asked Mohan, his nostrils flaring and his lip curling, "is our great guru going to achieve this miracle?"

Kishore was undaunted. "By the chanting of ancient prayers, by the mouthing of incantations, by the burning of rare fragrances and the casting of spells known only to my family." He spoke in a sing-song voice, as though the ritual for summoning Vanita's spirit had already begun.

Sundram placed palm against palm and directed his salutation towards Kishore before saying, "I am right, master-ji, to say that·this young man, who I now look upon as a son, will have to be with us tomorrow when you use your powers to summon the spirit of my dead child?"

I turned to Kishore and he said, "You, Menon, were the last person to be close to the girl. You were beside her when her essence was drained from her body. You must be with us when we recall it."

Kishore was clearly a crook who was taking advantage of the old man. Common sense decreed that I should align myself with Mohan. Yet there was something that made me want to be involved in summoning Vanita's spirit back to the world. I was being invited to participate in a dance. I could barely hear the music, didn't know the steps but I wished, wished more than anything else, to be a part of it. I did not understand why till Mohan spoke.

"Let us all be charitable and assume that this man has supernatural powers and can recall the spirit of my dead sister. What will we say to the dead child when we have her with us? What questions will we ask her?"

"Whatever you ask the spirit will answer," Kishore assured him. I knew why I felt elated, why I felt part of the game again. I also knew what I wanted to ask Vanita: I wanted to ask her who her killer was. One thing, however, bothered me.

I turned to Kishore. "How will Vanita speak to us?"

He looked at me suspiciously. "The spirit will speak through me."

"I know," said Mohan, now laughing openly. "I know exactly what will happen. Our friend here will go into some kind of fake trance. After a lot of chanting and shaking he will speak to us in a funny voice which we will all have to believe is the voice of my sister."

Kishore looked at him contemptuously, but his voice was even. "I will at the start of the ritual speak the mantras which are known only to members of my family. I will speak them in the order determined by the asterism of the full moon at the time of her death. If the invocation is successful her spirit will enter my body and will take over my whole person including my voice and my thoughts."

Mohan began to giggle and Kishore added, "You can laugh now but I can give you an assurance that by tomorrow evening not one of you will doubt that it is the girl that speaks through me." Leela, deciding that we had talked enough, began serving the meal. We ate in silence. From time to time, Mohan caught my eye and made funny faces. I continued to eat, unsmiling. I was excited at what was happening, shuddered at the turn of events which suggested that they were progressing, though in a direction I could not, as yet, understand.

We finished the meal and I stood up to leave.

Kishore said to me, "Tomorrow will be a day of exhaustion for you. Sleep early tonight, drink only milk and water tomorrow. Do not under any circumstances permit the emission of semen till after we have made contact with the dead girl's spirit."

Mohan laughed with genuine amusement. "I know that How Kum is half Malayalee and Malayalees are well-known for their prodigious sexual appetite. But Vani has not been dead one week and Malayalee or not I do not think that he has found a replacement for my sister."

Sundram reached out as though to strike his son, then let his hand fall to his side. I wanted to tell him that his son was wrong. Vanita was not just one of a number of women in my life. She was my first woman, my only woman. The woman I had waited for.

Before I could do so, Mohan said, "I'll walk you to the MRT station, How Kum. I will be needing a good deal of cold night air to clear my head of the rubbish a bogus guru has put into it."

His father looked fixedly at him and said, "I don't know

why you have taken to wandering about at night." He shook his head sadly. "A thousand times I have begged you to take a wife, so you can find contentment in a bed instead of walking restlessly around the town."

"Don't worry, father," Mohan retorted. "I give you an assurance, here and now, that no amount of wandering I do will lead to the emission of semen from me or on the part of anyone else." He paused to emphasise his point. "That is more than you could have said about your dear, dead daughter, isn't it?"

Sundram hung his head.

I was discouraged by Mohan's remark. I was being moved along a course, was beginning to recognise signposts. The night breeze moved the angsana to wave leafy hellos as I passed. Happy people bubbled up at me as I rode down the escalator. The train arrived as I willed it to and the doors opened to the touch of my eyes. I would find out why Vanita died. However painful, I would find out.

NINE

It stayed with me: this feeling of being on course. I realised that things would happen that would disturb the picture that was beginning to form in my head. These I must view as distractions, side issues to the main theme. But I would go with them and, in time, incorporate them into the total picture.

I was especially glad that I had come to see things this way till I opened the paper the following morning.

The front page of Saturday's *Straits Times* was taken up by details of more murders that had taken place in East Coast Park the night before. The victims, two girls in their late twenties, had been killed not far from where Vanita had died. One of them had been stabbed with a knife similar to that used in the earlier murders. The other had had her neck broken. Though both girls were described as being "in a state of undress", neither appeared to have been sexually assaulted. The newspaper story did not explain why they were naked except to state, somewhat coyly, that they were known to be very good friends.

I felt the excitement of the preset girls as I walked between them that morning. They went about their packaging silently, as always, but the tension in the air was inescapable. It caused my hair to stand on end and produced an uneasiness in the back of my neck.

I stopped to chide a preset girl for allowing a taloned finger to protrude from her plastic glove.

"I am sure you know that our regulations require that the food we pack is never in direct contact with skin." She was a pretty girl who I seemed to remember as a friend of Vanita's. I bent over to read the name-tag on her lapel. "Anita Chew, you must make sure that the protection worn is intact and that you wear gloves at all times."

"So we don't leave fingerprints, yah," she muttered before walking off to change the damaged glove.

I ignored the impudence but hurried through my tour of inspection. The phone was ringing when I got to my office.

"Menon," D'Cruz asked, "what d'you think of the news in the papers?"

"I don't know what to think."

"I'd like to talk to you. Put you in the picture, like."

"Now?"

"Yeah."

"I'll run down to security and get clearance . . .'

"No need for that. My inspector's uniform will get me past your bully-boys."

In less than an hour he was seated at my desk.

"Tell me what the papers left out."

He did.

The girls were lesbians. The butch had wanted a sex-change operation so that they could be married but the doctors had refused to do this, on the grounds that she was homosexual and not transexual. I looked puzzled. He explained. "Homosexuals love their own sex. Transexuals feel that they have been given the wrong sex organs and wish these changed." He laughed cynically. "No big difference when it comes to practical politics. This butch lady was really into love, big guy."

"Why d'you say that?"

"A female to male sex-change would mean that she was

prepared to give up sexual sensations altogether. And she was prepared to do this just so that she and her lady love could life openly as man and wife."

"I don't get it. Won't the doctors give her functioning sexual organs?"

"Functioning, sure. But only for her partner. She'd get a piece of bone covered with skin and muscle stuck between her legs. A couple of plastic balls to hang below this." He glared at the NO SMOKING sign on the wall before lighting a cigarette. "The whole caboodle would have about as much feeling as a lamb chop straight out of your deep-freeze."

I thought for a bit then added, "Clearly these girls had strong feelings for each other and didn't keep this secret. Their families must have objected."

He shrugged. "I guess."

"Could these objections have been strong enough for someone to want them killed?"

He shrugged again. "Could be. But my money's not on that type of killing." He began to tell me about the dead girls.

They had been going steady from the time they were in primary school. Stella Stevens, the "male", was Eurasian. Lee Bee Choo, the "female", was Chinese.

"Could there be a racial angle to the murders?"

He shook his head. "Race only comes into cunt'n'cock type sex. Know why, big boy?" I shook my head. " 'Cause that's the kind of fucking that produces funny-looking kids."

"And you don't think that anyone could have had strong enough feelings about sexual perversion to want to kill them?"

He threw up his hands. "No. If we killed all our weirdos we'd have no one left to hate."

I had come, more or less, to accept that Vanita's death

was central to what was happening and that everything else would have to be linked to it. The murder of the lesbians was bewildering.

"What connects Vanita's murder with that of these girls?"

"Sometimes you don't think too good, How Kum." It was the first time he had used my name. He stopped, resisted the temptation to pun and said, "You tell me, maestro?"

"Nothing I can think . . ."

The inspector gave in to temptation. "How Kum, you're so stupid." It wasn't a good pun and he looked at me apologetically before going on. "They were killed in the same place, at about the same time. The same type of weapon was used in three of the four killings."

"But one of the girls had her neck broken."

"Sure. But that was an accident." He lit another cigarette, aimed carefully and chucked the match into the wastepaper basket. "Poor Stella. She was a brave little soldier. Her lady love gets stabbed in the back. She jumps up to try and do something. Has to fight the bloke that did it barehanded. He still has the knife, mind you, and her breasts were slashed to shreds. I think she somehow managed to kick the knife out of his hands. It's unarmed combat now and the bloke's much stronger than our Stella. He gets behind her in the struggle, gets on a full-nelson and breaks her neck."

He stopped talking and looked at me.

D'Cruz and I are different. As different as two people can be. But the exact scene that was being played out in my head was being played out in his.

It is dark. The darkest of darknesses that precedes the dawn. A girl fights for her life. She is terrified. Not for herself but for her lover who lies bleeding on the ground. She knows she must get her to a doctor or the girl will die. The man is strong. He gets behind her. His hands slip under her arms, lock behind her neck and begin forcing her head downwards. She struggles but cannot free herself. She has only one thought before her neck snaps. One thought: she must save Bee Choo who is bleeding to death on the grass.

I thought of Vanita crying out in the night when the murderer struck. I had not risen to fight her murderer as Stella had done. I had slept on as her life's blood seeped from her body. As these thoughts passed through my mind, Vanita's ghost joined us and sat on the desk between me and D'Cruz. The Inspector was speaking and she was agreeing vigorously with what he was saying. I noticed this and began listening myself.

"I think that you now have begun to see that your girlfriend's murder is the main action in this case. The rest," he shrugged, "are sideshows, jokes, razzmatazz," he looked worried, "or, maybe a killer gone crazy."

"I think I am convinced that Vanita's death is central to the case," I said and paused. The ghost leaned back and applauded. "And I have a rough idea as to what you want me to do."

"Yes, How Kum. Poke around and see what kind of fires you can start." He seemed to look in the direction of the ghost as he said, "I did a little digging myself and came up with this priceless nugget. Seems like your friend Loong who was putting it to the victim . . ." He coughed apologetically. I shrugged. Vanita laughed. "Seems like this Loong had a father-in-law. And this geezer just snuffed it and left all the moola to Loong's scrawny little wife."

"How did you find this out?"

He grinned. "Twisting arms, rummaging in dirty linen, cashing in a few cheques. Call it routine police inquiries. Call it what you want. The important thing is that my sources are one hundred per cent reliable. They tell me that this Mrs Loong is so ugly that the sight of her makes you wish you were blind." He scratched his nose thoughtfully. "I guess she's not the kind of dame who'll tolerate competition. The same sources tell me that if the said Mrs Loong caught her beloved spouse waving the wick anywhere outside honourable family bedroom, she'd chew it off and spit it in his face before shoving him back into the gutter in which she found him. Am I correct, How Kum?"

I nodded and added, "There's one other thing. If the missus does give Loong the boot there's no way she's going to let him get near his kids."

A slow smile spread across D'Cruz's face. "I realised that Loong didn't like sticking it into hairy legs and vice versa. Even though she held the keys to the safe, fear of her discovering that he was into extra-marital sex was no reason for murder."

"But something I said has made you change your mind?"

"You bet your sweet life there is." I frowned and he explained.

"What you said about the kids, big fella. What you said about access to the kids. I got none myself, but I guess that those who do will go to some trouble to make sure that things are OK for their children. Chinkos carry this kind of thing to extremes. They think in terms of dynasties, see their children as pieces of immortality they have cornered for themselves.

"They are fanatically proud of them and see them as the start of something that will go on for centuries. The true-blue Chink has such a strong connection with his children that he'd think nothing of murdering anyone who threatened to break it."

"Vanita was not the kind of girl who would have done anything to have damaged his relationship with his children." Even as I spoke the words I felt a sharp stab of pain in my chest which expanded into a ball of agony. The thought that she should have even this kind of decency, this tiny loyalty to Loong, was unbearable. I forced myself to continue. "And if she was not going to betray him, what was the point of getting rid of her?"

"He could not be a hundred per cent sure of that. No one can." He lit a cigarette from the one he was smoking. "She could do it unintentionally, mention it to friends, casual like. Even make jokes about it. Then again, and this may hurt you, big guy, she could have used it as a lever to get him to do something for her. She may not have actually threatened him but, remember, the bloke is a fanatic about his kids.

"Suddenly ugly wife comes into big bucks. Not a few K here and a few K there but the multi-millions. It's a new ball-game as far as the future of his kids goes. We are talking Oxford and Cambridge now, we're talking Harvard and Yale. No longer does our Chinaman see his son as, at best, becoming the Chief Medical Officer of the Toa Payoh out-patient dispensary. He sees him as a Cabinet Minister, the Secretary of State. If shit-face finds out about his black bimbo. . ." he stopped, coughed on his cigarette and started again. "It's unlikely that ugly wife is going to let him be a part of all this if she knows he's been unfaithful to her with any woman at all."

"You are assuming that Mrs Loong suspected something was up between her husband and Vanita and, perhaps, other . . ."

"God only can guess what fart-face suspected or did not suspect. Wives generally guess more than they let on and I don't think our boy was the kind who would take chances."

I thought about what the inspector was saying. Much

though I wished it, I could not bring myself to believe that the supervisor had murdered Vanita.

I said, "Surely it would have been more to the point for Loong to have got rid of his wife?"

"Not really." He grinned again. "Police sources inform me that on Mrs Loong's death the money automatically passes on to one of the old man's nephews."

A strange thought struck me. "There's no possibility, Ozzie," the inspector looked pleased at my using his first name, "that the Loongs could have been in this together to save family face or some such thing?"

"The family that slays together stays together." He shook his head. "The hag's mean as miserliness and sour as sulphuric acid but she's not the sort who gets herself mixed up in violent crime." He stubbed out his cigarette on his shoe. The butt just made it into my wastepaper basket.

"I also called on Symons again and put the wind up his ever-loving backside."

"How?"

"I told him I didn't think much of the alibi provided by his mother. Said I thought he had motive enough as he and the girl were after the same bloke."

"God. You didn't mention me by name, did you?"

"Didn't need to. After flouncing around the room for a bit the bum-jumper admitted that he did fancy you but not enough to kill for, especially as you had not made up your mind as to which team you were batting for." D'Cruz became serious. "He seemed actually relieved that I had brought you up as a reason for his wanting to kill the girl. My policeman's nose tells me that there might be other reasons why he might want her dead. Reasons that he wouldn't like me to get near to. I felt that my latching on to your Vanita interrupting the free flying of fairies was just the red herring he was looking for."

He leaned back and stretched. "I've done my bit. Now you go in and stir things up some more and see what comes to the surface. But before you rush off and do that, tell me what's happening with the rest of the cast."

"Rest of the cast?"

"I want to know what's happening with the girlie's kith and kin," he looked into my face, "but maybe you would like to start by telling me what's happening at home. Your home."

I hesitated.

D'Cruz lit a cigarette and raised his eyebrows. I told him about Ma and Oscar being lonely without me and of the minor disruption that Vanita's entry into my life had caused. I mentioned Oscar's going walkabout on Friday and the fact that he had been hobnobbing with his old cronies again. I also mentioned Oscar's strange notion of finding out something about the murders from his old friends.

"Oscar, what did you say his name was?"

"Wu," I replied. "The same Wus that own the chain of department stores."

D'Cruz scratched his head and smiled slowly. "I think I know the guy we're talking about. I thought the family, embarrassed by his fecklessness, not to mention his drinking, shoved him off to England in the late sixties. Now you tell me that he's simply moved out of the Orchard Road area to downmarket Buona Vista. It's funny that he should be involved in the case. . ."

I was indignant. "Oscar has nothing to do with these murders. He's the gentlest person I know. He couldn't kill anybody."

"The second son of the Wu family is rich enough to buy anything he wants, murder included. But he needn't even have had to buy someone. Your Uncle Oscar has a reputation for being a nice guy. Always going out of his way to help this or that bit of riff-raff who found trouble for himself. There must be many hit men in town who owe him and will be only too happy to let him cash one of his cheques."

I laughed out loud. "You're not seriously suggesting that Oscar is involved in Vanita's murder, are you?"

"I'm not saying that any of the characters we talked about is. But I'm not saying that they are not either." He reached over and touched my hand. "We'll let Oscar rest till he returns from his walkabout. I'm sure he will have something that will surprise us all. Tell me more about the girlie's family."

I talked about the old man's involvement in religion and of his son's mockery. I told him about Kishore. Then I remembered the seance that was planned for the evening.

The inspector leaned forward, all alert. It may have been my imagination but his ears seemed to twitch. "Whatever you do, don't miss the ghost party this evening. Do exactly as they ask but keep your wits about you. Under no circumstances must you accept any food or drink they offer."

"Are you afraid this Kishore might try to poison me?"

"No. But he's not the sort of bloke who'd hesitate to spike your beer with some mind-blowing drug so you heard and saw things the way he wanted you to." He thought for a bit. "I would like to know details of what happens at this seance and the order in which they happen. I don't think much of ghosties but I like to keep tabs on crooks and cranks who raise spirits and especially how they go about the business."

He stood up. "There's one more thing. This Kishore is bound to have something of a surprise for all of you or he wouldn't be holding the party. He's going to make a ghost materialise. How I don't know. When the girl's spirit does make its presence known I want you to remember to ask it who did the murders and why."

I had planned all along to do this but was reassured that D'Cruz and I were still on the same course. "I did think of doing that," I said. I hesitated before I asked, "You don't think that there might be something to this ghost-raising business do you? That this Kishore might in fact be able to communicate with the dead?"

D'Cruz laughed. "My God, no. I'm an old-fashioned Catholic and believe that the Almighty has the good sense to keep the dead to himself." He grinned. "At least till Judgement Day.

"What you will be hearing or seeing at this seance will be coming from Kishore. He's a con-man and he's on the inside, as far as the Sundrams are concerned, and I'd like to know what might be in it for him. I'd also like to know how his plans affect the rest of the cast."

The inspector stamped on his cigarette. He had difficulty bending over to pick up the butt so he kicked it into the far corner of the room. "Even the most civic-minded of citizens occasionally litter," he muttered as he left.

I was brooding on the questions I would ask Vanita and the order in which I should do this when Loong came in. He sniffed, looked at the NO SMOKING sign and sniffed again before speaking.

"I have come to speak in private, Menon," he said, pulling up a chair.

I shrugged. "As long as you don't expect me to conceal any crime you may have committed, Loong." I was gratified by his look of alarm.

He laughed in the way that Chinamen are supposed to when they are hiding something. "No crime, Menon. Maybe a minor indiscretion only." His manner became obsequious. "You know my son, En Lai. He is sitting for O-level exams this year. En Lai has good brain like father but not fully matured yet. So exam results at the end of year may not be good enough to secure a place in Junior College."

I had opted out of the Singapore educational system a decade ago but remembered it well. It was a system that was competitive and unforgiving. If Loong's son did badly in his O-Levels, he would not be given a second chance. He would be debarred from entering a Junior College, which was the only way of gaining admission to a Singapore university. I understood the supervisor's problem but did not see how it had anything to do with me, still less with the murders.

"I don't see how your son's academic prowess or, to judge by what you say, his lack of it is something that I can help you with."

Loong's voice was hoarse, pleading. "En Lai is eldest son. En Lai have to carry the family name. The one who carry family name must succeed. If En Lai fails to get into Singapore University means must be found to send abroad to good-quality western university for higher education. He is eldest son, Menon, and must excel in chosen career." He stared into my face to make sure I understood his predicament. "Good quality foreign education is expensive and father's salary inferior." His face twisted with bitterness. "But very good fortune fall on Loong family. Mrs Loong comes from family with successful business background. Recently, Mrs Loong's old father die and leave fortune to only daughter. But only daughter very conservative and will harden her spirit of generosity if suspicion of scandal finds way into family home."

I suspected what he was building up to but was enjoying the proceedings and wished to prolong them. "I still can't see what all this has to do with me."

"You and dead preset girl become close friends. Maybe

she speaks of Loong and little playful mischief with her, yes?"

The enjoyment I was beginning to feel was replaced by pain. I thought of long afternoons in the Changi Meridien, of making love in air-conditioning, of calling room-service while they rested.

"You and your traditional Chinese ways make me sick, Loong. You may not be able to understand that I love Vanita and I was going to marry her. I don't care what she did with you or what she did with anyone else."

His eyes narrowed and he looked extremely cunning. "You are a wise and forgiving man, Menon. You still have wish to have the Sundram girl for your wife though she has passed through many hands. But my wife, Mrs Loong, has not such spirit of generosity. If she hears of husband's little mischief she will not provide funds for En Lai's education or, worse trouble, she will prevent father's access to son after son has become success." His expression became hangdog. "I must beg of you, Menon, for complete secrecy in matter of preset girl."

Suddenly, all I wanted was to get rid of the man. "I have no intention whatsoever, Loong, of telling your wife what kind of hanky-panky you get up to in the office."

I was confident that the inspector and I were working to the same plan. Even then, it did seem strange that what D'Cruz suspected had so quickly been confirmed. It seemed almost as though Loong were offering me a motive for the murder, one that though obvious, I mustn't take seriously. He could only be doing this to throw me off the scent, to distract me from a course that might lead me to the real motive for the killings. I did in the end discover what it was he wanted to hide. This did not, except in a very roundabout way, tell me the killer's ident- ity. It did, however, bring me closer to the woman I loved and so helped me come to terms with the eternity I had to spend without her.

It was difficult to pursue the thoughts passing through my head with the supervisor pumping my hand as vigorously as he was doing. "You may not be full Chinese, Menon, but you are a true oriental," he said, beaming, his voice suddenly genial. As he left he called over his shoulder, "And one hundred per cent trustworthy in all respects I am sure."

I was disturbed by the supervisor's visit. I would have liked him to hang for Vanita's murder. I had read somewhere that a man ejaculates as his neck snaps and this was the only kind of orgasm I wished for Loong.

I began to move things around in my head so that I could see Loong as the killer. He had presented me with the motive. He was a martial arts expert and it wouldn't be difficult for him to stab people through their chest walls or to break their necks. And I guess he had opportunity enough. None of us seemed to have thought of asking him what he had been doing on Friday night. I could see Loong as the kind of person who would unhesitatingly dispose of one human being who had become a threat to him. I could not see him committing five murders in a frenzy of bloodlust. Nor was he the kind of man who had the imagination to conceal one important murder under a mass of bodies. I had to look elsewhere.

I began with Vanita's family.

Sundram was not high on my list of suspects. Conventionally religious, he must have disapproved of the way in which his daughter carried on. It must have also caused him some embarrassment in the Hindu community of which he was a respected elder. Disapproval of her sexual conduct, however, was not a good reason for murder. If it were, most young women would not live to become mothers. What was more, Sundram loved his daughter intensely. This was obvious from the way in which he had transferred his affection to me after her death.

I began thinking of her brother.

He was an enigma. He claimed to have achieved the detachment from worldly things that Hinduism requires. It was not clear how far this went. Would he be detached enough not to mind being excluded from his father's will? Knowing that his sister would inherit when his father died was one thing; killing her because of it was another. And if money was the motive, killing Vanita would not secure the Sundram fortune for Mohan. Heart attack or no heart attack, his father was very much alive and could easily leave all he had to someone other than the son of whom he seemed to disapprove.

My mind wandered away from the Sundrams and I began to think of Ma and Oscar. My intuition had earlier told me that any suspicions I might entertain about their being responsible for the murders would be distractions, asides to the main theme. I still believed this, but something that D'Cruz had said caused me to examine that situation again. It was impossible that Ma or Oscar could have done the killings themselves. But as the inspector had pointed out, Oscar had money and enough influence in the criminal world to have them done for him. And there may have been reasons for him to arrange Vanita's death.

From just about the time I had reached puberty, I can remember Ma going on about my finding the right girl and settling down. She did not, I recall, seem to mind my taking such a long time to find such a person and wasn't in the front row applauding when I did.

A burning in my stomach distracted me from my musings. It was near lunchtime. Usually Choy, one of the cooks, sends a tray round to my room around one. I was

about to phone and ask for it early when I remembered
Kishore's injunction. The prospect of existing on milk and
water till the seance was an unhappy one made more so
by the fact that I didn't seriously believe in spirit raising
or the mumbo-jumbo that went with it. Nevertheless, I
was reluctant to prejudice the venture. I called Choy and
told the cook to send me a large glass of milk instead of
my usual tray. It had just arrived when the phone rang.

"Could you pop upstairs for a minute, HK?" said
Symons. "I'm having problems with one of our preset
girls."

I laughed. "Decided to go straight, have you?"

"You must know that I never mix business with
pleasure, How Kum," he retorted, his voice prim and
formal.

"Don't you now," I said thinking of our first meeting in
his office.

"Come at once," he ordered.

"I don't have your facility . . ." I began, then tiring of
the game asked, "What kind of problem?"

"I think that one of the preset girls, a young woman
called Anita Chew, may be infecting the food trays."

Anita was standing in a corner of Symons's room. She
was subdued and quite a different girl from the one who
had cheeked me in the morning. I guessed that Symons
had threatened her with dismissal. Speaking in his most
prissy voice, Symons said, "We have reports of three cases
of food poisoning from food which appears to have originated in our kitchens. I have checked the schedules, and
in all cases the only common factor I can find is the fact
that this preset girl was working the line at the time,
and could have infected the trays." He was clearly in a
bullying mood.

I said, "I take it you have only the reports of flight

stewardesses. No doctor's certificates, no microbiological reports."

He shot me a black look. "None will be necessary if I have proof, if you can tell me, that this girl did not, to your knowledge, comply absolutely with the very explicit rules of hygiene laid down by the management."

Anita turned a tear-stained face in my direction. I said, "I have on no occasion found this preset girl to do anything but comply exactly with our rules."

"I don't think we need to detain this person any longer," said Symons.

I was about to step out of the room when he said, "A moment, HK." His manner had gone back to being casual and he indicated a chair. "There's another matter which I feel we should discuss."

"I hope it doesn't concern my sex life."

He laughed. "Only peripherally, in that it involves the Sundram girl."

"What the hell did you ever have to do with Vanita . . .?" I began.

"Hang on HK," he interrupted, laughing. "You know I don't mix my metaphors. Nor is it anything to do with what that beastly fellow D'Cruz suggested to Mamma." He shook his head. "The scoundrel had the nerve to insinuate that I may have killed the girl because we were going for the same fellow. Upset Mamma terribly. Thank God she had already had several of her medicinal brandies when he made his appearance.

"The damned impudence of the man. He went on to suggest that, not only were we after the same man, but that I may be," his voice became shrill with indignation, "bisexual and interested in the slut myself. Confused the dear old Mamma by talking about people being AC-DC. For a while Mamma thought he was an electrician being impertinent."

"What else did the inspector get up to?"

"Just about called Mamma a liar to her face. Said that her word about my being home on Saturday night would not be enough. 'Needed corroboration' were his exact words. Mamma's spirits were fortified enough to tell him where he could put his corroboration." He looked slyly at me. "Did the girl ever say anything to you about me?"

"Why in heaven's name should a normal girl like Vanita want to talk about an out-of-date fairy like you?" I knew I was losing control and this is the last thing I wanted.

"You were aware of her liaison with Loong, the supervisor?"

"Listen, Symons," I said, doing my best to keep the tremor out of my voice. "I wanted to marry Vanita and spend the rest of my life with her. I was interested in her future, not her past."

"Cool down, HK, and get off the horse." I looked confused. He smiled and added, "The high and moral kind. And tell me if the girl ever mentioned some kind of arrangement that Loong and I had with our meat suppliers?"

The air-conditioning at Nats is absolutely silent. Suddenly, the compressors began to hum, whispered a warning, told me to look where I walked and to place my feet carefully or I would find myself somewhere other than where I wanted to be. Less than an hour had passed since I talked to Loong and I was being offered another motive for Vanita's murder.

When I first joined Nats, Symons had given me an impressive-looking file. This was marked STAFF ONLY and he insisted that I read it and return it to him as soon as I had done so. Mostly it contained boring information on how the organisation worked. It did, however, tell me something about our system of tenders. Every three years we advertised for meat suppliers. We provided specifications of the type of meat that was to be supplied, the amounts, and how often deliveries were to be made.

None of the merchants knew what their rivals were bidding. This information was considered top secret. Tenders were decided upon by a board made up of several of our directors as well as some of the city's eminent businessmen. None of them knew much about the meat business or the airline servicing industry. Anyone who had inside information on the price range the board were thinking of could win the tender. Having won it, he could possibly increase his profit margin by providing meat of inferior quality to that described in our specifications.

In making their award, the selection board was strongly influenced by what the manager of Nats advised. It was the duty of the supervisor to ensure that the meat supplied conformed to specifications. Nats ordered millions of dollars of meat each year. I remembered the inspector's words about looking to money first as a motive for murder.

Symons had asked his question almost as an afterthought. I wasn't deceived by his casualness and repeated it to give myself time to think. "You want to know if Vanita mentioned an arrangement you and Loong may have had with our meat suppliers?" I looked up and smiled at him.

"Yes, HK. Did the girl say anything at all along those lines?"

"Vanita did say there was talk about leaks in the tender system that favoured one of the suppliers in town." His face froze and I decided to chance my arm. "She also said that perhaps Loong had a hand in things, for some of the specs were not quite right. . ."

"Oh God, oh God," he said, banging his fist against his head. "I told the idiot not to get the girl involved. Now he's told the girl and she's told you and God knows who else."

He hung his head. "I guess it's only a matter of time before the police begin one of those horrid investigations and, I know, those corruption squad thugs are only too pleased to expose all the details of one's private life." He began to rock backwards and forwards like a crying child. "If anything is made public, Mamma will certainly have a heart attack."

If the brandy doesn't get her first, I thought, as I left the room, but could not help but feel a little sorry for the man. The Corrupt Practices Investigation Bureau, called the CPIB, was well known for its thoroughness and the ruthlessness of its officers. If Symons were guilty of corruption involving our national airline, he would certainly spend some time in jail, and he would risk murder to avoid this.

But the whole business of Vanita knowing anything about irregularities in the meat tenders had been a lie. What was more, Symons had not thought that she would talk till I lied that she had. Vanita's involvement with Loong and Symons was not the cause of her death. It was nevertheless something that I wanted to find out more about.

I walked out of the building and round by the hangars.

The murders were the main theme. There were several subsidiary themes which were different but were related to the main. These appeared, altered the score a little, then disappeared only to surface somewhere else later. Vanita's involvement with the meat tenders was one of these.

I let the themes, major and minor, drift slowly through my head. it would be a while before they would come together to produce the kind of rush one experiences at the end of a symphony. But I could wait, for I could smell the sunlight glinting off the grass and hear the sweat trickle down the bodies of the men in boiler suits as they worked on the engine of a jumbo jet. The world was right again.

I entered my office and was happy to find it empty except for the glass of milk standing on my table. I had just finished drinking this when the phone rang. It was Kishore. He asked me to be at Cairnhill Circle by five forty-five as the seance was scheduled to begin precisely at six. The time had been determined by various astrological parameters. The same parameters had decided that it should end at eight.

Perhaps it was the lack of food, perhaps a confusion induced by the day's events, but I kept telling myself that, in addition to other things, I must not forget to ask Vanita's ghost what Loong and Symons had been up to.

TEN

I wanted to make sure that I got to the Sundrams early. Instead of bussing all the way as I usually do, I travelled overland from Changi to Eunos and there caught the MRT into town. It was near the rush hour but the train was empty. Most people were at this time travelling away from the city rather than into it and for most of the journey I had the compartment to myself. I was glad of this for I wished to be alone with my thoughts.

Vanita had not been in the office when I got back to it. This seemed only right for I expected her to be waiting for me at Cairnhill Circle.

I must have been foolish with hunger for I was becoming increasingly convinced that Kishore could actually summon Vanita's ghost. What was more, I was certain that the presence he invoked would be capable not only of answering my questions, but of otherwise responding to me. It was difficult to believe, even in my present light-headed state, that I would be able to see and touch her but I was sure that I would speak to her and, who knows, even get to smell her body. Anticipation made me dizzy. I was breathing heavily and was in a state of high sexual excitement. A middle-aged woman entered the compartment. I didn't realise that my state was obvious to her till she looked over her shoulder when she left the train. She seemed relieved to see the doors close behind her.

I got off at Orchard. It had been sunny when I left Changi and I was surprised by the change in the weather.

The sky was black and a premature dusk had fallen on the city. I could smell the lightning suspended in the clouds, taste the slight panic as people scurried about, clutching shopping bags or brief-cases, bumping into each other in their hurry to get home before the storm broke. I joined them and rushed along Orchard Road and got to Cairnhill Circle at five-thirty. It was dark. Night had fallen early to hide the entry of Vanita's spirit into the world.

Kishore let me in. Behind him stood Leela. She glowered at his back but gave me a conspiratorial smile and followed this with a nod. As I followed Kishore in, she nodded again. I thought there was something she wished to say to me. She had been Vanita's confidante. The warmth I felt for her was included in the longing I had for Vanita. I must, I told myself, find time to speak to the old lady alone after the seance.

"You, sir, have concurred with the constraints I prescribed as necessary for invocation of the girl's spirit?"

"Of course, Mr Kishore. I have had only a glass of milk all day and as to the other thing. . ."

He smiled. "I understand. The object of your affections no longer has a material presence, so you have been forced to contain your desire till another vessel for your carnal effluences is found."

I didn't quite like the way he put it but nodded as he led me into the dining-room. This was in near darkness, lit only by an oil-lamp in the centre of the table. Things had been arranged so that Kishore sat at the head of the table with me on his right and father and son on his left.

"It is important that the person who last had physical contact with the girl sits, at all times, near my right hand, which is the hand I will use to try and grasp her spirit," explained Kishore as we took our places. "The dead girl's atman is even now in the process of uniting with the Divine All Presence. It is with reluctance that it returns, even temporarily, to this earthly plane. The jewel that flies towards the light has no desire to return to the corruption of the lotus. To draw it back requires the memory of its last carnal contact, so that the desire that remains from unburnt karma acts as a fleeting temptation for its return."

All I knew about seances I had learnt from the movies and I asked, "Do we hold hands in a circle?"

"No," Kishore said, with surprising vehemence. "Any bodily contact between us will act as an impediment to the atman emerging from the world of the spirit. Above all," he looked steadily at Mohan, "there must be, more than any other thing, a craving, a desire for the girl's spirit to be with us. Hostile influences will force it away." He raised his hands and addressed us as a group. "Breathe in slowly and deeply. Fill your hearts with the air of goodness." He paused while we did as instructed. "Now fold your hands over your chest and remember that, whatever happens, you must not speak to each other or make bodily contact."

He lit several incense sticks. These he placed on the table beside him. Miraculously, they stayed upright. It took a good bit of peering to detect the little blobs of wax in which they were embedded. He held a piece of camphor to the flame of the lamp. The room was filled with acrid fumes. A brass decanter appeared in his hands from out of nowhere.

He stood up. "The man Menon, the dead girl's lover, the man who last had carnal communion with her, must drink first."

I remembered D'Cruz warning about food or drink being spiked and asked, "What's in the decanter?"

Kishore looked at me contemptuously and said, "There is water from the well of the temple, so some part of a holy place is here with us, and this water from a sacred place has been perfumed with the essence of roses."

I felt Vanita's spirit hovering like the lightning outside the windows and would have drunk a mixture of hemlock and heroin to have her in the room with me. I leaned towards him and Kishore poured a small amount of fluid into my mouth. The strong smell of roses did not conceal the earthy taste of well-water.

"Then the father of the dead girl must savour this mixture of earth and fragrances, then her brother." He poured the water into the mouths of Sundram and Mohan. "Now we must all, with one heart, remember the girl. The bells that chimed in her voice, the flowers that floated in her breath. Remember, you who loved her, the sweetness of her presence and the beauty of her person." He began chanting in a whisper, his voice undulating, notes high and low threaded together by the ghost of a melody.

The chanting numbed me. Carried me on a wave into the past, to the time when we first made love, to the time when I first set eyes on her.

When I first saw her, Vanita was sitting in a row of preset girls. I realised she was different, someone special to me. I wondered how I would tell her this. She looked at me each time I passed. Looked at me from under heavy lashes. It was curiosity, I told myself. What other reason could this long-haired beauty have for even glancing at one as unprepossessing as How Kum Menon. Yet, every time I passed, her eyes caught and held mine.

Then, one evening, I found her at the bus-stop. She had been late and missed the transport that Nats provided for preset girls. I smiled. I hoped that she saw it as more than a smile of recognition. She smiled back. Vanita is not one for coyness. Her smile was certainly more than an exchange between people who work in the same office.

Then she began speaking. I heard for the first time that voice with its mixed up highs and lows, its unpredictable tones: a voice like a boy's at puberty. And when I heard it, I felt the movement of the tumbler even before the key was in the lock. A new world was opening for me.

So entranced was I by the voice that I didn't get what she was asking. She repeated her question. "Are you married?" I shook my head. "Thank God," she said.

"Why d'you say that?"

"I used to look at you and think 'you should be mine'. Now I know 'you will be mine'."

For the next three evenings, we rode the bus into town. On the fourth, Vanita suggested we spend the night together.

She was at first surprised that I was a virgin, then happy. We were opposites, counterparts made to be one. I was unhappy about my inexperience but she said this was not something I should worry about. She had experience for two. She laughed and assured me that, though a virgin, I need not be afraid; that she would be gentle with me. I laughed too. Fascinated by the intricacies of her body, I forgot to be ashamed of the blandness of my own.

Now my thoughts made me breathe heavily. Under my folded arms I could feel the pounding of my heart. Kishore's chanting had become louder. I didn't know what he was saying but recognised aums and shantis. Several times, in a breathless aspirational voice, he mentioned yonis and lingams. How different were the Sanskrit words from the assertive, earthbound cunt and cock.

I warmed towards Kishore. The man was saying prayers which involved me and Vanita, and in them he had not failed to include a very important aspect of our relationship. I watched him sitting bolt upright, his chest heaving, his voice getting louder. I began rocking to the rhythm of the chant and my head swam a little with the fumes of incense and camphor. I listened carefully to what he was saying, hoping I would catch more words to which I could relate.

The change was gradual. I cannot say exactly when it occurred. Drops of sweat formed under my arms and trickled down, getting colder as they descended. Under the table my knees trembled. There was no question about the voice: high tones mixed with lows, unpredictable like a boy's at puberty. Vanita's spirit had entered Kishore's body.

"I have been summoned here by powers I cannot resist. The movement of my atman has been impeded as it rises towards its ecstatic and inextricable union with the Spirit of the Universe. I must be told why my progress has been halted."

Kishore mumbled for a bit then said, in his own voice, "We have asked your spirit to pause on its journey towards union because the man from whose body you sprung, the man whose blood you share, and the man who has lain in your body have requested it. Many questions are unanswered and they have need to speak to you but it is you who must say who you wish to commune with."

"It is my lover I desire to commune with. He who taught my body the delights that only union with the Godhead can surpass."

"Will you permit him to address you directly?"

"You hear my voice, How Kum. Talk to me."

Vanita was in the room with me, sitting near my left hand. My mind went blank.

"Speak to her, Menon," Kishore hissed. "I cannot be sure how long we can detain the spirit."

I found my voice. "It is really you, isn't it, Vanita?"

"You hear my voice. You should not have doubts."

"Oh, my darling."

Kishore mumbled something under his breath and Vanita began speaking again. "I will speak of things that only you know. I will tell you secrets shared only by you and me." She stopped speaking for such a long time that I was in terror that she had gone away.

Then Kishore breathed in deeply and Vanita began speaking again.

"You gave my carnal presence great pleasure. So great are the memories of this pleasure that the wise man in your midst has used it to tempt me back to the earthly plane. The pleasure was greatest when I rode you and rushed to my destination of earthly ecstasy. You were my horse except that it was your spear that was embedded in my body."

"Oh, Vanita!" My arms began to reach in the direction of the voice.

"Keep your hands folded," Kishore snapped. "If you don't, the spirit will immediately leave my body."

I replaced my arms over my chest and the spirit began to speak again. "There are things that you must do. Things that must be done before my atman can find shanti, the eternal peace."

I wanted to be sure that I would have further contact with my love and asked, "Will you come back again, my darling?"

"I will strive to return but only if you see that what I ask for is done."

"What is it you want us to do, my darling?"

"You must advise father, How Kum. You must tell him that a person close to him, one of his own blood, is filled with false ideas. You must make him understand that his kin will only deceive him. You must tell him that the guru he follows knows the true path and will lead him to the light. This is so especially in matters of money where

ties of faith are more important than ties of blood. Father
trusts you and you must make sure that he does as you
bid him."

"Your father is here, my darling. Speak to him and tell
him what you want him to do."

"Father has come to trust you, How Kum. You must
see that he does as I ask."

"I will, Vanita. I will, my darling. But I have questions
of my own that I must ask."

"I am slipping away, How Kum. The ecstasy of spiritual
union with the Godhead draws me away from this earthly
plane. You can ask me one question then I must depart.
Depart never to return unless my wishes are obeyed in
all respects."

All the questions I had planned to ask, questions that
I had so neatly arranged, got out of line and swirled about
my head. I shook it violently and one question rose to the
surface.

"I must know who killed you, my darling."

There was a long silence then Kishore began chanting
again.

"Who killed you, Vanita? You must tell me."

"Those things are not of importance to me any more,
How Kum."

"But they are to me, Vanita."

The silence was so long that, once again, I thought the
spirit had departed. I was beginning to shift about in my
seat when she spoke again, her voice fading even as she
did. "You ask who murdered me and I must say that I
can't tell you because I don't know myself. Such things
no longer concern me." The end of the sentence was barely
audible.

I could have kicked myself. How could Vanita have
known who had killed her. She was asleep and lying face
down on me when she was stabbed.

The volume of Kishore's chanting increased. He thumped his chest, gasping as he did. "Depart, depart," he shouted. "We will trouble you no longer now."

His voice became softer and he began to sing in a high plaintive voice. The words of the Sanskrit hymn touched my face and trickled down it like teardrops. I felt Vanita's spirit leave even as I became aware of Leela entering the room.

"Shall I put on the lights, master?" she asked Sundram.

Kishore was bathed in sweat and the electric lights gave the gleam in his eyes an increased intensity. "We have all seen what we have seen with our own eyes, heard what we have heard with our own ears." He looked directly into my eyes, held my gaze the way a hypnotist would. "You especially, Menon, can tell us whether the spirit spoke the truth."

I looked down partly from embarrassment and partly to avoid the effect his eyes were having on me. "She spoke the truth," I muttered.

"And she spoke of things that only she could know."

I nodded.

He said, "Then it is your sacred duty to see that what the girl wishes comes to pass."

I looked up at Sundram, His face was streaked with tears. I was not the only one moved by Vanita's voice. "I will do as my daughter wishes," he said.

Mohan, his voice hoarse with suspicion, turned to me. "What she said about . . . riding you is correct?" I nodded and he continued. "It is all difficult to explain. But," he looked at his father, "I don't think we should rush into any kind of action till. . ."

"Till what?" asked Kishore, doing nothing to hide his triumph.

"Till we . . . ," he stopped to think. "Till we hear from the spirit again and have asked it more questions."

I hated Mohan then. Hated his doubts and quibbles. His need to doubt. "You heard your sister, Mohan. She made it quite clear that she will not make further contact till her wishes have been carried out." I turned to Sundram. "I think your daughter means you to use your money for religious purposes, sir."

"It would have been her money, anyway. I broke with tradition and left everything to her. I have not made much of a secret of my intentions."

The look on Mohan's face was terrible. He couldn't stop his mouth from working and his eyes rolled about. "There is so much that can be done, father. We should spend our money on education, to free our religion from superstition, not increase the rubbish that already befuddles it. You, above all people, have the means to do so much to make Hinduism what it should be. You, father, more than everyone else. . ." He choked in his indignation.

Leela left the room and returned with a glass of water. Mohan took a sip of this. It calmed him and he said, "I don't know how he did it, father, but it was a trick of some sort." He turned to me. "You must realise that it was some kind of trick."

I turned away and Leela caught my eye. "Shall I let Mister Menon out, Master?" she asked.

"Yes, Leela. Do that."

The maid took my hand and led me out of the room. I was surprised but not displeased by the familiarity.

She looked over her shoulder when we reached the front door and said, "You were good to Vani. Very good to her." She reached into the folds of her sari and produced something in a brown envelope. "You keep this."

I felt the package before slipping it into my pocket. It was a tape cassette. I had no doubt that it contained recordings of the bajans Vanita used to sing. I would listen to them later. Much later. Right now the echoes of her voice were so strong in my head that they drowned everything else.

ELEVEN

I got home just before nine. Ma fussed as she always did when I was late for dinner. She liked me to eat freshly cooked food, not food reheated in the microwave. Muttering to herself, she watched my dinner go round and round till the "ping" informed her that it was done.

"Any news from Uncle Oscar, Ma?"

She shook her head glumly. "Nothing. He'll turn up when he turns up." Then her face brightened slightly. "I found my missing kitchen knife, though. Oscar had used it to cut the string round a packet of books and left it behind a book-shelf."

Though I had persuaded myself that I had no need to suspect Oscar and Ma of having anything to do with Vanita's death, I was glad the knife had been found. That little sideshow was over.

As I chewed on the chop grown tasteless from its sojourn in the microwave, I realised how murder gives a spurious significance to random happenings. Events, which ordinarily would have been meaningless, become sinister and full of menace. I would have to be careful not to be misled by isolated incidents, must learn to look at the drift in the tide of events, find currents, recognise direction, before I even thought of interpreting what was going on. I recalled how I had first chanced upon the notion of looking for direction in things; remembered the moon red as blood surrounded by clouds looking like bruises; remembered waking to find Vanita dead beside me. Swallowing became difficult and I pushed away the half-eaten chop.

"I told you," said Ma, "these machines take the taste away." She emptied my plate into the garbage. "Come and watch the nine o'clock news with me, son."

Normally Oscar watched the evening news with Ma and, however much he had drunk, usually managed to stay awake till it was over. Ma emphasised the fact of his absence by sitting at the far corner of the sofa. I knew what she wanted me to do and slowly moved across till our bodies were almost touching. Then I let my hand sneak round her shoulders.

The killings of the lesbians dominated the local news. The details of the murders were recapitulated. After this the parents of the two girls were interviewed. They swore that the victims did not have an enemy in the world. There was, in neither questions nor answers, any implication that the girls had been anything other than good friends.

When the families had said their piece, the Deputy Commissioner of Police appeared to assure the public that everything that could be done was being done to find and apprehend the culprit. The DCP was a young man, handsome in a smarmy kind of way and overly confident. He moved his hands about a lot when he talked and flirted outrageously with the girl who was interviewing him. He seemed the kind of man D'Cruz would have difficulty getting on with.

The murders, he explained, were not of a kind we had experienced before in Singapore. They had been classified as serial killings. This meant that their perpetrator was not an ordinary criminal but a psychopathic killer.

The pretty, young interviewer stopped him here to ask, "Perhaps, Commissioner, you could explain for the benefit of our viewers what this implies, as far as members of the public, as far as the ordinary man is concerned."

If D'Cruz was watching, I am sure he would not have failed to notice that the DCP forgot to remind the girl that he was the Deputy Commissioner, not the Commissioner of Police.

Instead he leaned towards her, his arms open, his smile wide. "I find talking to people I can't see a very inhuman business. Can I just speak as though I was talking just to you?" The interviewer nodded and he continued, "This person, for we do not have definite evidence as to whether we are dealing with a man or a woman, is clearly not someone like you or me." His hand fanned the air before it touched the interviewer on the shoulder.

"This person has a psychopathic nature which, from time to time, compels him to kill. He kills without reason and without provocation. His victims are not people who have done him harm, not persons he has reason to dislike. They are unfortunates who are selected simply because of certain fantasies going on in the killer's mind. These fantasies have nothing to do with the real world and serial killers do not have a motive, as you and I understand the word."

He smiled and touched the interviewer's shoulder again. He was assuring the girl that, whatever happened, he would be at her side protecting her. Then his face became serious and he shook his head several times as he warned, "Members of the public are requested to avoid parks and such places after dark unless they are in large groups."

What he said next was a surprise to me and would have had the inspector, had he been watching, jumping out of his seat.

"This kind of killing," he looked piously upward, "praise the Lord, has not, till now, occurred in our city. A good thing," another pious upward glance, "but it has its draw-backs. The East Coast Division, who are investigating these murders, do not have the necessary expertise to deal with crimes of this nature." He smiled beatifically all round as though by doing this he removed the insult contained in his words. Then went on, unsmiling, to add to it. "The officers dealing with these killings are OK when it comes to dealing with your routine robberies, rapes and murders. But in situations like the one now facing us they are completely out of their depth. The man . . . ," he smiled, threw up his hands disarmingly and started again. "The person responsible for these deaths is not so much a criminal as someone with a terribly sick mind.

"I have been interested in crimes of this nature and am lucky to have obtained the services of an expert in this field. His name is Dr Quincy Sio. Dr Sio is a highly qualified psychopathologist who has worked for several years in the Behavioural Science Unit of the FBI. He is a man of singular talents as you will shortly see."

The interviewer explained that an interview with Dr Sio had been arranged, to follow immediately after the newscast.

"My God," Ma whispered. "I hope Oscar is not trying to catch this madman by himself."

Oscar was a drunk, out on a wild-goose chase, but to Ma he was a knight risking himself to do noble deeds. I tightened the arm round her shoulders. "Don't worry, Ma. Uncle Oscar won't try anything on his own. He'll get help and he knows where to get it if he needs it."

The interview with Quincy Sio was quite the most amazing I had seen. Our television interviews are usually dreary affairs. Men in jackets and ties answer questions with which they have been familiarised so that things move to conclusions foregone long before the end of the interview. It was clear that Quincy wasn't going to allow this to happen.

"Before you waste air-time asking me a lot of damn-fool questions about myself, let me tell you who and what I am, and what qualifies me to talk about the kind of problem that your city is experiencing." He extended a hand to prevent the interviewer from interrupting. "For starters, I am, give or take a few decimal points, the world's foremost authority on serial killers."

Quincy was a small man with a boyish face and a bow-tie which he touched now and again as though it was a good-luck charm.

He spoke in a manner that many Americans adopt when they are in countries they consider less developed than their own. Quincy detailed the numerous serial killings whose investigation he had been involved in. No details were too gruesome to be mentioned. The drinking of blood, cannibalisation of sexual organs, the garnishing used when testicles were microwaved.

Quincy maintained that all serial killers were motivated by perverted sexual drives and had no control over their actions. As such they should be regarded not as criminals but as psychiatrically ill. They should be treated rather than punished. I felt it was all a load of rubbish and was incensed at the thought of Vanita's murderer being shown any kindness. Ma, on the other hand, had her eyes glued to the set and seemed to believe every word that Quincy uttered. I am sure that many Singaporeans felt the way she did. Then, the last person I expected to be taken in by the likes of Quincy phoned. It was Jafri.

"Did you catch that, How Kum?" His voice was higher than I have ever heard it. "If you didn't I have it on tape."

"I saw it, Jafri . . ."

"Really marvellous chap this Quincy. Really up there

with state-of-the-art criminology. Has all the upfront details of technology you don't even find in sci-fi magazines." He paused, drew a breath, and went on. "Met him today with the DCP, who is himself a very forward thinking person."

I was stunned by the change in Jafri's voice, the change in his idiom. I asked, "Was D'Cruz at this meeting?"

"Sure thing. The DCP had to have the investigating officer present. And I'll say this. The old-fashioned inspector sure didn't like the way things were going and kept a low profile for most of the time. No doubt about it. Our Ozzie sure doesn't go with modern criminology."

"What about you, Jafri?"

"I'm with Quincy one hundred per cent. And you should be too, How Kum, if you are really keen on getting Vanita's killer to treatment."

"Well, I'm not sure. I'll think about things and . . ."

"But not for too long, How Kum. Quincy is visiting with us for dinner tomorrow and we'd like you here as well. I've asked the inspector too, so he and Quincy can battle it out before an impartial jury, though I have no doubt at all that Quincy is right."

I agreed to have dinner with them the following evening but more than one thing worried me. Jafri seemed to have changed more than in his voice and the way he spoke. The man, on whom I had always depended for rationality and objectivity, mentioned providing Quincy and the inspector with an impartial jury, forgetting that he himself could not, under any circumstances, be part of such a body.

Zainah is a marvellous cook. Generally, the Malays tend to tone down strong tastes with the liberal use of coconut milk. Jafri's wife, however, managed to combine Malay softness with the more virile flavours of the Middle East and the sharp sauces of India, and I always looked forward to a meal at the al-Misris' home.

I gazed at the food before us with an anticipation I had difficulty hiding. Central to the meal was the beriyani made of several varieties of rice, each differently stained. Accompanying this was a leg of lamb roasted in its own juices and heavy with spices. Then there was a rich kurma, all but hiding the chicken drumsticks inside it, and an assortment of vegetables and pickles. Jafri, in the way of his ancestors, did not drink and usually did not offer his guests alcohol. Today, however, beer was provided to wash down the meal, perhaps because D'Cruz was present. Quincy was there when I arrived. In the flesh he appeared even smaller than he seemed on television. Both growth and ageing appeared to have been halted just before puberty, and there was a Peter Pan quality about the man. The effect of this was increased by his high-pitched voice and his overly energetic movements. Unlike most Americans he was undeterred by the calorie or cholesterol content of the food. He ate voraciously and talked almost continuously.

D'Cruz on the other hand was subdued. He ate little, talked less and smoked a chain of cigarettes which he did not seem to be enjoying. He seemed somewhere else and, at the start of the evening, did not question even the most outrageous claims that Quincy made.

"It has clearly been established that serial killers, like the one we are dealing with, have abnormal limbic systems." He looked at the inspector who was frowning at his cigarette. "I don't think you got much anatomy in police school except to know where the kidneys are so you can throw punches at them." He permitted himself two short bursts of laughter. "The limbic system comprises the nuclei of the hypothalamus, the hippocampal gyri and the olfactory apparatus."

He paused and muttered, "I wish I had brought my set of neuroanatomy slides . . ." then carried on in his normal didactic voice. "At this point in time, this organ system is looked upon as the nucleus of all criminal psycho-pathology."

Believing he had given us enough to work on for a while, Quincy leapt from his chair, cut himself a large slice of lamb, stuffed it into his mouth and began chewing it. The movements of his jaw were short and exactly timed. As soon as he had reduced the piece of lamb to manageable proportions he began talking again. "As I said, I can't go into real details without my slides but I'll do the best I can." He swallowed the lamb to prepare himself for his extempore exposition.

"The limbic system is triggered off by smell. Even he," he jerked his head in D'Cruz's direction, "will realise how important smell was for the water-living animals from which we all stem and from whom our nervous systems are derived. Smells, carried to us on water, brought messages of good and bad. Told us if an available mate or a dangerous enemy was close." He stopped to stare at D'Cruz, whom he had targeted as the stupidest boy in the class. "It doesn't take a high-grader like our police-man here, to tell us that smells, whether we are aware of them or not, influence our emotional reactions greatly. And smell," he gripped Zainah's shoulder, "is a sensation that is primarily involved in the sexual function. It initiates and sustains it. It is the most primitive of our sensations, the sensation we are least aware of and the most powerful."

He paused, more because he was out of breath than for dramatic effect. "And serial killers, I cannot repeat often enough, are essentially sick people, sexually sick folk."

Quincy, who had not released Zainah's shoulder, began pumping it as though in congratulation. She reached for a glass of water to disentangle herself from his attentions, attempting to catch her husband's eye in the process.

Jafri was unaware of any presence other than Quincy's. When he had spoken to me on the phone, I felt there was a change in Jafri. There was a whining quality about a voice that had, over the years, been so full of self-confidence and assurance. His manner too was fawning as he said, "You have explained, very adequately to me, the intimate connection between the olfactory sense and sexual function. I think my friends here would appreciate it if you could explain to them something of the nature of the affliction these unfortunates suffer from, and why you and your group see them as sick rather than criminal."

Quincy, having been forced to relinquish Zainah's shoulder, picked up a glass and began rolling it about in his hands. "Let me begin by telling you folks something about the well-known serial killer, Henry Lee Lucas. Now, our boy Henry was way ahead of the class. At ten he was having sexual relations with animals and his younger brother. Even without scientific know-how, does this not sound like his sexual physiology was disturbed? And would it really come as a surprise to hear that he committed his first murder-rape when he was fifteen?" He helped himself to more lamb and, his mouth full, asked, "And would you not say that a man who killed his victims, cut them to pieces and had sex with bits of their bodies, had an abnormal brain?" He beamed around the room.

Zainah pushed her lamb into one corner of her plate.

Quincy continued. "Then consider the case of Bobby. I mean Bobby Joe Long, of course. We have documented proof that Bobby had sex at least three times a day with his wife as well as masturbating at least five times."

"The boy sure didn't leave himself much time for saying his prayers," D'Cruz muttered.

Quincy didn't spare him a look. "We're looking at eight orgasms a day and that definitely spells brain damage. You don't need CT scans, magnetic resonance imaging, PET scans or even EEGs to confirm that."

"None of the victims of our so-called serial murderer was sexually assaulted," said D'Cruz in a flat voice.

"Ah, my dear Watson," he laughed to himself, "a good name for you, my old-fashioned policeman friend." He leapt from his chair, seized D'Cruz's hand and began shaking it as though they had just been introduced. "We modern criminologists see the murder itself as a sexual act. The victims were stabbed, weren't they?" He nodded to himself several times. "Even you, dear Watson, can see how closely the act of stabbing resembles coitus."

"Most women I know," the inspector mumbled into his beer, "would rather be fucked to death than stabbed to death."

Quincy did not appear to have heard him. "The knife, you see, represents the erect penis, the gaping wound the vulva, the track into the body the vagina. And rest assured, our killer had an orgasm, with or without ejaculation, at the moment of the slaying."

"Can you have an orgasm without ejaculation?" asked Zainah, her eyes wide.

"You do all the time, don't you?" Quincy retorted, but without the slightest trace of humour.

"I mean men, lah," she countered, only her use of the vernacular betraying her embarrassment.

"Certainly," said Quincy. "Psychologists today view the orgasm more as an electrical discharge from the temporal lobe than a seminal discharge from the penis."

"One of the girls had her neck broken," said D'Cruz.

"But her breasts were slashed. The equivalent of Henry rubbing himself off on bits of his victims' bodies."

"What about there being more than one victim on two occas . . ." D'Cruz began.

"Like Bobby, our killer has a great sexual appetite."

Speaking in his new voice, Jafri said, "Tell them how you propose to find the killer, doctor."

"Primarily from their biosocial make-up. It is clear that this kind of man will have a history of severe childhood repression and trauma. Gary, for instance, was forced by an older sister to perform cunnilingus on her when he was a little boy."

I was irritated by Quincy's habit of referring to killers by their first names and asked, "Gary who?"

"Gary Schaefer, of Springfield, of course," the doctor replied.

"But you have other ways of detecting these sick men, haven't you, doctor?" Jafri prompted.

Zainah butted in before Quincy could answer. "I don't think there are many people who have oral sex with their sisters, uh?"

The doctor rewarded her perceptiveness with a smile, nodded, allowing her to go on with the rest of her question. "And those who do go down on their sisters are not likely to tell the world about it, yah?" A nod of approval from Quincy. "So, if we don't know how many men were forced to have oral sex with their sisters, we have no way of saying what percentage of them would become serial killers." She paused and looked around her before continuing. "What I mean is that many men who have oral sex with their sisters may not become loony murderers later in their lives."

I was surprised by how sharp Zainah was. D'Cruz shot her a look of gratitude. Jafri, however, didn't seem to take her point and said, "But there are other signs of this disease, aren't there, doctor?"

"There sure are," the little man replied. "C. Robert Cloninger of the University of Washington School of Medicine has shown that the disorder is a genetic one. His work on adoptees has demonstrated that children whose biological parents are criminals are four times more likely to become criminals than those children whose parents are law-abiding."

"So all we have to do," said the inspector, barely concealing a snigger, "is to go through the records of our Social Welfare Department on adoptees and find out which of these had criminal parents. Then we find out which of the adoptees were forced to go down on their sisters and, hey presto, we have our murderer."

Jafri glowered at D'Cruz. "Listen, Ozzie. Doctor Quincy here is a scientific criminologist, whose efforts take us to the limits of our understanding of the criminal mind." He altered his tone. "But there are ways, aren't there, doctor, of physically identifying these unfortunate creatures?"

"Sure thing," the doctor replied. "The work of Dr Sarnoff Mednick of the University of Southern California has confirmed Cloninger's theory of the genetic basis of criminality. Apart from the typical neuropsychiatric disturbance, these criminals are likely to have attached earlobes, webbed fingers and very long limbs."

"Not tongues?" asked D'Cruz with a look of exaggerated innocence.

Quincy looked puzzled. He thought, and shook his head several times. "I don't believe anyone has looked into glossal abnormalities in pathological killers. Perhaps a long tongue could be correlated with maldevelopment of the brain, some abiotrophy of Broca's area. I must get one of our research teams to look into it." He leaned across and thumped the inspector's back. "You know,

Watson, you're not so dumb as your beetle brow makes you look."

D'Cruz exploded. "Listen Quincy, doctor, or whatever you call yourself. I don't know how you persuaded the DCP . . ."

"DCP?" Quincy raised his eyebrows.

"The Deputy Commissioner of Police," Jafri dutifully explained.

". . . the DCP," D'Cruz continued, "to let you in on my case. But one question burns my arse more than too much hot curry. And it is this. How the hell are we going to find this killer with his webbed fingers and spiked balls or whatever?"

Quincy was unperturbed by the outburst. "Elementary, my dear Watson. I have already set the wheels in motion. Even now, teams of social workers are tabulating data and feeding them into computers which I have specially programmed. Programmed to elicit the information we require. We are looking at the records of known sex-offenders, of juvenile malcontents, psychiatric patients and abandoned children." He bounced in his seat and farted loudly. "Within forty-eight hours, seventy-two at the outside, we will have unearthed suspects who warrant further investigation. And this, dear Watson, is more than what you have come up with in a week."

"Tell How Kum what you may need him for," said Jafri.

"We in the Behavioural Science Unit of the FBI have, from time to time, come up with two suspects with identical psychopathological profiles and similar conditioning. In such circumstances, a person who has been close to the criminal at the time of a killing can usually indicate to us which of the two is guilty. You, How Kum, are the closest anyone has come to the killer."

"How on earth will I be able to identify the killer?"

D'Cruz, who was sitting next to me, whispered, "The hairs on your balls will bristle, big fella."

"Do not worry," Quincy assured me. "When the time comes you will know."

TWELVE

Because Quincy had to keep what he called his "psycho-sensitive antennae" alert, dinner at the Al-Misris' home ended at exactly ten, and I woke early the following morning. It was a Monday. Through the thin walls of our flat I could hear Ma pottering around. Dusting, moving furniture about and occasionally turning on the vacuum cleaner. It was eight days after Vanita's death and she was very much with me.

She sat naked on the edge of my bed and crooned to me. I was in a state of high sexual excitement and, to make matters worse, my bladder was full. I should have slipped into the toilet and relieved myself, perhaps doubly, but I enjoyed the condition I was in. I toyed with the idea of listening to the tape Leela had given me. Maybe, if I listened to my beloved singing bajans, I would fall asleep again and dream of making love to her. The seance was over and there was no need to avoid the emission of semen. I was just drifting off when the commotion in our living-room woke me.

Ma's voice was raised and she seemed to be weeping. I heard Oscar's voice and that of a third person. The man's voice was familiar but not one that I could immediately identify. I became fully awake when I did. It was D'Cruz. I dressed quickly.

The trio were at the dining table drinking coffee. There was the usual bottle of brandy beside Oscar's cup. I did not realise till cups were re-filled that D'Cruz too liked a little brandy in his coffee.

"I was drinking with the law till early this morning and I thought it was a good idea to ask him home," Oscar explained as I entered the room.

"I didn't know you two knew each other," I remarked, keeping down the note of disapproval in my voice.

"Every cop of my vintage knows the great Oscar Wellington Wu." D'Cruz sounded drunk, which may have been why I had a problem identifying his voice.

"And the inspector, good policeman that he is, knows where the said Oscar Wellington Wu goes to ground."

D'Cruz had apparently traced Oscar to an all-night coffee-shop in Toa Payoh. I hated this sprawling mass of concrete. It was the first of our "new towns" but was now sufficiently old to contain dark establishments in which sinister men sat drinking till the small hours of the morning.

"Been asking hither and thither, old chap," said Oscar in my direction, "but didn't get the tiniest whisper of what these killings are about."

"As I have been trying to tell you all night, Oscar, these are not one of your gangland slayings of the sixties." The inspector looked terribly tired. He had obviously gone in search of Oscar as soon as he left Jafri's home. "I am also sure that this is not the work of a madman who kills instead of fu . . ." he looked apologetically at Ma ". . . instead of sexually assaulting his victims."

"I'm in agreement with you on that score," said Oscar. He looked at me. "Yes, I've heard all about the pundit from California. The hostelries I favour may be humble but they are possessed of," he smiled, "you may say possessed by, television."

I disliked Quincy but had to admit that a serial killer on the rampage was, as yet, the only logical way of linking the five murders we had on our hands. "I can't say that I like the little squirt any more than you do, but there could be a grain of truth in what he says."

D'Cruz turned bleary but contemptuous eyes on me. "If you believe that that pint-sized freak is anything more than a con man, you need to have your head examined."

I was riled by his contempt. "You can say what you want about Quincy, but you seem to have no theories of your own. What for instance do you propose to do? Right now, I mean."

He looked around him wearily. "Right now, I'm going home to bed. The missus will be awfully worried about my staying up all night."

"And you, young man," said Ma, taking Oscar's hand, "are going to have a good hot bath before I put you to bed myself." The tears in the corners of her eyes were quite dried.

They needed to be alone. I showered quickly and rushed off to work.

Mondays are bad days at Nats. This one was worse than most. There was a minor 'flu epidemic in town and many of the preset girls claimed to have symptoms of the disease. They had done so after they had clocked in, thereby ensuring themselves a day's pay whether or not they were sent off sick. In addition, several girls were genuinely down with the 'flu and there was a real possibility of our not being able to meet our commitments. It was company policy not to use staff who were in any way infectious and Loong was in a quandary as to who to retain and who to send off work.

He insisted that I should decide between the girls who were ill and those who were malingering. I protested that I was not a doctor but this did not impress the supervisor.

"Keeping our products hygienic is your job, Menon," he snapped, "and I will consider it negligence if you do not comply with my orders."

Feeling awfully foolish, I went down the line of giggling girls, feeling their brows and taking their pulses. When I came to Anita Chew she turned her eyes upwards and said, "There has been another case of food poisoning and I wasn't on duty when that tray went out, so you'd better tell that bum boy to look elsewhere if he needs someone to blame." I was relieved. The episode with Symons had not caused her to lose her spirit.

I had no sooner pronounced the whole row fit when the public address system summoned me to the manager's office.

"There's been a further case of food poisoning, HK. If this gets to the ears of our competitors, we might as well close Nats down, for all the business we will get."

"Have you looked at the duty schedules to see who might be responsible this time?"

"I thought that was your business," he retorted. "The flight crews' reports have been on your desk from early this morning."

"I know," I lied. "And there is no common factor. Certainly the girl Anita Chew cannot be held responsible. She wasn't on duty when these trays went out."

He fussed about the papers on his desk, rearranging them into several neat piles. I was sure that Symons had not summoned me to his office to discuss food poisoning. After a bit, he said, "You know that business I mentioned about the meat tenders?" He tipped his head and looked at me sideways. "About there being loose talk about preferences in awarding them?"

"Yes," I said as nonchalantly as I could.

"No need to worry about it any more. I had a word with our Chairman. He assures me that he has been more than impressed with my impartiality and will stake his reputation on it." He smiled confidently. "Perhaps you will be so good as to convey this piece of news to your inspector friend." His smile widened. "I believe he drops in to see you from time to time."

I rushed back to my office. I remembered that I had forgotten to tell the inspector about any hanky-panky that Symons and Loong might have been up to in the selection of meat tenders. I was about to call him when the phone on my desk rang. It was Jafri. He wanted me to go immediately to a government-run psychiatric clinic on the outskirts of town.

"What's so urgent, Jafri?"

"Dr Sio and his team have sifted through a whole mass of data and come up with a couple of hot possibilities."

I didn't look forward to meeting Quincy again and said, "I might have difficulty getting off work . . ."

"If you have any problems on that score, I'll get the DCP to call your manager and get you time off."

"No need, Jafri. I'll be there in an hour."

The computer print-out informed me that Lenny Drigo was a compulsive masturbater. This habit was noted when he was in infant school. It continued throughout his school life and became really awkward when he reached puberty and began ejaculating. An added inconvenience was that Lenny preferred to masturbate with his genitals exposed.

In infancy his mother, who was unmarried, had beaten him severely to discourage the habit. She had also tied his hands behind his back and taped a plastic cup round his genitals. None of this stopped Lenny. He had managed to free himself and carried on as before.

The anonymous author of the print-out believed that

Lenny was open about his affliction because he had not, as a child, been given clear moral directives about sexual conduct. The fact that he was illegitimate indicated that his mother too was without any socio-sexual values, and that this aspect of his personality had been genetically transmitted.

As he grew older, lack of restraint became outright exhibitionism and he had been arrested several times for indecent exposure. He had also been charged once with assaulting a minor. The female in question had, on further investigation, proved to be a thirty-five-year-old midget, and witnesses had come forward to testify that they had seen her fondling Lenny's genitals in a crowded bus. He had also been arrested on one occasion because the crotch of his trousers was blood-stained. Laboratory tests proved the blood was not human but bovine, and Lenny later confessed to liking to wrap a piece of raw steak around his penis.

He had, according to the single-page print-out, other psychopathological tendencies besides the ones detailed. There were a series of arrests for shoplifting and petty theft and one for inducing a minor to commit a crime, the crime in question being to hide a bottle of liquor Lenny had lifted from a supermarket. I reached the end of the sheet and put it down.

"You will see . . ." Quincy frowned with the effort of remembering my name. "You will see, How Kum, that we find in this dossier the exact kind of personality the serial killer we are looking for will have."

We were seated in a large, air-conditioned room. It was tastefully decorated and comfortably furnished. Quite different from the room in which D'Cruz had interrogated me but somehow more frightening. Dr Lum, whose room it was, had on his desk a stack of volumes and an impressive looking computer. This endlessly produced patterns of amazing complexity on a colour screen.

The psychiatrist, noticing my interest, said, "The way subjects interpret the patterns on the monitor clearly indicates to us the direction their disease is taking. We study them on a bi-weekly basis."

"How would a normal person interpret these patterns?" I asked.

"I don't see what that has got to do with the scientific study of psychiatric disease," he retorted.

Quincy butted in. "We are not here to investigate you, How Kum, but to get your impressions of the suspects."

"Suspects?" I asked. I had only one computer print-out in my hand. "Are there several?"

"For the moment, only two have been identified. I want you to soak up Lenny's vibrations first. Let them tell you whether or not he is the killer. Relax," he shouted, leaping from his chair and briskly massaging my shoulder. "Your extrasensory perceptive psyche cannot work if you are tense. To make things simpler, we won't clutter your head up with data about the second subject till you have formed an impression of Lenny."

"How have you connected this Lenny Drigo with these crimes?"

Quincy looked puzzled. "Isn't that obvious from the psychobiosocial dossier we have complied?"

"I think, Dr Sio," said Jafri helpfully, "that How Kum is still unfamiliar with modern criminological methods. He wants to know about motive, opportunity and that sort of thing."

"I see." Quincy laughed and punched his palm several times. "No need for that kind of detection today. We have," he indicated the print-out, "pieced together the man's complete inner make-up. It is clear that he has a powerful and perverse sex drive, that he is congenitally a criminal and will therefore express his uncontrollable sexuality in criminal ways."

"But none of the victims were sexually assaulted," I protested.

"I repeat that killing, to this kind of person, is essentially a sexual act. Once aroused by proximity to sexual activity they reach a point of no return . . . and kill." He turned to look at Jafri who was drinking in his every word. "One of the most important features of the case and one," he nodded sagely, "not noticed by your police force, was that the victims were killed during or shortly after they had been sexually active." He stared at me. "Our friend here had completed intercourse when his partner was stabbed. Esther had semen of a man, though not the man she was with, in her vagina at the time of her death. The two lesbians were undoubtedly indulging in cunnilingus when they were attacked."

I asked, "So you think that the killer was a peeping Tom driven to some kind of sexual frenzy by watching others making love?"

Quincy's eyebrows showed that he didn't quite approve my use of non-technical terms. "I guess that's the way that a non-scientific person would put it."

"How then, do you account for the fact that in my own case and that of Esther Wong, the murders were committed long after sexual activity was over?"

"Good question," he shouted, leaping from his chair and bowing in my direction. "You assume that the build-up of stimuli was visual. It would be correct to say so in some instances. However, in most cases the stimulus is not visual."

Jafri looked at me peevishly. "Can't you remember what the doctor told us about the limbic system?"

I shook my head and Quincy said, "I explained how serial killers have disorders of the limbic system. This

links together the hypothalamus, the hippocampal gyrus
and the olfactory tracts, thereby controlling both our emo-
tion and hormonal responses." He nodded severely at me.
"I explained, at dinner the other evening, that the system
is basically one of smell, which is the main trigger of
sexual attraction and reaction."

The smell of Vanita's body suddenly came back to me.
It was strong, overpoweringly so. It could not have originated in the atmosphere of Dr Lum's room which was
deodorised and air-conditioned. It must have somehow
burned its way into my limbic system.

I felt a slight sympathy for what Quincy was saying. A
sympathy which his next remark destroyed. "One has
only to watch dogs drawn to a bitch in heat and copulating
with her serially to understand the power of the sense
of olfaction. There is, however, definite scientific work
done to demonstrate the influence of smell on the
hypothalamus."

He paused. "The hypothalamus, as we all know, is the
centre of the body's endocrine functions and determines
the timing of all sexual activity: the onset of puberty, the
timing of ovulation, menstrual cycling, coital frequency,
the occurrence of menopause. It has been shown, in a
carefully controlled experiment on nuns, that ovulation,
in these celibates, could be triggered off by the smell of
semen which, unknown to them, had been smeared on
their pillows. Now, if the smell of semen can make nuns
ovulate, think what it can do to a psychobiosexually
deranged killer. The first two of our killer's victims would
have had semen trickling out of their vaginas."

"What about the two lesbians?" I asked. "It's hardly
likely that they would have had semen dripping out of
their vaginas."

Quincy was undisturbed. "Not semen, but vaginal
secretions. This has a distinctive odour and has the ident-

ical effect as semen on certain psychopaths and disturbed limbic systems."

He paused, having settled the argument to his satisfaction. "We must now come to the matter in hand. I am satisfied that we have established a watertight psychological case against Lenny Drigo. To keep this inquiry absolutely objective and scientific, we will not show you the data we have on our second subject. You make up your mind first as to whether or not you think Lenny is guilty."

"And how will I make up my mind?"

"I'm going to bring Lenny into the room. Study him and see if he produces any feelings of revulsion or fear in you. You may speak to him if you wish but do not question him directly about the murders. I will, when the time is right, want to do that myself."

"What if he asks me questions?"

"That is most unlikely," Dr Lum assured me. "We have taken the precaution of sedating him heavily with valium, so that he is of no danger to us. He is," he added in explanation, "suspected of committing five murders."

Before allowing Lenny into the room, Quincy reminded me, "Take note of any feelings of fear or revulsion the subject arouses in you."

Lenny Drigo was a scrawny creature whose face was creased and pitted by acne. His hair looked as though he had cut it himself. Lenny shuffled in and took the chair that Dr Lum had placed in a far corner of the room. Even at a distance, it was clear that a strong ammoniacal odour clung to the man. It was the smell that one encounters in the lavatories of boys' schools. Lenny sat with his legs widely apart. A hand which was deeply in his trouser pocket moved rhythmically. Dr Lum's sedative, whatever else it did to Lenny, was no more successful than his mother's efforts in eradicating a lifelong habit.

"Do you register any feelings of revulsion, fear or hatred for the subject?" Quincy asked in a voice loud enough for Lenny to hear.

I felt nothing but an overwhelming pity for the man. I shook my head.

Quincy directed his attentions to Lenny. "What feelings do you have for women?" he barked.

The hand in the pocket stopped moving momentarily and Lenny replied, "I don't know, doctor." He spoke in a very low voice.

"Denial of gender hostility is always indicative of on-going psychosis," Lum hissed.

"Why don't you know?" Quincy was clearly not going to be put off by the subject's evasiveness.

"I've never tried a woman, doctor," said Lenny, the hand in his pocket beginning to move again.

"What would you like to stick into a woman?" asked Quincy.

"Into her mouth or where?" asked Lenny, clearly puzzled by the question.

"OK," Quincy conceded. "What would you like to stick into her mouth?"

Lenny thought for a while, then smiled broadly when he felt he had worked out the correct answer to the doctor's question and said, "An ice-lolly."

"Transference to symbolic representation," commented Lum, "is semiotically diagnostic." I must have looked as puzzled as Lenny, and Lum explained. "The ice-lolly represents the penis and the act of sticking it into a woman's mouth is symbolically one of degradation."

"Do you ever think of fellatio?" Quincy's tone was ingratiating.

Lenny shook his head. "I don't know her, doctor."

"Notice the immediate association between a demeaning act and a woman," Lum pointed out to his colleague.

Quincy nodded agreement. "Right," he said. "Enough psychodata in this session alone to associate him with the crimes." He turned to me. "But we like intuitive confirmation from someone who has actually been at the scene of a killing." I shook my head and he said, "Too bad. We'll see what you can do with our next suspect." He handed me another print-out.

From this I discovered that the suspect Oh Kwee was the last of six children. His father was a carpenter and his mother a washerwoman. He dropped out of school at sixteen and was apprenticed as a motor mechanic. He was dismissed from his apprenticeship because of the theft of some spark plugs and fuses. Soon after this it became known that he was a catamite.

"What's a catamite?" I asked Lum.

"A man who indulges exclusively in receptive anal intercourse. Often this is for financial gain," he replied in a disinterested voice.

I continued reading.

It was not established when Oh Kwee began hiring himself out to S & M groups. However, it was clearly a sadomasochistic episode that resulted in him being admitted to the Singapore General Hospital with peritonitis. This was found to have been caused by rectal perforations with a sharp object. He was also diagnosed as suffering from both syphilis and rectal gonorrhoea. Psychological profiling showed that he had a very low self-opinion. This was consistent with him allowing himself to make a living by being sodomised. There were genetic markers to the personality type. The suspect had a bullet-head, indicating severe brain abnormality. It was also to be noted that he had exceptionally long arms and pointed ears with attached lobes. He was much darker than his siblings and his name, Oh Kwee, which in the Hokkien dialect means "black devil", became, in this context, of significance. His hatred for women stemmed from his having to compete with them as a male prostitute, and from the fact that he blamed his mother for his name. That he had allowed himself to be systematically brutalised indicated a vicarious desire for violence. However, the suspect had not, thus far, been actually implicated in acts of aggression, sexual or otherwise. This was, more than likely, because he had been under adequate surveillance.

Even though his name gave an indication of his complexion, Oh Kwee was surprisingly dark, almost negrito in colour. He was short, with well-rounded hips which he swung about as he walked. He shot me sidelong looks while Lum asked him numerous questions in Hokkien. Oh Kwee answered these amiably and with much gesticulating.

At the end of the interview, the psychiatrist turned to Quincy and said, "There is no doubt in my mind that he has a marked hostility towards the female sex. This hostility could well turn to violence but he has it well concealed from himself. As things now stand, he is unaware of his hostility, and I would suspect that he would be amnesiac for acts of violence committed against women."

Quincy seemed a little dejected by what Lum said. Then he nodded several times and said, "It must be evident, even to your out-of-date police force, that four of the five victims were women. What is more, the murderer passed up the opportunity to stab a man," he glanced at me, "who by his own account was in a deep, post-coital slumber."

Jafri smiled ingratiatingly and said, "I'll draw this gender preference to the attention of the relevant authorities."

"Do that," Quincy instructed, before turning to me.

"What now interests me is the effect the second suspect has had on How Kum."

"None whatever," I announced happily.

Quincy's face fell. "No fear reactions, no sweating, no palpitations?"

"None whatsoever."

"We should have had him on a polygraph," he said to his colleague. "Then we could detect changes in his physiological parameters of which he is not aware."

"As things stand, I see no option except to wait for the arrival of Madam Zoroastris, who will be in Singapore in a few days. We have worked together on several cases like this and, I might add, with one hundred per cent success."

I asked the question that was on the tip of all our tongues. "Who is Madam Zoroastris?"

"One with more powers of perception than has been given to any human I know. Zelda Zoroastris hails from England but now lives with me in California." He allowed himself a tiny smile. "We shall reconvene as soon as the dear lady is in town."

When I returned to the office I found, to my disgust, a stack of documents on my desk, all of them tagged IMMEDIATE. I knew I would be working overtime and called Ma. Instead of being upset, as she usually was when I was late home for dinner, she seemed happy about it.

"Your Uncle Oscar and I will wait for you," she said cheerily. "I'm cooking a laksa and the longer the gravy simmers the better."

Ma's laksa was something to look forward to. No restaurant got the mixture of coconut and prawn sauce right, nor did any cook I know prepare the noodles to a point where they were just soft without being soggy. The dish had to be painstakingly produced, and I knew why Ma was making laksa tonight. It was Oscar's favourite dish. I also realised why Ma didn't mind my being late. Though Oscar was sixty and they had lived together for twenty-eight years, their relationship remained tender and touchingly physical. The thin walls of our flat assured me of this often enough. My resentment at the stack of documents on my desk diminished slightly.

I got home a little after eight and was surprised to find D'Cruz there. He was drinking with Oscar. Ma was clearly less than ecstatic about his presence, and sniffed several times as she bustled about getting the meal on the table. The inspector's unexpected visit had, no doubt, cut short her reconciliation with her man, for the two had clearly been drinking for some time.

As soon as I came in, D'Cruz put down his glass and said, "I came to speak to you, How Kum. I hear you have had some sort of a session with our midget con-man."

"Yes," I said apologetically. "He wanted me to ..." I stopped. I wondered what Quincy wanted me to do.

"He wanted you to do what our temporarily deranged Arab is doing. He wanted you to lick his arse and tell him what a clever boy he has been to have unearthed those two," he couldn't control his laugh, "killers." He laughed again. "Anyway, tell me what happened?"

I did. When I finished Ozzie said, "You play along with him for a while. That's the only way I have of keeping tabs on the little squirt.

"The DCP is a well-lubricated political cunt who's playing some game of his own. I don't give a shit what happens to him. What's got me as cross-eyed as an idiot in Disneyland is the way our normally level-headed Arab is behaving."

I told Ozzie what Zainah had said about Jafri being dissatisfied with his profession, and the doubts he had expressed over conventional notions of justice.

"Only an ostrich with its head stuck up its arse is completely happy with any system of justice. Being unhappy is one thing. Believing the kind of shit the little squirt from California is spraying all over the place is another." He finished what was left of his drink and rolled it around his mouth. "I'll see what I can do to get our Arab's brains unscrambled."

Oscar realised that the inspector had completed his business and put down the glass he had been nursing. "I did, dear boy, suggest earlier that this was some kind of mass slaying. If I remember correctly, I referred you to Jack the Ripper." He picked up his glass and pointed to the inspector's empty glass. D'Cruz shook his head and Oscar continued. "After my sortie into the other world, I am convinced that this is not some kind of gangland terror stunt, nor is it the work of a lunatic. I am also of the opinion, dear boy, that your lady was the murderer's real target." He smiled weakly. "I cannot give you chapter and verse but that is the overall opinion of my friends."

Ma began serving the laksa. We ate in silence for several minutes. We began talking again when our bowls were empty and after D'Cruz and Oscar had complimented Ma on her cooking.

"I don't know what goes on in California, but murderers in Singapore kill for a purpose. Usually it's money." D'Cruz hesitated. "Except for my Tessie who was killed by an animal out of lust. And I'll say this here and now. Whatever he's got wrong with his limbic system or his hippocampus or whatever, that bastard's going to swing for it when I catch him."

A strange look crossed Oscar's face when D'Cruz started talking about his sister. I had never seen it before. I wondered if it was fear. Then, as if to change the subject, he said, "Though I did say that this dear boy's lady seemed the murderer's target, I cannot for the life of me think of a motive for her murder."

"Look to money first," the inspector advised.

I remembered the business about the meat tenders and told D'Cruz about them. I also told him about Loong saying that there was nothing he wouldn't do to safeguard the interests of his son.

D'Cruz brooded over my statement for a bit. "I think I may have exaggerated the Chinko and son situation a little. The business of the meat tenders is, however, interesting. Except for one thing. You lied when you said that Vanita had information that everything was not squeaky clean about awarding tenders. . ."

I interrupted, "I thought about that and believed that Symons had no motive for her murder. Then I thought again and wondered if Loong had not confessed to Symons that he had in a weak moment told Vanita about the tenders. They would both want her dead because of what she knew, and Loong had additional incentive for wanting her dead."

"Very good, big guy. Except for one thing."

I nodded. "That there were five murders instead of there being just one. Which brings us back to Quincy's mindless lunatics."

Oscar, who seemed to have suddenly become terribly drunk, said in a slurred voice, "You are forgetting, dear boy, the insights I gained by my sojourn in my other world. Insights which tell me that, however much you wish to believe it, your lady's death was not a mindless affair. In fact, it was very much a matter of mind."

Suddenly everything about Oscar irritated me: his drunkenness, his old-fashioned language, his long-windedness. I spoke in a voice so quiet that I could barely recognise it as my own. "Uncle Oscar, you brought me up to speak the truth always."

"Indeed, dear boy, so press on with what you want to say."

"The friends you talk about, the pimps and prostitutes and outdated scoundrels, have nothing to do with the world of today. They have no right to have opinions about Vanita's murder. They are just a bunch of has-beens like you. . ."

D'Cruz clapped a hand on my shoulder. "Hang on, big fella." The grip on my shoulder tightened. "This man has been more than a father to you. . ."

"It's all right, dear fellow," said Oscar, leaning unsteadily forward to remove Ozzie's hand from my shoulder. "This boy of mine has been brought up to be unafraid of speaking the truth, however painful it may be, and to whoever." He sat back in his chair and took a swallow of brandy. "And I think he has a right to say his piece about these murders." He looked blearily around him but his manner was not that of a hopeless drunk. He continued, "There was something I wanted to avoid bringing up till this present mess was cleared up. Something that has waited for a long time and will keep for a little longer."

He rubbed his eyes with the back of his hand. "Oh God, I must be drunker than I thought. Whatever else, I do not want you, How Kum, to see your Uncle Oscar as an absolute no-good." He sipped his brandy for a while. "I may not have anything to contribute towards the solution of the present crop of murders but I did discover something about one that took place long ago. So my going 'walkabout' was not entirely a pointless exercise."

I was so intent on what Oscar was saying that it took me a while to notice the change that had come over D'Cruz. His eyes had sunk beneath his brows and his breathing had quickened. Once more he had become the brute who had interrogated me in the room marked SIR. His voice too had become hoarse and unreal. "You haven't found out anything about Tessie, have you Oscar?"

"I'm not quite sure yet what I am on to but. . ."

"If you've got anything at all, I've got to know about it. You understand. . ." D'Cruz had risen slightly from his seat.

Oscar shook his head. "I was moved by the drink and this boy's contempt." He touched my arm. "I should have waited for a more opportune moment, till the picture was clearer."

Ma stood up and moved behind her man. She slid her arms round the front of his chest and squeezed him to her. "You are responsible to neither of these men, Oscar my love," she said, looking me straight in the eye. "This is your home, this is my home. Here you can say and do exactly as you like."

Though his voice became more gentle and he was back in his seat, Ozzie was not going to be put out by Ma's action. "Listen, Oscar, I've been with Tessie's ghost all these years. You must give me a chance to catch the man that did it." Some of his old venom returned. "You must give me a chance to catch the bastard that did it and hang him."

"I have, dear friend, just the tiniest hint, just the swirl on the surface of the sea, not even the tip of the iceberg. I wouldn't even whisper about it, and, but for the way this boy of mine feels," he patted my hand, "I would have said nothing, nothing at all."

"You do exactly as you want, Oscar . . ." Ma began.

"I'm sorry, madam," D'Cruz cut in, "but if this man here has knowledge about a felony, it is my duty to warn you that it is against the law to keep this kind of information from the police."

"Are you threatening him?" Ma shouted.

"Not threatening, just telling him what the law says." Then suddenly he collapsed. In a voice softer than I believed D'Cruz capable of he said, "I'm begging him, madam. Can't you see, I'm begging him."

"If you're begging," said Ma with a waspishness I didn't think she possessed, "you can't be choosing when and what he is to be giving."

"Bravo, Lili," said Oscar, applauding loudly.

"Whoever this person is, or these people are, who know something about my Tessie, I'd like to meet them with you." D'Cruz had begun to sweat. "I'm a policeman . . . ," he changed his mind, "I know more about this case than . . ." he stopped again. "Oh God, Oscar, I just gotta know."

"Of course, you do, Ozzie old chap. That's not in question. The question is whether the people I know will talk with you around."

"My Oscar is right, Police Inspector," said Ma, pulling herself upright but still keeping a hand on Oscar's shoulder. Suddenly a thought struck her and she smiled. "I think you, How Kum, should be with your Uncle Oscar when he meets these people."

I began to protest. I had no wish to be involved in yet another murder investigation. Then a weird thought began to form in my mind. There could be a possible connection between the murder of Tessie D'Cruz and Vanita. I realised, nevertheless, that unless I understood everything about Tessie's death, I would never come to terms with Vanita's. It was the murder-rape of his sister that had caused D'Cruz to assault me and to bring our lives together. I could not, now, wash my hands of the circumstances of Tessie's death.

"Okay, Ma."

"I would be more than happy to have the dear boy alongside when we come to resolving things but I'll have to make the first contact myself." All traces of drunkenness had left Oscar, and he looked at Ma as though he was a sixteen year old in love for the first time. "It won't take long, Lili. And I assure you there will be no danger involved. It's just a matter of getting a trusted old friend to set things up."

Ozzie seemed to have given up completely. "Will it be possible for you to tell me what you plan?"

"If you put your hand on your heart and swear that you won't interfere with my . . . with our plans."

The inspector seemed to have regained some of his composure. Smiling slightly he stood up, placed his right hand on his heart and said, "I swear."

Oscar pushed aside his glass and leaned back. "We were discussing the present troubles when someone, I forget who it was, began talking of all the unsolved killings we had had and suggested some absurd way in which they all might be connected. I didn't think there was much mileage to be gained from that kind of runaround, but the group enjoyed it and we gassed about things for a while. Then Uncle Choo, who is usually silent about everything except football, piped up and said that he knew something about one unsolved murder, and it certainly didn't have anything to do with any of the others."

Uncle Choo was one of the few of Oscar's friends that I knew something about. He was one of those great soccer coaches who could pick up a bunch of scallywags and, in no time at all, make them into a great football team. His methods were notoriously unorthodox and ranged from witchcraft to getting wives to deny husbands conjugal rights, but the players trusted him more than God and loved him more than their women.

Choo was a diabetic who smoked heavily and considered it cowardly not to indulge in the food he enjoyed. When gangrene struck and one of his legs had to be amputated, Choo said that it was too much to expect a man to change the habits of a lifetime simply because of the loss of a leg. In six months the other leg had to go too. He now propelled himself or was trundled about in a wheelchair, but still frequented his old haunts and carried on with his old ways. It seemed unlikely that he would know anything about murder, the present lot or one that occurred years ago.

Oscar, reading my mind, said, "I was surprised too, How Kum, when Uncle Choo claimed to have inside knowledge of a murder-rape. I felt that any opinions the legless wonder expressed outside of football were to be discounted, but the coach insisted that a footballer was in some way connected with the death of the D'Cruz girl, and his boys had no secrets from him."

Suddenly Ozzie's control snapped. "Are you trying to tell me that some crazy, football-playing animal mur-

dered my Tessie and this Uncle character has been an
accessory to the fact all these years. I have half a mind
to walk straight out and pull in this coach person for
interrogation."

"Don't," said Oscar, now sober and severe. "Judging by
what I hear of your methods you will certainly kill him
and, just as his players were loyal to him, Choo is loyal
to his players. He won't talk, whatever you do to him."

"So what . . .?" D'Cruz began.

"I'll tell you what," said Oscar in tones I had never
heard him use before. "I talk to Uncle Choo and set up a
meeting between me, him, How Kum and the man who
might have information about your sister's death. When
we are satisfied that the information is relevant and that
the party is willing to speak. . ."

"When do I get into the act," the policeman shouted.
"When the blokes are wiping their dicks and the girls are
pulling up their knickers?"

"All right, I'll talk to Choo. Then the four of us, How
Kum included, can meet. If your behaviour is exemplary
throughout and, if we are quite sure that it is necessary,
we will call in the man you have so much been wanting
to meet."

Ozzie looked terribly down in the mouth. I felt sorry
for him. Not Ma however. In clearing the table, she
removed his glass, which Oscar had recently replenished.
She wanted Oscar to herself tonight, and she wanted him
reasonably sober.

FOURTEEN

Nothing happened on Tuesday and Wednesday. The play was by no means over. This was merely the intermission. The curtain was down, but behind it I could hear the sounds of furniture being rearranged, backdrops changed. At Nats there were rumours of strange men visiting Symons and Loong. They were doubtless from the CPIB and sent by D'Cruz to stir things up and shuffle them about for the next bit of action. Vanita's ghost, too, had taken time off and left me to myself, so the pieces in my head could be reassembled.

On Thursday morning, the phone on my desk rang. I knew that the intermission was over even before I picked it up.

It was Mohan.

"Are you free for dinner tonight?"

"Yes. Your father wants to see me?"

"No, no. I want to see you. There are certain matters for discussion between us. Matters that should not be allowed to stand and cool for too long."

"What do you want to discuss, Mohan?"

There was a long silence. "I think that must wait till we are face to face."

"Where shall we meet?"

"If it is to your liking, we can meet at Komala Villas in Serangoon Road." He added, "In the air-conditioned dining chamber upstairs."

I like the Indianness of Serangoon Road, the homely

smell of garbage and spices, the contrapuntal beauty of women in saris and wizened men in dhotis strolling in narrow lanes. I got to the tiny restaurant and slipped up a narrow wooden staircase to the room where I was to meet Mohan. He was talking to a waiter when I arrived. It was early and we had the place to ourselves.

"The people working here are employed from India and are a tardy lot. I took the liberty of ordering for both of us so that the meal would not be unduly delayed. To ensure we are able to sample everything properly, I have ordered two full dinners."

He indicated the two large banana leaves that had been placed on the table. I love eating with my fingers off banana leaves and grabbed every opportunity to do so, despite Ma considering it proof that the blood of the "Malayalee scoundrel" ran strong in my veins.

"I am not a vegetarian," said Mohan, shovelling a mouthful of rice and pickle into his mouth, "and do not believe that being so is essential to Hinduism." He swallowed what was in his mouth and began fashioning another ball of rice. "However, the cuisine here is excellent and one must, in this world, seize all opportunity for pleasurable experience. That is the true message of Hinduism."

"I must say that I thought the Hindus believed in denying the body in much the same way as Christians do."

"That is the kind of rubbish that the missionaries spread to make our beliefs seem not unlike their own." He laughed merrily. "Take sex, for instance. There are the glorious carvings in our temples which talk to us of beauty of copulation, the delights of the conjunction between flesh and flesh which is the only experience in this life which can, even in the tiniest of ways, resemble the ecstasy of union with the Infinite. Sexual congress has a Divine purpose, yet there are some among us who insist on chastity and continence being all important to those aspiring towards the Godhead. Krishna, the most sacred of our avatars. . ."

"I'm sorry, Mohan, but I am really quite ignorant about Hinduism. I'm afraid you will have to explain quite a few of the terms you use."

"That, my dear How Kum, will increase the pleasure of dining with you. It will also introduce the matter I want to discuss.

"To return to the avatars. Avatars are reincarnations of the God Vishnu. There are three basic Hindu Gods. First there is Bhruma, the primary consciousness. Then we can consider Shiva. Shiva is the creator and destroyer, for creation and destruction are the same process. The last God I mention, though he is by no means the least in importance, is, of course, Vishnu the preserver." He swept up the food on his leaf with his palm, before going on. "It is not difficult to see that these so-called gods are in fact primary natural forces. Hinduism, to my way of thinking, is an elegant form of theoretical physics."

"Sorry I let my ignorance disturb your train of thought, but you were saying something about sexual attitudes." Vanita had told me that Mohan's interpretation of the Hindu sexual code had scandalised her father even more than her own behaviour. I wanted to hear more about this family disagreement.

"Krishna was a sexual enthusiast and, if legend be true, a sexual athlete. He recommended that both men and women have four relationships going on concurrently. This would ensure, as must be pretty evident, that relationships were not ruined by boredom. Further, he advised men to make sure that women had five or six orgasms to their one. This would keep the male-female bond a loving one.

"Then the missionaries got into the picture and corrupted us with their nonsense." He sniffed several times. "All this rubbish of having one God, one king, one spouse, one orgasm, one sexual position."

"Your sister agreed with your views?"

"What Vani believed was a mystery even to herself."

"She didn't believe in a sexual morality . . . the traditional kind, I mean?"

"I don't know for sure but I hope not. How can a simple animal pleasure be noble or base. It is how we use these acts that gives them the values that we attribute to the acts themselves." He waved to a waiter for more rice. "Can there be any ethical principal involved in my having more rice. Would I be a morally superior being if I chose to deprive myself and left this table only half satisfied? As the Epicureans put it, dum vivimus vivamus, 'while we live let us enjoy life'. That is what dharma is about. The celebration of life in all its forms, not its mourning in rituals and sacrifices."

"What then is a moral action?"

He shrugged. "To think one capable of answering that question is to be stupidly arrogant. We attempt to be one with the forces of nature by understanding them. We do this by keeping ourselves unattached to too many man-made values. Through non-attachment comes enlightenment, from enlightenment a feeling of oneness with the universe. This feeling of being one with everything that exists is all we are capable of achieving."

"And what does one have to do before one arrives at this enviable state?"

"One struggles for detachment, one pursues knowledge, one fights against maya, the illusory component in life, and prevents it from dulling one's perceptions. One refuses to be involved in the petty things, the squabbles, the entanglements that make up the lives of most people." He mopped up the remains of his food and folded the leaf along the spine to indicate to the waiter that he had finished. "We are, you and I, no more than a shudder of electrons; a tiny disturbance in the ether." He picked up the bill. "Let's walk as we talk."

Mohan led me away from the crowds and into the back streets lined by old-fashioned shop-houses. Families sat in their front rooms. It was early evening, the time for eating, watching television, lying around and scratching each other's backs. I slowed down each time we passed one of them. I felt the warmth from within reach out and touch me, understood the smiles which invited me to join them. They were strangers but I was attached to them. Mohan's philosophy did not allow for this kind of thing. He was unmoved by everyday things; unwarmed by the common and ordinary that binds us together. More than that: he was not merely oblivious of everyday goings-on, he went to great pains to distance himself from them. These thoughts crossed my mind, at first idly, then with increasing purpose. It began to dawn on me that the man walking beside me was the killer. Killers have to be distanced from people, from those they kill.

When I was a little boy, I first noticed toad's eggs. Females laid them in gutters and monsoon drains during the rainy season. The eggs are bound to each other by a gum and, thereby, a continuous sheet is formed which could not be swept away by the rains. I have always felt that the gum protects the egg, keeps it in touch with its fellows and makes it less lonely in a frightening world.

We too have a gum no less protective and no less strong because it is invisible. We call it attachment. It glues us together, protects us not merely from the world outside but from each other, for it makes us see the death of others and their pain as identical to our own.

By not being attached, Mohan had broken loose of this gum. He had made himself free to follow what he called "the dictates of dharma", which, as far as I could tell, were the liberty to do what he saw was the right thing for himself. I was not interested in whether or not his understanding of Hinduism was true or false. All I was concerned with was how it affected the workings of my life.

I knew I was not deciding it was moonrise simply because I saw a red ball perched on the edge of the world. Thinking back, I realised that I was seeing, if ever so slowly, the ball move up and out of the sea. Tiny incidents began to come together.

Early on, D'Cruz had emphasised that the killer had to be physically strong to have driven a knife through the chests of Lip Bin and Esther. Podgy and effeminate he may look, but I had realised how strong Mohan was when he held the mayurasana position for several minutes, supporting the weight of his entire body with one hand. There were other things, more incriminating, more like evidence. Mohan mentioning that he knew where Vanita and I spent our nights though I was sure she had not told him this; Sundram complaining about his son wandering about all night and him actually leaving the house with me on the evening of the lesbians' murder.

I didn't hate Mohan. In fact I felt a melancholy warmth for this man who had distanced himself from other men and sought to free himself from the pain and passion that made life worthwhile. He claimed to love his sister but his was not a philosophy that allowed for the sticky attachment that love entailed. Perhaps, in killing her, he had proved to himself how detached he really was.

Mohan interrupted my thoughts. "That scoundrel, Kishore, is persuading father to go sanyasin hoping that this will give him the family fortune without him having to wait for father to die."

"What's sanyasin?"

"When a man reaches the final stage of his life, when he does not need the solace of a woman, nor finds pleasure in the acquisition of wealth, when all his worldly obligations are fulfilled, he sets out to find himself. He has by this time no needs, not even the need to find himself." He laughed, enjoying the paradox. "Yes. That is in fact the case. The first step in finding oneself is losing self-awareness. I do not see father as having reached this stage, do you?"

"I really don't know."

"You must see, How Kum, that father is more concerned with preserving identity than losing it. He even believes in the egotistical Christian rubbish about the preservation of the personality after death. That's not the frame of mind in which one goes sanyasin."

"What sort of mood should one be in?"

"A truly holy man has no thought for the future. His entire consciousness is committed to the present." He stopped walking and put a restraining hand on my shoulder. "Listen to this lovely sanskrit hymn." He began crooning. His voice was more high-pitched than his sister's but the cadences of the song were identical to the bajans that Vanita sang.

"Look to this day for it is life;
the very life of life.
In its brief course lie all
the realities and truths of existence:
The joy of growth,
The splendour of action,
the glory of power.
For yesterday is but a memory
and tomorrow only a vision.

"You can see, How Kum, that Hinduism asks nothing but that we glory in the actions that confront us, looking neither backwards into what prompted them nor forwards into what we can gain from them."

"That must make life very difficult to live."

"In one sense it is impossible for life to be lived in this way. Yet if you contemplate the proposition a little, it is the only way in which life can or is actually lived."

"So you make no plans for the future?"

"I plan but only to enjoy the pleasure of planning, detaching myself, as much as I can, from the end-point of my plans. The vedas teach that we are entitled to the labour but not to the fruits thereof."

"What then is the point of any action?"

"The point of doing anything is to enjoy doing it in the knowledge that we are doomed to action. Our lives are laid out in our karma. We act, not because we choose to, but because of events enacted long, long ago in our history."

"And we are not in control over what we do?"

"What we see as choice is simply a recognition of imperatives whose origins are deep and untraceable."

I realised that Mohan was telling me in Hindu jargon what Quincy said in sociological mumbo-jumbo. By Mohan's book it was karma that made us bad. By Quincy's, it was perverse genes. In both, choice and its twin, responsibility, had been removed. I began to understand why I felt no hatred for this man who had killed the woman I loved. It is difficult to hate someone who is debarred from hating himself.

Mohan continued the exposition. "Once the fact of karma is grasped, things become simple. We act as situations demand and see ourselves as blameless."

"Are there many people who believe like you?"

"Not enough, but a group is being formed, a resurgent

force, that will bring our religion in line with thinking in the modern world."

As illustrated in the thinking of people like Quincy Sio, I thought but said, "Perhaps you could introduce me to this group some time."

"No sooner said than done, my dear How Kum. We meet on Thursdays and I had invited you to dinner in the hope that you might meet the group." He added apologetically, "There are only three stalwarts at the moment, for wisdom is the least infectious of human conditions. But we will grow, given time, and," he paused and looked into my face, "sufficient funds."

I knew that Mohan was our killer and the philosophy he expounded made me more certain of this. Now he was telling me what he needed Sundram's money for.

We came to an old-fashioned drinking house in which several elderly men sat swilling arak. An incredibly thin man dressed in a pair of black shorts appeared to be the landlord. At a table beside him sat two young Indians.

"Ashok and Tilak," said Mohan, introducing them. They shook my hand but greeted Mohan with a namaste in true Hindu fashion. "I have been familiarising How Kum with our views," said Mohan, as we sat down.

The three Indians spoke a mixture of Hindustani and English. Mohan, from time to time, stopped the conversation to tell me what was going on. From their discussion it was clear that they looked on themselves as leaders of the Hindu renaissance. They had contacts with like minds in India and frequently referred to a group called the Araya Samaj, which had aims similar to their own, though Mohan and his friends were confident that their own ideas were in advance of those put out by the Indian organization. Much of their talk centred around the problem of getting funds to begin activities in Singapore. Two well-known Indian business men had reneged on their promise of a donation. Their lawyers had advised them that Mohan's group constituted a secret society, the support of which was illegal.

"Secret," said Mohan who had begun to speak in an authoritarian voice, "perhaps, but not exclusive. We would accept anybody into our fold as long as he was prepared to abide by our rules."

"Would you accept someone who was a criminal?" I asked.

"Let me quote you some lines from the *Bhagavad Gita*, that great discourse between Krishna and Arjuna:

> He who shall say, 'Lo! I have slain a man.'
> He who shall think 'Lo! I am slain.'
> These both know naught!
> Life cannot slay.
> Life is not slain.

"I choose the exact lines that refer to killing, because your mind still dwells on the murder of my sister, does it not, How Kum?"

"Would you be prepared to accept a murderer into your group?" I pressed.

"The slayer and the slain are the same," said Mohan, nodding sagely. "We are only agents and cannot seek to judge."

I stood up and took my leave. In the course of the evening Mohan had shown me that he had motive, means, and opportunity for the murders. What was more, he had a philosophy which provided automatic absolution. I would let D'Cruz work on the details of evidence. I had forgotten that many sub-plots remained unresolved. I did not realise then that these were as important to the course of my life as the main theme.

FIFTEEN

Vanita haunted my dreams. I awoke randy and the feeling stayed with me as I rode to work. Even the sight of Mary Lourdes waiting in my office did not rid me of it.

"Two men came very early," she informed me, in a conspiratorial manner. "They questioned them, then took them away in a police car."

"Took who away, Mary?"

"The supervisor, Loong, and that pervert Symons."

"Were you waiting here to tell me this?" She nodded, and I added, "Why?"

"Because I think you'll want to know who else was involved in whatever they were up to."

"Who else was involved, Mary?"

"The Jezebel who corrupted you."

A queasy feeling in the stomach all but replaced the randiness with which I had come into the room. Perhaps I shouldn't have told the inspector about the meat tenders. The last thing in the world that I wanted was for the police to unearth scandals that affected Vanita. "Are you saying that Vanita was in with Loong and Symons in fixing the meat tenders?"

"She was sleeping with the supervisor."

I let that pass and said, "But she was just a preset girl. How could she be of any help to them?"

She shrugged. "All I can say is that she knew what was going on and she kept quiet. She must have been getting something out of it."

"Are you suggesting that she was blackmailing the two?"

"Who can say?" She shrugged again. "Maybe you. After all, you knew her very well too." She paused to allow this to sink in. "I thought I'd tell you what I know to show you that I'm your true friend."

As soon as Mary left, I called D'Cruz then Jafri. Neither was contactable. I had the afternoon off and left my office immediately after lunch. Vanita's ghost rode the train with me and I began to feel randy again. She teased me about the state I was in and suggested several ways in which I could be relieved. Her suggestions only made matters worse.

When I reached Orchard Station I realised that, if Jafri wasn't at work, he was probably at home, which was just round the corner from the station.

Zainah let me into the apartment. She was again alone. I looked around and wondered where Jafri was. Zainah noticed this and said, "Not in the office, not at home, but Zainah knows where her husband is."

The lilt had gone out of her voice and her eyes were puffy. I wanted to put my arms around her and comfort her.

"Where is he, Zainah?"

"Where else. Like always nowadays he spends all his time with that Quincy. At home, too, he talks only of criminal psychology and abnormal sexual needs." She made a sound between a laugh and a sob. "What about normal sexual needs, I ask, but he just tells me not to joke about serious matters."

I followed her into the living-room watching, with the attention that sexual arousal produces, her bum moving inside the tight sheath of her sarong.

"What's he doing with Quincy?"

"You ask me?" She shook her head and plonked down

on the couch beside me. "Now somebody else comes too. Some Madam Zoroastris who does some borak with psychic forces. Any nonsense is good enough for my Jafri these days. I don't know what's happening." She began to cry.

I put an arm around her. She sobbed violently and snuggled against me. I smelled the soap-and-water freshness of her body, felt its curves shuddering against mine. I put both my arms around her and pulled her against me. She turned her face up and pressed it against mine. Her lips tasted of tears. Her tongue had a clean, sweet flavour as it searched the back of my mouth and her nipples seemed to know their way into my fingers. She reached between my legs to touch the part of me that strained most urgently towards her. As I began to press her down on to the couch, I heard a key in the lock. I pushed Zainah away from me and crossed my legs.

Jafri seemed more relieved than surprised to find me in his home. "I'm glad you're here. I tried your office and your home without effect. Quincy has asked me to bring you round to meet Zelda Zoroastris. We need to re-run our investigations in the presence of someone who is familiar with telepsychic phenomena."

Again I thanked God that Jafri was so mesmerised by Quincy's bullshit that he failed to notice the state that his wife and best friend were in. Out of the corner of my eye, I saw Zainah discreetly arranging her blouse.

"Have you informed D'Cruz, Jafri?"

"I was with Quincy and Zelda." I frowned at this familiarity but Jafri, who seemed to have become quite insensitive to the attitudes of the people around him, failed to notice my disapproval and continued blithely, "We have made contact with Ozzie . . ."

"Telepathically?" I asked.

"Try not to be frivolous, How Kum," he snapped. "Some

terrible murders have happened on our island, our police seem to have drawn a blank, and Zelda is here to see how she can help. I need not, I hope, remind you that your girlfriend was the first of the killer's victims."

"When is this meeting scheduled?" I pronounced the word the way the Americans do. It was a last-ditch effort to make Jafri smile. It failed.

"Right now," he replied. "Ozzie has agreed to be there too. One would have thought that he would have jumped at the opportunity to get initiated into modern criminological techniques, but it took a lot of pressure to get him to agree to come at all." He shook his head several times.

Before I could protest, Jafri had grabbed my arm and was hurrying me through the door. I noticed that neither look nor word had passed between husband and wife. I wondered if Jafri would mind my taking up with Zainah if he had no use for her.

Madam Zelda Zoroastris was an impressive woman by any standards. She was at least six foot tall and nearly as broad. Her bosom ballooned out well ahead of the rest of her and from its depths issued a rich contralto, which seemed somehow to be detached from her person. "Good to know you, Houk," it said, resonating against my face.

"He likes to be called How Kum," said Jafri, as though describing an allergy.

"Houk's good enough for Zelda, and what's good enough for Zelda. . ." She turned to Quincy and they said in chorus, "is good enough for the USA."

"Mamma Zel likes things her own way," Quincy explained.

I didn't see any point in protesting.

"You lay things out the usual way, poppet," she said to Quincy, "and Mamma Zel will get the show on the road."

The psychiatrist Lum was fiddling with elaborate electronic apparatus in one corner of the room. Much of this was unfamiliar to me but I did recognise video cameras and the kind of microphones used in movie sets. Quincy noticed my interest and said, "Yes, siree. We encourage visual recording so all is clean and above board." His cadences had begun to echo those of the large woman.

"Do we have a member short?" asked Zelda. "I understood there were to be three observers: the doctor, the lawyer and the police chief."

"Not the chief," Jafri said apologetically. "Just the inspector who . . ." he groped for a word, "who began investigations in this case."

"He ain't materialised," said Zelda, rolling her eyes.

We heard a commotion outside and D'Cruz walked in closely followed by a tough-looking man in a white coat.

"You tell this gorilla that I am part of the investigating team," he said to Quincy.

"My dear Watson, of course," said Quincy, nodding in the direction of the tough.

The inspector looked terrible. He had shaved badly and his shirt looked slept in. His normally tiny eyes seemed to have grown in size but, instead of improving his appearance, this gave him a wild, haunted look. I noticed that his hands shook and his fingernails were dirty. He glanced in my direction and, avoiding eye contact, said, "I understand you're going to perform, maestro."

I nodded and said, "But I'm not sure how."

"Hang loose, Houk," Zelda commanded. "Technique's been long established. All kinks have been ironed out. This investigation will go as smooth as oysters on ice."

"How Kum," Quincy informed her, "has already contacted two of the suspects. No objection to that, is there Mamma?"

"None as long as my baby is happy." She reached out,

grabbed Quincy and crushed him to her bosom. Her baby seemed happy to be where he found himself and stayed in her embrace till his breath ran out.

Zelda clapped her hands and shouted, "Documents."

Computer print-outs were handed round.

I had read two of them and did not bother to read the other two.

Quincy noticed this and said, "Gotta do your homework, man."

"I think I'll take these two without knowing anything about them."

He began to shake his head till Zelda boomed, "Houk may have a point, poppet. Just let him get the vibes without the words."

"How do we go about things?" asked D'Cruz.

"Like so," Zelda replied, in an authoritative voice. "We get the four suspects into the room. Houk's the only one who knows the killer's vibes, right?"

"I was close when the first murder was committed," I said weakly.

"Close as into the skin of the victim, I understand," said the large woman without the slightest change in her voice. "So here's how we fix things. Houk sits on one side of the screen," she indicated a plastic screen in one corner of the room, "our four suspects on the other. I ask them to contemplate the murders, refreshing their minds with details of the killings. Remember, these guys have soft limbic systems and get easily amnesic.

"Then I put my hand on their heads, one at a time. As I do, I ask Houk if he's getting any vibes. Even if he doesn't consciously feel anything, there will be frequencies oscillating between him and the murderer and I'll recognise them." She turned to Quincy. "Don't I always, baby?"

"Never fail, Mamma," he confirmed.

"But we're not one of your Indian fakers . . ." Zelda began.

"Fakirs," said Jafri, pronouncing the word correctly.

"Fuck who?" Zelda was genuinely puzzled.

"Fakirs," Jafri explained. "Religious men."

"Fuck whatever," said Zelda impatiently. "We're not one of them. We believe in science." She turned to me and put her hands on my shoulders.

The smell of perfume was overpowering. This seemed to arise not from her body but from her face which was on the same level as mine. The tiny cracks visible in the heavy make-up didn't change the fact that it was a striking face with large hypnotic eyes which were a surprising mauve. "We're scientists, Quince and me. We don't simply rely on my special gift. I will feel the reverberations between Houk and the killer as sure as I'm feeling his skinny shoulders, but that ain't gonna be good enough for science.

"We gotta measure what's happening in this bag of bones here and document our findings before we can think of ourselves as being scientific." She released her hold on me.

Quincy bounced forward. "I got the polygraph and accessories right here, Mamma."

"I know my baby never fails me," said Zelda. This was occasion for a further prolonged embrace between the two. When this was done she said, "We'll get Houk hooked up in the chair before calling in the suspects."

I had, all along, looked on this unlikely pair as creatures to be ridiculed. I was prepared to play along with them as long as I was not involved in any discomfort or danger. Now I wasn't so sure.

I looked nervously at the mass of electronic equipment. "I hadn't realised that all this was going to be necessary," I protested, doing my best to hide my anxiety. "No

one told me anything about being connected to electric
wires . . ."

"Not to worry, darling," said Zelda. "We have to immobi-
lise you so recording baselines remain steady. The seat
may look like an electric chair but the juice flows out of
you, not into you."

With difficulty I caught Ozzie's eye. "Don't worry, How
Kum," he said. "If you get electrocuted I'll make sure
these two hang." Jafri made disapproving noises but did
not stop the inspector saying, "And I'll take great pleasure
watching. Them hanging. Not you getting electrocuted."

"Not a chance of that," said Quincy. "The wires conduct
tiny impulses out of How Kum's body – these are ampli-
fied then synchronised before they are codified by the
computer."

I was placated but not completely. "What are you measuring?"

"The usual parameters," said Quincy. "Pulse, blood
pressure, EEG, EKG, galvanic skin response and that
kind of thing. The genius is in how we link them together
and correlate them with Mamma's extrasensory perceptions."

A collapsible chair was produced and my arms and legs
were strapped to it. A metallic band was placed over my
head. I caught the inspector's eye. He gave me a tiny nod.
For reasons of his own he wanted the show to go on.

The four suspects were brought into the room. In
addition to Lenny and Oh Kwee, there were two others
named Awang and Ah Sin. Their skins were rough and
burnt a deep brown from long exposure to the sun. They
were clearly convicts and I wondered how two men,
already incarcerated, could be guilty of crimes outside
their jails.

"Aren't those two jailbirds?" I asked Quincy.

"Well done, How Kum," he replied. "I can see that your

extrasensory antennae are out and ready for action. It was good thinking your not wanting to see their data sheets."

The plastic screen was pulled into place and the four men led behind it. Zelda, Quincy and Lum stayed on the far side of the screen as did the suspects. Ozzie and Jafri remained on my side of it.

"We are almost ready to begin, Houk," Zelda boomed. "Just let your mind go slack so it is open to influences."

"The parameters are steady," said Lum.

"Now drift back, Houk," Zelda instructed. "Drift back to the time of the murder. You and the victim are making love, faster, faster, faster . . . then the quiet. Now you are at peace, asleep beside the love object . . ."

"Pulse rate's risen and there has been a slight fall in skin resis . . ." Lum said.

"Sharrup," Zelda shouted. Then added in a quieter voice, "I was just making contact with the oscillations from Houk's aura." She addressed Quincy. "Now, baby, feed in the interference patterns I usually use. And you," – this to Lum – "just observe the changes as they occur but keep your lip buttoned."

"Sorry," he apologised.

Zelda Zoroastris now began speaking slowly and rhythmically, her contralto expanding to fill the whole room. She was addressing the suspects.

"You are by the sea and it is dark. You have been watching the lovers all evening. They have made love many times and you can smell their juices. You have been hard for a long time. Too long. You know what you have to do. You have brought your weapon with you. The woman is asleep with her back to you. You know they are both naked. You raise your weapon and push it into her, just as the man was pushing his weapon into her. In–out, in–out and you feel yourself coming just as he did. The man is still asleep and you walk out to the beach. Your weapon is still in your hand." The voice became louder. "I mean this weapon, the knife I now hold in my hand."

"Christ and fucking spiders," said Ozzie in an explosive whisper. "How on earth did she get hold of the murder weapon without my knowledge?"

"Couldn't get hold of you," Jafri replied, "So the DCP got forensics to release it for this experiment."

Both men fell quiet as Zelda began speaking again. "You walk along the beach for a while. Then you feel you are getting hard again. You must find someone else. The couple are asleep, near each other and fully dressed. But you can smell love juices on the woman. You know that she has been making love." Zelda's voice rose the way an opera singer's does at the end of an aria. "Yes, she has been making love . . . fucking, fucking, fucking, while you are hard and always by yourself. You creep up to her and raise your knife. You stick your weapon into her and you come. Your hand is wet with her blood. The man awakes. You want to go away and he stops you. You don't want to fight but what can you do . . .? You raise your knife again.

"A week passes and you are calm. Not at peace but not troubled. You go back to your life. Then the urge begins to return. The hard-ons start again and sometimes they make walking difficult. People on the street are staring at you and you know what they are looking at. The whole world can see what's going on between your legs. You touch yourself again and again, play with yourself but you can't get rid of it. Then you buy yourself another kitchen knife.

"It is night in the park again. There are many groups around but no lonely couples. Your hard-on is now painful and the pain is increasing, moving up your chest, threatening to choke you. Then you find a couple by themselves. They are naked, rubbing against each other. The woman goes down on the man, kneeling between his legs. Her head is moving up and down and her naked back is facing you. The air is filled with a woman's smell, a strong smell but there is no man's smell to go with it. You want to wait till the man comes before you plunge your weapon into the girl giving the blowjob. Then suddenly you realise why you can't smell a man. They are both girls.

"You are bursting with pain but you wait. You know you are most satisfied when you come at the first thrust. You wait, and the girl on the grass begins to groan as she comes. You plunge your weapon into the girl with her back to you. You can feel yourself squirting as her blood gushes on to your hands.

"You are at peace now. The only thing you want to do is to leave but the girl on the ground jumps up and attacks you. You try to explain that you are finished and you want to leave. But she won't listen. She rushes at you, pinching, punching, trying to get her hand round your throat.

"You slash at her body with the knife but this doesn't stop her. She kicks the knife out of your hands. You get behind her and put your arms round her waist. You just want to control her. You mean no harm. But she struggles. Without wanting to your hands slip under her armpits, your fingers lock behind her neck. Your knee is somehow in her back and you bend her forwards, down, down, down till suddenly you hear c-r-a-c-k and her body is as limp as your dick."

From behind the screen came Quincy's piping voice, "You have all seen how Madam Zoroastris has used her psychic powers to recreate the crimes from the killer's point of view . . ."

"Psychic, my arse," D'Cruz hissed. "The bloody DCP has probably given her photocopies of the investigation papers."

Quincy continued, "She is now locked into the thought processes of all the five subjects involved in this experiment."

"Five?" D'Cruz repeated in a soft voice.

Quincy heard him and said, "Yes, five. For the purpose of scientific study, How Kum is classified as a subject whom we like to call the recipient. Madam Zoroastris will be involved in his thought processes as well as those of the other four."

"What should I do?" I asked.

Quincy replied, "Just let your mind go blank while the psychic makes physical contact one by one with the four subjects on this side of the screen."

"What could I expect to feel?"

"A psychic thrill, not unlike fear. Very rarely, and only in subjects with very strong tele-psychic propensities, does this feeling amount to blind terror."

I made my mind go blank as best I could. Nothing happened. Behind the screen I could hear Zelda moving slowly around.

"Say 'yes' as soon as you feel anything," Quincy piped.

"Nothing," I said, feeling slightly disappointed. "I feel nothing at all."

Zelda spoke in a faraway voice. "The recipient is resistant. I'm aware of very strong oscillations from one person from this side of the screen." She sighed. "Run the programme, Quince."

"I will, Mamma. I will."

"You, Dr Lum, watch the screen carefully for any alteration of the recipient's parameters."

"I will do that, madam," said Lum dutifully.

"I have located agitatory vibrations in one of the subjects," said Zelda. "I will now touch the person from whom these vibrations emanate and you watch the screen to see what happens to the recipient's parameters."

I examined myself very carefully as she did. I felt no fear or excitement, nor even a little flutter of expectation. The same could not be said for Dr Lum.

"This is really quite remarkable," he said, his voice shrill with excitement. "As soon as the psychic makes contact with this one suspect, the recipient's parameters show great turbulence. The main change is in the EEG, as expected."

"Note," said Quincy, "the concomitant change in his galvanic skin response and a slight but definite tachycardia."

"This is most convincing," said the psychiatrist.

"The objective signs are clear enough, though the recipient is unaware of anything happening, even the slight change in his heart-rate. I might add that this is due to the excellent interceptive faculties Madam Zoroastris possesses. She is interfacing with the oscillations between How Kum and the suspect but, such is her skill, that neither is aware of it." Quincy's voice was all admiration. "However, we are practitioners of science not witchcraft and, to make absolutely sure that this is not some random phenomenon or some glitch due to variations in your Singapore voltage, we will repeat the process and show that the disturbances in How Kum's parameters only occur when contact is made between our psychic and one of the suspects."

There was a murmur of admiration from Lum as the process was repeated. "Even Dr Freud couldn't be more scientific than this. Every time Madam Zoroastris makes contact with this particular subject we record changes in the recipient's heart-rate, blood pressure and EEG."

"So we've got the murderer, have we?" asked D'Cruz in a matter-of-fact voice. "Because if we have, I'll free How Kum from all these bloody gadgets." He began undoing the straps and wires.

"We don't approve of judgemental terms like 'murderer'," said Zelda as the screen separating us was removed. "We prefer to call this kind of person psychobiologically damaged rather than labelling him a criminal."

"Psychobiologically damaged, my arsehole," said Ozzie D'Cruz. He added, "And yours too for good measure, madam." The inspector had clearly recovered his composure and was beginning to take command of the situation.

Zelda seemed exhausted by her performance and said, "Tell him, Quincy baby, that dirty talk is a definite sign of sociopsychopathic behaviour."

The little man nodded. "It has clearly been demonstrated that aggressive language is a precursor to overt acts of sexual violence."

The inspector was not impressed. "You can take your psychosociobiologico-sexual whatever and ram it up any hole from which you see shit coming." He snapped his shoulders back several times as though spoiling for a fight. "I have come here to solve a murder . . . , several murders, in fact. I was informed by a man I used to respect that these new-style criminologists would tell me who the murderer was. Perhaps they can." He let out a breath as though it was cigarette smoke. "OK, you three scientific criminologists, which of these poor slobs is the killer?"

It was Lum who spoke. "From the data recorded on the polygraph it is clear the killer. . ."

"Dr Lum," said Zelda sharply. "You are no doubt unfamiliar with our procedures. It has always been our practice to let the killer identify himself."

Lenny Drigo was the only one who seemed interested in the proceedings.

Zelda stared at the four for several minutes before saying, "I have, of course, already made a positive identification of the killer. It is now up to the maniac, the sex maniac, to tell us who he is."

"I'm the man, sir," said Lenny in the general direction of D'Cruz.

"My God, Lenny," said the inspector with a laugh. "You're a wanker, son, not a murderer."

"He's the man though," said Zelda, nodding her head slowly. "He was identified by my psychic sensibilities which the polygraph confirmed."

Ozzie turned slowly to Jafri. "Ask them, my learned friend, to be quite sure of who they mean because in this country murder, whatever its psychosociological cause, is punished by hanging."

"Listen, Ozzie," said Jafri, irritated at last by the inspector's baiting. "Not only have the newer techniques identified our man, he has himself confessed. What more do you want?"

"An explanation for this," he replied, fishing from his pocket a sheaf of papers which he handed to Jafri. "These are the IPs, the investigation papers, concerning one very minor nuisance called Lenny Drigo.

"You can see from these papers that, on both nights when he was supposed to have been in the park murdering people, he was in the Central Police Station lockup." He turned to Zelda. "Perhaps he did it by telekinesis. Maybe the knife jumped up and killed people because of psychosexual impulses beyond his control."

Jafri frowned at the papers and gradually his face went blank. Then he nodded and said, "I see."

"What do you see, Jafri," I asked. "What was Lenny locked up for?"

"For indecently exposing himself," he replied. "Lenny, it appears, is a habitual offender. The police would not have done anything about it except for the fact that the lady who reported him on both occasions was a close friend of one of our Ministers."

"Poor Lenny," said D'Cruz. "He's not even a flasher, he's just a wanker. And if you saw his equipment you'd see that he hasn't got much to flash."

"But he confessed," said Jafri without conviction.

"Like eyes are balls he confessed. Lenny thought we were accusing him of being a sex maniac and in his eyes he is. He was brought up to believe that masturbators grow hair on their palms, that they go blind, that they become madmen. Of course, he confessed. And there is one other thing that needs to be considered."

"Which is?"

"He's the only one of that sad lot that speaks English." He looked slowly round the room till his gaze rested on Jafri. "I rest my case."

SIXTEEN

Jafri steered the BMW carefully through the rush hour traffic. He had been silent after we had left Quincy and his handsome face was expressionless. When we got into Holland Road, the traffic thinned a bit and he said, "The Arabs have a saying: if you've been a fool, the wise thing to do is to tell everyone, for only then will they realise that you are not still a fool." He looked at D'Cruz who sat in the seat beside him.

Ozzie said, "Case closed."

I leaned forward, "Con-men or not, they seemed to be able to interfere with my pulse rate and some of the other things they were measuring."

"And you didn't feel any different for the changes taking place in your body, right?" Ozzie laughed. "You remember Zelda making sure that Quincy had put in her usual computer programme? Well, this saw to it that, after a specified period, it cut out the recording coming from your body and replaced this on the computer screen with something prerecorded. It did this at intervals which were based on something Zelda could count, like your heart rate. The interference would appear irregularly, after five heartbeats the first time, after ten the second and so on. The only requirement was for Fatso to know when it was going to come, so she could at that precise moment put her hand on poor Lenny's head. The hand on his head had nothing to do with the change in the pulse rate or EEG."

When we reached Buona Vista Road, Jafri said, "I'll drop you off here How Kum, and Ozzie, wherever he is going. . ."

"I'll get off too," said the inspector. "There are a few things that I have to discuss with big guy here."

As soon as we were settled I told him about Symons, Loong and the investigation the CPIB had begun. I also told him what Mary Lourdes had insinuated about Vanita's possible role in the business.

"I'm very unhappy about Vanita being involved in any way in an investigation of this sort." As I spoke I looked over his shoulder and saw Vanita's ghost perched on the window-sill.

He laughed. "Even the CPIB boys aren't vindictive enough to tarnish the name of a murder victim." Over his shoulder the lady in question nodded agreement. "You, How Kum, should be burning your arse out trying to find out who killed her instead of worrying about her reputation."

Vanita applauded.

"But I know who killed her."

Ozzie smiled. "Whatever you may want to believe, it's not those two villains from Nats."

"It isn't Loong and Symons I was talking about, Ozzie." I paused deliberately. "Our killer is Vanita's brother, Mohan."

The inspector put down his beer glass with a thump. "What makes you say that and why so confidently?"

I told him.

He brooded on it for a while then said, "We still have a problem about motive. Killing the girl wouldn't secure the fortune for the brother. The old man could still leave everything to the temple or, worse, to that scoundrel, Kishore."

"Kishore was not very much in evidence till after Vanita

had been killed. Mohan may not have realised quite the kind of influence he would have on the old man. He may have believed that with Vanita dead, Sundram would simply leave everything to him."

D'Cruz lit a cigarette and I found him an ashtray.

He said, "I have difficulty seeing this Mohan as a mass murderer, however neutrally his philosophy views suffering and death."

He drew on his cigarette. "But I think that I have made it clear how much I value your opinions in this case." He paused. "You see things differently from other people, you make pictures out of little pieces. And pictures sometimes make more sense than bits and bytes of logic." I was a little surprised that the inspector understood my impression of the world as clearly as he did and seemed to be using my own words to describe the way I saw things, but said nothing.

He continued, "What is more, murder investigations are always full of ghosts. You are familiar with the ghosts in this case. I am not." From the window-ledge, Vanita applauded. "Speaking of ghosts, you never did tell me what happened at the ghost-raising party that Kishore conducted."

I told him what happened at the seance, how Kishore spoke with Vanita's voice, though as far as we knew they had never met, and how the man had intimate details of my sex life.

"You are sure the man had never met or spoke with Vanita?"

"Absolutely."

"And these bedroom secrets that he got hold of . . . could anyone other than your girlfriend know about them?"

"How? They are terribly private things."

"People talk about their love life, you know. Even boast about it."

I was indignant. "Not me, inspector."

He laughed. "Maybe not you, but your girlfriend could have told the girls in the office about this marvellous fellow she'd got hold of."

"And they all rushed off to tell Kishore and did it imitating Vanita's voice."

Ozzie threw up his hands. "OK. It's impossible to work out a trick till it's been explained to you."

On the window-sill, Vanita was clapping her hands and swaying her body rhythmically. It took me a while to understand what she was getting at.

"There is some kind of tape-recording, a collection of Indian songs that Vanita used to sing to me. Leela, the family maid, gave it to me but I don't think they could have anything to do with what we are discussing."

He looked at me slyly. "Then why did you bring it up?"

I couldn't tell him that a ghost behind his shoulder had prompted me to, so I said, "I haven't listened to it myself and feel a little guilty about this. If you like I'll pass it on to you later."

"Do you have any objection to my listening to it with you?"

"None at all, though I doubt you'll like Vanita's taste in music."

"Why don't we listen to it now?"

Ozzie sat on the edge of my bed and we listened to the tape on my little compo. After a few bumps and long hiss Vanita began speaking.

"I don't know why I waited so long about it, my little tape-diary. I usually get on with things if I want a fellow. I had my eye on him for a long time. He looks at me in a funny way as he walks down the line of preset girls and I don't see him looking at any of the other girls like that. I look at his face then down his legs to tell him that I like him that way too, but I think he is very shy. I should go up and ask him for a date but I think he is so shy that I will frighten him off. I don't think he is very experienced. He looks so innocent, but you never can tell. Wow, it'll be great if I was to be his first girl. Forget it. That's not poss. Simply not poss. He must be nearly thirty years old. Old man Loong says he's worked with Nats for nearly eight years." There was a short hiss before Vanita began talking again.

"Lucky my working overtime and getting the late bus. Just the two of us and he had to talk to me. A bit shy at first but no sweat once we got going. He says such strange things sometimes. Not crazy like. Just strange. After a few minutes I told him I had watched him looking at me. Didn't say anything, so I said that I looked at him too and told him what I wanted. What I really wanted. He didn't seem surprised. Said that's what he wanted too. Silly boy. He should have told me long ago and we wouldn't have wasted all this time."

The tape went quiet.

Ozzie looked at me inquiringly. I nodded. This was Vanita's most intimate diary and I was happy for him to listen to it.

The voice began again.

"Well I was right about one thing. He's not just inno-cent. He's brand new and I'm the lucky girl that broke the seal. My friend, Anita, says that with men it's not called deflowering, it's called defrosting. Just like an ice lolly. He looks like a Chink, but down there he's no Chink. The best equipment I've ever seen, and under my expert tuition he has learnt to use it well. I think he got a shock when I got him hard the second time round, turned him on his back and rode to glory. No shyness after that. Very loving and will do anything. Not like that shit Loong and his 'Chinese culture does not allow man to spend time with head between woman's legs.'

"And How Kum is so loving about everything that the action just flows. I think I am falling in love. I must be in love. How can it be so good if I'm not in love. I must keep him to myself. He thinks I'm perfect. Well, I am, and I will never let him near another woman, so he'll always think I'm perfect. Even after I've had our six children and I'm old and loose, he'll still think I'm perfect. I'm so, so happy. I know this is the man I want to grow old with."

She began to croon a bajan.

Ozzie looked at me. "Now we know how Kishore did it. The voice, the sord . . . the intimate details. He must have found this tape, listened to a bit then copied it before replacing it."

The song over, Vanita began itemising the events of her life. I knew she loved me and now I had it in heart-rending detail. I yearned for her, and, for the first time in my life, understood the meaning of absence. Vanita was talking about the house we would live in, the children we would have. I didn't mind Ozzie listening to the details of our sex life, but my grief I wanted to keep private, and I was having difficulty in holding back the tears.

He realised this. "I don't think this bit concerns police work."

I nodded. He leaned over and turned off the machine.

I would listen to the rest of the tape alone and in the silence of my room.

"I could use more beer," said Ozzie.

We returned to the living-room.

"We know how that villain Kishore did it but I don't think you are going to find the motive for the murder on that tape." He sipped his beer. "And, whatever you say, I don't go in for people committing murder just because they've junked up a philosophy that is neutral about killing, any more than I go in for the theory that people commit mass murder because they are mad dogs with defective limbic systems.

"Nevertheless, I'll give this Mohan character a closer look. I'll do this, for no other reason than my trusting your intuition, How Kum."

Before I could say anything, the door opened and Ma and Oscar walked in.

Oscar put down the shopping he was carrying and said, "I have news for you, Ozzie." He poured himself some beer. "I've done my homework and have made the arrangements for tomorrow. I think we are on the verge of solving the murder that has bothered you for so long."

"You mean you know who killed my Tessie?"

Oscar rocked his head from side to side. "Not know but may be on the verge of knowing."

"I guess you know I spent the whole of last night rummaging among your old friends. Couldn't turn up a thing. Your buddies are tight-arsed clams when it comes to giving information to a police officer."

Oscar laughed. "Heard whispers of your efforts." He shook his finger at the inspector. "Join me for a drink tomorrow night and you will be a wiser man."

"Where?"

"The Mitre Hotel. Used to be a lovely place but is now a little the worse for wear. Just like most of us." He shot Ma a glance. "All except you, my flower, whose fragrance improves with the years."

"You are talking about that old place on Killiney Road?" asked D'Cruz.

"The very one," Oscar replied. "Meet there at six-thirty for a sundowner."

Ma put a hand on his shoulder. "How Kum goes with you."

"If he wishes," said Oscar.

I wanted to. Very much. And it was not just out of curiosity.

SEVENTEEN

I was a little anxious when Symons called me to his office the next morning. He would, by now, have discovered my role in the interest the anti-corruption squad was taking in him. Though I had come to dislike the man, it is distinctly uncomfortable to be cast in the role of a Judas. I delayed seeing him for as long as possible and dropped in just before lunch.

"Finally plucked up the courage to see me have you, HK?" he said as soon as I walked in.

"The CPIB were on to you anyway, Symons," I countered.

"I'm not going to argy-bargy with you, HK. All I can say is that I never showed you anything but loving kindness from the first day you came to Nats, and cannot say that I am not hurt by your disloyalty." He affected a wounded look. "I am, however, pleased to inform you that we have not been found guilty of a felony, only a minor indiscretion for not following procedure to the letter of the law. A warning is all we received."

"I'm glad," I said, and meant it too, till I heard what he said next.

"You may have some inkling as to the role your erstwhile lady-love played in all this." He smiled sweetly. "I understand from various sources that you knew she was on to things."

"She guessed that things were not all hunky-dory. . ."

"Oh, more than that, my dear fellow, more than that."

"She wasn't on the take from you and Loong." The strain in my voice must have been obvious. "I'm sure of that and you must be too."

"We didn't pay her. That's for sure, but there may have been others that did."

"I don't see what you're getting at."

"Don't you, my dear boy. I did warn you, years ago, about the dangers of these mixed relationships but I guess you were too innocent to understand."

"Just come out and say what you are trying to say, Symons."

"If you must know," – he sighed heavily – "we are dealing with quite big fish in the business world and big fish need decent bait. Just making a few bucks was not enough for some of them so we threw in some flesh as well." He grinned at my discomfiture.

"Loong said the girl was game and virtually insatiable." He turned his nose up. "A condition, I understand, not uncommon among the female sex, as their orgasms have no proper point of termination. I don't, as you will under-stand, speak from experience." He laughed unpleasantly. "Loong suggested that we introduce her to our more important suppliers."

"And what was Vanita supposed to do?"

"Tenderise their tougher portions and in the process find out what was in it for us, if we were prepared to overlook certain fine points in procedure." He saw the look of pain on my face and added in a conciliatory voice, "She was not the only one of the preset girls who was on the game, you know."

"What do you mean 'on the game'? " I shouted. "Are you trying to tell me that Vanita was a prostitute?"

"Steady on, dear fellow," he said, alarmed by my tone. "I'm not in a position to make judgemental statements about female sexual behaviour. I am simply stating the facts as objectively as I can." His face became unnaturally solemn. "All I'm saying is that your girlfriend got more than love out of the liaisons we arranged for her."

"You mean she took money from these men?"

"Oh dearie," he said, flapping a hand playfully in my direction, "you are much too coarse. She didn't charge by the hour and I don't think that actual cash changed hands."

"But if she didn't get money, what did she get out of it?"

"There are things that can be converted into cash."

"Like expensive gifts?"

"Like tips on the stock market and arrangements with banks to enable you to follow your fancy."

By the time I left Symons' office, the picture was clear. The girls were introduced to chosen men whom they entertained. In the course of this they ascertained whether or not their "dates" were prepared to fall in with Symons' and Loong's schemes. The men rewarded the girls in ways they considered suitable.

I spent the rest of the day thinking of Vanita in the arms of strangers, hard-faced men who made perverse and cruel sexual demands on her; men who were turned on by pain and humiliation. Images, ugly and wounding, entered my head in what appeared to be an unending stream. I spent so many hours scratching at the sore that, by the time I got home, it was numb from chafing.

Ma was at a mah-jong game and Oscar had left early for the Mitre, doubtless to get in a few quick ones before our appointment. This suited me just fine. I lay naked in bed and listened to Vanita's tape. Beyond the point about her wanting to grow old with me, the voice changed. It became clearly more determined.

"I know father wants to leave me everything but I don't want that. I don't want his fortune. I don't want anybody's fortune. How Kum has been asking me to marry him. I have been playing a little hard to get, but nobody can call me a cocktease. I know that I want to marry him but I want him to be sure too, so I am keeping him dangling for a bit. And there's another thing."

There was a hiss and a short break, then Vanita started again.

"I'm funny about money. I can get as much as I want from father but I don't want it that way. I want to get it on my own. I don't want father's money because he hates How Kum. Hates him because he looks so Chinese. Sometimes I worry if he is planning to pay someone to hurt him. I go mad at the thought of anyone wanting to hurt my darling. I want to protect him with my body, keep it snugly around him, so no one can reach him and do him harm."

I remembered Vanita's body lying on mine. I wanted to scream with grief. On that terrible night of the full moon, there were three murders. There should have been four but Vanita was lying on me, and I was spared simply because the murderer couldn't reach me. I forced myself to go on listening.

"I won't take father's money. I have a way of making some myself. Loong introduced me to the scheme. We get information for Loong and Symons when we entertain these guys. These fat cats don't actually pay us money but fix it so we get new issues of stock, bank loans, tips on the market and even the horses which are going to win at Bukit Timah.

"I will stop as soon as I have enough for the little house near East Coast Park. The one How Kum and I want, so we can come to the park when we tire of our beds. I can't tell him about this now. I don't think he will understand and I fear he will be terribly hurt. Whatever I do, I don't want to hurt my darling. Maybe when we are very old I will tell him, and he will know how much I really love him."

This was followed by more endearments of the soppy schoolgirl kind. It ended with a promise to record all her feelings in greater detail so we would have more to listen to when we grew old. When the voice stopped, there was an emptiness in the room which was unbearable. I wanted Vanita. Wanted her badly, ragingly. As I rewound the tape, I felt her in the room with me. I looked round and saw her on the far side of the bed. Her eyes were full of tears. She knew that only the touch and smell of her body could ease my pain. I put my head down on my pillow and wept noisily. An hour passed and I felt better. I was beginning to understand Vanita and, in time, would not be pained by what she had done. She had done it for me. I should be looking for a moonrise. I showered. I had an appointment with D'Cruz and Oscar.

Killiney Road slopes gently upward from state-of-the-art Orchard Road towards River Valley Road where the houses have a dishevelled, old-fashioned look. I got off the MRT at Somerset, and walked up this narrow street which connects the present with what remains of the past. There were still a few old buildings along Killiney Road, dilapidated shop-houses, ancient coffee shops, a bungalow built at the turn of the century with a walled garden surrounding it.

A large board with red letters directed me to the Mitre Hotel. I followed the arrow which led to a tiny lane. At the end of the lane was a spacious pre-war house. This was surrounded by an enormous garden, the most out-standing feature of which was a row of traveller's palms. I found Oscar and D'Cruz in the front room of the house. A faded sign on the wall assured me that this was the

SALOON BAR. With Oscar and D'Cruz was an elderly man in a wheelchair. Both his legs had been amputated at the knee. Wooden pegs were attached to what remained of his lower limbs. They were too short to serve any purpose except to emphasise the fact that he was a double amputee.

"You haven't met Uncle Choo, have you?" Oscar said, "though you, of course, know all about him." I nodded and extended a hand. "My . . ." Oscar fumbled, "my step-son, How Kum."

"Everyone who has heard of football has heard of Uncle Choo."

Choo looked at me suspiciously. "You think so, yah. You really think so?" I nodded. But this didn't stop him from adding, "Sometimes I think the great days were for nobody."

Ozzie intervened. "Before we get the great man to regale us with the highlights of his career, let us get him to tell us about the murder he claims to know something about."

Suddenly all the lights went out. Power failures in Singapore are rare things and most places are not equipped to deal with them. The Mitre, however, perhaps because it had memories of a time when such things were common, was. Within minutes, a waiter supplied us with candles, assuring us as he did. "Don't worry. Black-outs in the Orchard Road area don't last for more than fifteen or twenty minutes."

Choo, unperturbed by the interruption, took up the conversation and said, "I keep telling you, policeman, that I won't say anything, till you swear on whatever Gods you believe in that you won't poke around and cause trouble."

"I'm a policeman, as you say. Then how can I not investigate if I have evidence of a crime?"

"Ozzie," said Oscar, pleading, "all Uncle asks is for an assurance. He says that, though a crime was committed, the criminal has been adequately punished. He wants your assurance that you won't go upsetting innocent people with unnecessary investigations." He nodded in the direction of the bar, and a young man came over with a tray of drinks. "Uncle has a witness who can tell you something you've been trying to find out these past fifteen years."

"If someone knows anything about how my Tessie died, he should have come forward fifteen years ago. If he didn't do so, then the shit-eating bastard must be charged with being an accessory after the fact. That kind of turd could also be an accessory before the fact and, if so, is guilty of abetting a criminal by concealing an intended crime. Who knows," he said darkly, "he may even have been an accomplice."

"You look here, mata-mata," said Choo, using the bazaar Malay term for policeman in an effort to bring D'Cruz down to earth, "if you want to be so smart, you go solve your own murder." He laughed, and, as he did, his stumps waggled disconcertingly. "After all, you've had fifteen years to work things out." He touched the sides of his wheelchair as though about to make a move. The inspector stood up to stop him.

I had an idea. "Why not let Uncle Choo begin telling his story," I suggested. "If at any point it looks like he is in danger of having been party to concealing a crime, I will warn him. He can then decide whether or not he wants to continue."

I was surprised when the coach turned to me. "You, young fella, have you heard of the twins, Linga and Loga?"

I must have been about ten when the Indian twins

Linga and Loga had first burst on the Singapore football scene. "L and L", they were dubbed by the newspapers, who nevertheless went on to explain what their names meant. The *linga* was the symbol of Siva the Hindu god of destruction. He was also the God of Creation and *linga* was the Sanskrit word for phallus. Loga was a contraction of ullagam, the world. Not the universe but the normal, everyday place in which we found ourselves. Perhaps the newspapers had wished their game upon the lads, for the twins, identical in every other way, played vastly different brands of football.

Both were inside forwards. Linga destroyed defenders, sending them scarpering hither and thither, and Loga, capitalising on the confusion, set about, in a practical workaday manner, creating goals. Linga was considered to be the genius; temperamental, inconsistent and yet capable of unbelievable brilliance. He turned games round in a matter of minutes but his performance was so variable that there was, from time to time, speculation as to whether or not he was on the take.

His personal life in many ways reflected his game. There were bouts of drinking, and he had been up for driving under the influence. He was involved in innumerable fights and an equal number of love affairs, one of which ended in a paternity suit. His brother, on the other hand, led a life of such rectitude that no one knew very much about him. It was said that Loga spent so much time looking after Linga that he had no time for a life of his own.

I looked at Choo. "Of course I remember Loga and Linga."

D'Cruz leaned forward in his seat. "They lived quite near us in Katong. Then, I understand, they moved to upper Bukit Timah. I never got to know them myself, though the whole neighbourhood talked about the boys, especially about the wild one, Linga." He smiled. "I was too busy those days getting bruises on my butt from senior officers kicking me around to get interested in neighbourhood heroes."

"Do you remember how Linga died?" the legless man asked.

D'Cruz frowned. "I can't say I do." He shrugged. "For lots of reasons, my memory for that whole period is as buggered as a fairy's bum."

I couldn't understand the inspector's lapse of memory. I was thirteen at the time, but Linga's death was something so spectacular that no one in Singapore could have avoided knowing about it.

Oscar explained. "I think, Ozzie, you were too involved with Tessie's death to think of anything else."

"You don't know about Linga's death, policeman, but Uncle can throw light on the matter."

No sooner had he said this than the lights came on again. Choo applauded loudly, as though he had been responsible for the timing of the re-establishment of the power supply. Uncle Choo waited till another round of drinks had been served before he took up his story again.

"At the time when Linga died, Uncle was head coach of the Singapore Football team and there was nothing about football or footballers that didn't reach this." He pointed at his ear. Choo said he had been worried because Linga had been playing badly for several months. The boy was also drinking heavily and the selectors were thinking of dropping him from the side. There was a further matter that worried the coach. The young man had suddenly severed relations with his many girlfriends and become celibate.

"No good," he said. "I tell boys that if they are used to girls, they must not stop. 'No good,' I say to Linga. 'Must not stop going with girls or you get too tense for football.' "

Choo's advice had, apparently, little effect on his star player. The coach communicated his worries to Loga. Linga's twin was himself disturbed by his brother's conduct. Apparently, Linga had decided that he would keep off women till he found the one woman who was meant for him. The twins were strict Hindus and their widowed mother was unfashionably traditional. That being the case, she would expect to choose her son's wife. Linga didn't go with this and was, much to his mother's distress, looking for a bride himself. The conflict between mother and son made the drinking worse and Linga was clearly into drugs as well.

A narrow-gauge railway links Singapore with Malaysia. The line runs northwards up Bukit Timah. Mostly the railway lies in a deep ravine. In places, however, it surfaces and one of these places was just behind the twins' home. The night-mail bound for Kuala Lumpur leaves the station near the harbour at ten. It makes no stops till it reaches Johor Baru on the mainland of Malaysia. A drunken and heavily drugged Linga was lying on the track at the back of his home. The train amputated his legs as it made its way north. Though he had not died immediately, there was nothing to show that he had attempted to move or to save himself after he had been hit. It was difficult to believe that he was not awakened by the injury. There wasn't enough alcohol or opium in his blood to make him that anaesthetised. Most people believed that Linga had committed suicide and, for reasons of his own, wanted to feel the pain of dying.

"His legs," Choo shouted, "cut off. Legs that could have taken him to Wembley or the World Cup." He waved his stumps in disbelief.

Ozzie, who had listened to the tale in silence, said, "What has the suicide of this football no-good got to do with my Tessie?"

"You promise no problem and I bring somebody who will tell you."

"Why are you prepared to introduce this man to me now after keeping quiet all these years?" The inspector seemed genuinely puzzled.

"Because Oscar good to Uncle. When," he swept his palm over his stumps, "I lose legs, Oscar get best doctors to try to save maybe one. Oscar pay all medical bills. Oscar pay only because Uncle once-upon-a-time a good football coach. Now Oscar says he wants to know about murders, all murders, old and new. Uncle only knows about old things but Uncle will talk if no police trouble."

"You will get this person who knows something about my sister's murder here if I promise I won't involve him in a police investigation?"

The coach nodded. "Loga waiting nearby on telephone. I call, he come."

D'Cruz threw up his hands. "OK," he said. "OK."

Choo signalled the barman who brought him a cordless phone and wheeled him out of earshot as he made contact with Loga.

Ten minutes later, a man came walking up the narrow lane that led to the hotel. It was dark, and all I could make out as he walked towards us was that he was tall, taller than I remembered. As he drew closer, I saw that he had remained trim, the way he had been fifteen years ago. He moved with that economy of movement that all good athletes possess. This was so pronounced in Loga's case that his walk was almost a shuffle. Oscar waved to the barman as he sat down but Loga shook his head. There was a sadness about the man that touched us all.

It was several minutes before D'Cruz asked "So this is the man I've waited fifteen years to meet?"

Loga said nothing.

Oscar shot the inspector a warning glance. Ozzie took the hint and looked to Choo to direct proceedings.

"You talk, Loga," said the man in the wheelchair. "You tell things like you tell me."

"They know how Linga died?" Loga's voice was almost a whisper. He leaned towards us when he spoke, as though afraid that we might not catch what he said.

"We know the background," D'Cruz assured him. The inspector's manner was uncharacteristically gentle and he seemed strangely diffident. "You tell us what Tessie has to do with all this."

"Do I tell him everything, Uncle?" Loga asked, putting a hand on the man's wooden stump. His coach nodded and the footballer began to speak.

"We are identical twins, yes, but my brother Linga is the opposite of me. He always does things as he likes, when he likes." His practice of referring to his dead twin in the present tense was unsettling but did not distract us from the story he told. "Even in football we are different. He moves quickly, thinks fast. I am the tortoise, slow and steady."

"Like the yin-yang drawings, opposites forming a perfect circle together. . ." Oscar began then regretted his interruption and reached for his drink.

Loga didn't appear to notice. "Like I say, he always moves fast, in football and in other things, but we think like one. Towards the end, Linga moves faster and faster. Things are not like usual. Even Loga cannot understand what is going on in Linga's head. Linga says that he doesn't want many women now, just one, one special woman. This is strange, for you know what Linga used to say about women, Uncle?"

Choo said, "Too well, I know what he said about women. He said, 'if milk is free, why buy a cow'."

"Now he stops trying for every girl. He says he is

searching for the one special girl. I know that he will not
be satisfied with one. Linga has very powerful sexual
urges. Sometimes I know his desire is uncontrollable. I
know, because sometimes it is as if his need enters my
body. When he doesn't get what he wants, he becomes
violent. I fear this, for Loga's heart feels the frustration
and anger that burns in Linga.

"But mother is happy. She says that Linga's time to
settle down has come. She will find him a good Indian
girl, a virgin.

"Linga is happy, at first. Then he starts drinking. I tell
myself not to worry. He is often like this. Now he starts
the drugs. At first, he is just fooling, trying to frighten
me. I am close to my brother. I know what goes on in his
head. He is thinking that if he gets bad, really bad, we
will all be happy when he stops for whatever reason. All
the time, mother is trying to arrange a marriage for him.

"One day, Linga comes home and tells mother to stop
looking. He has found the girl. Is she Hindu like we are,
mother asks, is she a virgin? Linga laughs. She is not a
Hindu. She is a Christian, but she is a virgin. That he
can guarantee. And she will stay a virgin till they are
married in church.

" 'Church,' mother shouts, 'what church? We are
Hindus.' But the girl he loves is a Catholic, Linga says.

"He must marry her, he says. There is no woman that
loves him as much as this girl. I know that he desires
her. I am his twin. I feel what he feels. It is like one part
of me is doing the same thing that Linga does, one part of
me that I feel but cannot control. He wants her and can't
control his desire. I know that he may break down, that
his love can turn to violence. He says he can wait till the
girl tells her family and they are married. But that is not
true for the beast inside him I feel. I feel it is just like I
used to feel the ball as Linga hit it into the goal. Some-

times, I cannot tell if the burning inside is in me or in my brother." He stopped talking and looked around the table. "Maybe it doesn't matter. Maybe we are one person, we feel joy together and pain together. We should have died together."

I noticed that something was happening to Ozzie. Even when Loga shifted slightly in his seat, the inspector's eyes followed him. He seemed on the verge of wanting to say something. It was Choo, however, who spoke.

"When you play, Uncle can see it is like one person playing inside two bodies, the combination is so perfect."

Loga looked at him but did not smile or in any way acknowledge what the older man had said. His soft voice had lost all emphasis. It had become mechanical, like the movements of a sleepwalker.

"I don't see Linga for days. Mother is worried and asks me to go and look for him. I don't know what to do. I feel the tension building inside my body. I must do something about it or I will burst. Then late one night, I wake up. I feel as though two people are fighting inside me, I feel pain, then I feel the joy of release. My body is at peace. The tension that fought inside me is gone."

D'Cruz again seemed about to ask a question, then stopped himself, and Loga continued.

"The next morning, Linga comes home. Our mother is happy. We are all happy. Then I read in the papers about this young girl, this Theresa D'Cruz. She is murdered but, before that, the papers say, she is raped. My brother is calm, but I am boiling inside. I know that I am feeling what he should be feeling. I am feeling this because of something he has done."

Ozzie was leaning so far forward in his chair he was barely sitting on it. He asked, "What made you connect your brother with this murder?"

Loga did not turn or otherwise acknowledge the inspector's question. He just continued his recital. "I know that something happened that night, and the girl was like the one Linga talked about. She is a Catholic, she is a virgin. I know she is not raped. She is, maybe, pushed to the ground, but she is not raped. I don't think I can rape a woman, and what I cannot do Linga really cannot do."

"But there was medical evidence. . ." D'Cruz began.

Loga ignored the interruption. "A young girl loses her virginity. There is blood but this doesn't mean that she did not consent to the act. There is pain too, but this doesn't bother her too much. Then there is fear. Her family are strict Catholics. If it is known what she has done, there will be shame. If she gets pregnant, this will be worse. And if this man does not marry her, there will be dishonour for the whole family.

"The girl begins to accuse her lover of being only after one thing. She is wild with fear. She uses language that surprises him. Words that an innocent girl shouldn't know. He tries to calm her. Tells her that this little act makes no difference to what there is between them. She will not be calmed. She begins to strike him. She begins to scream. He covers her mouth but this doesn't stop the screaming. He puts his hands on her throat and presses gently but the noise continues. It is shrill, screeching, so loud the whole town can hear it. He squeezes harder and the screaming stops. She is not fighting him any more. Her body is soft. She has fallen asleep. He calls but she will not wake up. He kisses her but there is no response. He shakes her shoulders, slaps her face but nothing happens. He feels her throat where his hands were. The pulse is no longer there. He tries to give her the kiss of life, but maybe he doesn't know how, and she does not wake."

For the first time, Loga seemed to admit to an audience. "What can poor Linga do? He didn't mean to kill the girl. He only wanted to make love to her and now he has a

dead body on his hands. He realises that people will say
that this is murder, that this is rape. He knows how
people look on a sex criminal. Nothing he can say now is
going to help him. He has his widowed mother to think
of. She will die if she has a rapist for a son.

"So Linga does the only thing he can do. He leaves the
body naked. He takes her panties and ties them tightly
round her neck. Let the police look for a sex criminal. No
one knows of their connection. It was a secret. No one
will think of Linga as a rapist. Why should he rape?
There are so many women in town that he can have. But
Linga never found peace. His head is full of noises, his
heart thumps with anguish. Even drink and drugs do not
stop this. He thinks of the trains. They fly past every
night. If he lies on the track, the train will pass over him
like a wave of peace.

"He knows he will not have the courage to kill himself
so he begins to drink from early in the morning. He will
chew some opium later. He watches the clock. He knows
the night-mail passes at half-past ten. At a quarter past,
he is lying on the track. He feels the rails shuddering,
like Tessie shuddering under him as he is about to enter
her. He pushes harder and harder. He hears Tessie
scream and her voice is the whistle of the train." Loga's
body went slack and his voice died away.

We were all silent. D'Cruz broke the silence. His voice
was much too loud but it was less disturbing than the
question he asked. "Why did you have to kill her, Loga?"

Choo said, voice indignant, "Loga didn't kill the girl,
policeman. Linga kill her."

"Oh, no. This one here is the murderer."

I was puzzled. "What makes you say that, Ozzie?"

"The newspapers called her Theresa. Only someone
who knew her very well would call her Tessie." I looked
sceptical. "It's true, in traditional Indian families even

spouses address each other formally. And for one who was not actually present, he knows too many damn details."

"Linga and Loga are the same. Two parts of completeness. One kills, one dies, one plans the goal, the other kicks the ball."

Oscar asked, "I don't quite understand, my good man. Are you admitting to killing the inspector's sister?"

"The girl dies. She is not murdered but I am responsible for her death."

Oscar continued, "Why have you agreed to tell us all this?"

"While my mother lived, I could not bring shame on her. Last month she died, so I am free to rid myself of a burden I have carried these past fifteen years."

"Well, Ozzie," said Oscar. "What we have heard leaves me quite speechless. Is the case closed? Can fifteen-year-old cases be reopened?"

D'Cruz looked at Loga. "What do you want to do with yourself?"

"The woman I loved is dead. My mother and my brother are dead. It only remains for me to join them."

"How?" asked D'Cruz. "Are you going to lie under a train too?"

The tall man smiled for the first time. "There are high-rise buildings now and there is always the sea. I can't fly and I can't swim."

"Choose the sea," D'Cruz advised. "They say it's not frightening. Just like going to sleep, they say."

EIGHTEEN

"But why do we have to go to the Sundrams' place now?"

"Walk along and I'll tell you."

We were walking down Killiney Road.

As soon as his story was done, Loga left as quietly as he had come.

Ozzie sat silently for several minutes, then suggested he and I visit the Sundrams. Then, sensing our disappointment at his reaction on meeting his sister's killer, said, "What did you expect me to do? Strangle the man with my bare hands, grab a knife from the bar and cut his balls off. . . ."

"I can't say we expected the reaction we did get," said Oscar.

"I guess when I heard the full story, I realised I didn't quite want revenge as much as I thought."

"Didn't you want to punish the man?" I asked.

"I don't know. Maybe he's been punished enough, maybe he'll be punished where he's going, maybe he's done nothing that calls for punishment." Then Ozzie did something I didn't think him capable of: he sighed. "I sure as hell saw the whole thing arse-end up. Hearing it the way he told it made it sound more an accident than anything else. So I guess Tessie can now sleep in peace. Big Ozzie has found her killer, though he's more of a lover than a murderer.

"I've had some fresh thoughts about the present crimes, so, while Oscar and Legless sit drinking here, How Kum and I will go for a little walk." He gave me no chance to protest and dragged me out of the Mitre.

As soon as we were outside he said, "While I got Tessie's murder all ballsed up, I think I'm near solving your girl-friend's killing."

"You don't agree with me about Mohan."

"No. I think I know who and why but not how." He put a hand on my shoulder before continuing. "I think the old man's our murderer and he did it because of you."

"But Sundram accepted me."

"Only after the girl was safely dead. Hearing Loga talk about his mother reminded me of how deep prejud-ices go."

"But the old man doted on Vanita."

"I know people do the darndest things for love. I know of one upright Christian mum who cut off her baby boy's balls to prevent him from sinning, forgetting how she had got him in the first place. As for your Vanita, she seemed hell-bent on bringing shame to the family one way or another. The last straw would have been her choosing to marry a Chink." I felt him smile. "Because, however much you may not like it, that's what you look like."

"Even if Sundram is guilty of his daughter's murder, you can't see him going on a rampage and killing four other people? And he can't possibly be strong enough to drive a knife through a man's chest."

"True. But what the rich cannot do, they can get others to do for them."

"Come on, Ozzie. You talked like this when you wanted me to suspect Oscar. You can take out a contract on one life but you can't ask a hired killer to go round a park knocking people off willy-nilly. And, are you suggesting that Sundram got several people killed just to throw the police off the scent?"

"Of that I'm not sure. Maybe he was on a moral kick.

Got so ashamed of his daughter's behaviour that he felt he would be doing the world a favour ridding it of people who did their fucking outside the marital bed."

I remembered the look of pain on the old man's face when his son had taunted him and said that his own, Mohan's, nocturnal wanderings, unlike Vanita's, would not lead to any loss of semen. I remained silent.

D'Cruz said, "I'm not sure of many things. What I am sure of is that we will find the answers to many of our questions in that house in Cairnhill Circle."

The house was in total darkness when we arrived. I rang the bell but nothing happened. Then I remembered that Leela had gone to India and there would be no one in if Mohan and the old man were out.

"Ring the bell again," Ozzie instructed.

I did. Nothing happened.

Ozzie turned the knob and to our surprise the door was open. "Let's take a look. People in Singapore never leave their doors unlocked. Something about this place stinks like a bucket latrine."

The sitting-room was pitch-dark. I realised that I was afraid. Not of physical harm but of something else. Usually, I regard darkness as an envelope of comfort. Now I had no doubt that it could also be a hiding place for evil. I was aware of being surrounded by a spirit of malevolence. So strong was this feeling that my feet became glued to the ground. Ahead of me I could just see the inspector moving forward. I forced myself to follow him. D'Cruz walked with a crouch, his arms held in front of him. Suddenly I felt that I needed light in much the way that a drowning man needs air, and reached for the switches on the wall. The inspector slapped my hand down before I touched them.

He pulled out a pen torch, shielded it with his palm before turning it on, and we moved forward. In its glow

I could just make out objects in the room. Everything was as I remembered. I released the breath I had been holding and inhaled deeply. There was the smell of incense in the air. It was clear that Sundram had been praying. We went into the kitchen and then into the two downstairs rooms. Nothing seemed to be amiss. When we reached the bottom of the stairs we heard the noises.

They were difficult to describe. They sounded a little like someone falling down a flight of stairs but ever so slowly, with the thumps never getting closer. The intervals between thumps were long but absolutely regular. It was impossible to imagine what was making them, though an inner voice told me it was something horribly unpleasant.

The sounds got louder as we climbed the stairs and seemed to be coming from Sundram's room. The door was ajar. Inside the room, the smell of incense was overpowering. The room itself was vast and dark: in infinite emptiness. I sensed rather than saw a shadow suspended from the ceiling and swirling round and round. It was the source of the thumping.

We had been moving in darkness and I assumed this had some purpose. I was surprised when Ozzie snapped, "You know where the switches are, turn on some fucking lights."

I reached behind me and did.

It was an old-fashioned house and its roof was supported by heavy wooden beams which are concealed by an asbestos ceiling. Anything heavy would have to be supported from these beams, and not the ceiling. Overhead fans have heavy motors. Special U-shaped clasps are screwed into the wooden beams to support them.

Sundram was hanging from one of these clasps by a length of plastic cord. His neck sagged on to his chest and a trickle of spittle stained the front of his shirt. The fan was on low and, as it turned, one of the blades caught his limp form and slammed it against a nearby cupboard. His face was peaceful and his eyes were closed. He looked like an old man who had fallen asleep at a party. A chair lay on the floor beside a table on which it had recently stood. It was clear the old man had hanged himself. Ozzie jumped forward and grabbed Sundram's legs so his neck was no longer stretched. "Get me a knife," he ordered.

I went in search of one, turning on all the lights in the house as I did. I had some difficulty finding one. As I searched I wondered what it was that had triggered Sundram's suicide. I no longer had any doubts of his guilt. Perhaps the inspector had somehow indicated that he was on to him. I felt sorry for the old chap. He seemed such a poor thing hanging from the ceiling with his head on his chest. It didn't seem fair that a man of his age should choose to die in pitch darkness and alone. It had somehow ceased to matter that this same old man had murdered his own daughter to stop her marrying someone who looked a little different from him, and had followed this up with the murder of four strangers. I finally found the knives stashed away in a bottom drawer behind a pile of linen.

"You are taller than me," D'Cruz whispered as though afraid of waking the dead man. "Get on the table and cut him down."

I did as instructed and the inspector gently lowered the body to the ground.

"Do you know anything about CPR?" he asked. I looked blank and he said in a louder voice, "Cardiopulmonary resuscitation, you idiot."

I shook my head. "OK. Open his mouth and breathe into it when I tell you to."

I was revolted at the prospect but refusal was imposs-ible. Ozzie positioned himself astride the dead man's belly and, using the heels of his hands, began rhythmically compressing the centre of Sundram's chest. When he had done this four times, he asked me to breathe deeply into his mouth. We went on like this for about ten minutes. The inspector was bathed in sweat and my face was smeared with the old man's saliva.

"I've never seen this work but, unless we go through the motions, some smartarse lawyer is just about going to accuse us of murdering the old bugger ourselves."

"Murdering?"

"Yes. We are dealing with murder, How Kum." We looked at each other. "You really amaze me, big fella. From gut feeling alone you work out who the killer is, and when the proof of your case jumps up and bites you, you don't see it."

"Explain slowly, Ozzie."

He sat down beside the body and began talking. "This is the kind of fake suicide that only an amateur would try to pull. When a man hangs, he dies either because his neck snaps or because he chokes to death. You will agree there are no signs of strangulation on this old man's face. So death has to be due to a broken neck.

"If you see a gallows, you will realise that it takes quite a drop to pull apart the ligaments that hold the neck bones together. The drop in this case is nowhere near enough to do that. What is more, once the ligaments have been torn, the neck has to be acutely flexed and the head forced forwards so that a small bone, called the odontoid, pierces the medulla oblongata and produces instant death. The hangman's knot is what forces the head forward. You will notice that there is no such knot behind this man's head."

"If he didn't strangle and didn't break his neck, how, in heaven's name, did he die?"

"I didn't say he didn't break his neck. I am saying that

it could not have been broken by such a small drop. I am saying that Sundram died in much the same way as the lesbian, Stella Stevens, did. The killer broke the old man's neck with a full-nelson then strung up the victim to make it look like suicide.

"I am really quite insulted that the bastard thought that I would fall for this kind of rubbish. But murderers, when they reach this stage, become so arrogant that they go on and believe exactly what they want to believe."

I brooded for a bit. "There's one thing that you haven't explained."

"What?"

"How did Mohan manage to string his father up with the fan going full blast?"

Ozzie's grin began slowly then widened. "This is where we, the dumb mata-mata, the old-fashioned flat-footed police, come into our own."

He paused for effect and smiled. "There was a blackout of the whole Orchard Road area when we were at the Mitre. Mohan kills his father just before or during the blackout. When he comes to stringing him up, the fan wasn't moving. He must have got out of the place before the lights came on, for it would be impossible for even the most arrogant of murderers to think that the stupidest of policemen would believe that a suicide would, or could, string himself up from a hook from which a ceiling-fan was turning. Then our murderer must have turned off all the light switches to heighten the effect of black despair leading to suicide. One of the touches of excessive high drama that seem to be typical of this case. Very Tamil. But he forgot the fan switch." He paused and scratched his head. "Oh, yes, he left the door open to impress upon me that someone was alive and looking after the house when he left it."

"What happens now, Ozzie?"

"I'll call the station and get them to send round the forensic boys and the technicians. Then we'll sit tight-arsed and wait."

"Don't you put out APBs, alert all your services and the public that a dangerous criminal is on the loose?"

"You've been watching too much television, How Kum." He laughed. "OK. As a concession I'll ask our people to look out for him at the airport and railway station. But the main action will be parking our bums here till he shows up."

"What makes you so sure that he will show up?"

"He's an arrogant bastard. A person who thinks he could fool even a child with that fake suicide must be really so arrogant that he's out of touch with the real world. Our Mohan's going to breeze in here pretending nothing's happened."

"You're sure he will turn up?"

"As sure as I am that I will move my bowels tomorrow." But D'Cruz was wrong. Mohan did not show up. I waited till three, then said that I was tired and was going home.

It was easy enough to get a taxi. As I boarded it, the inspector said. "Contact me immediately if Mohan gets in touch."

I promised I would, but I didn't. When Vanita's murderer did contact me, I discovered that I wanted him all to myself.

NINETEEN

"You forgot about your Uncle Oscar last night," Ma said as she poured me my coffee the next morning.

"Oh God, Ma. So many things happened." I sipped a little coffee before asking, "How did he get back?"

"A nice gentleman called Loga brought him home. Mr Loga said that he had been with all of you at the Mitre Hotel. He said that Oscar introduced him to Inspector D'Cruz, who he had been waiting to meet for several years. He had not thanked Oscar for this and, when he returned to do so, found both your uncle and coach Choo so drunk that he took it upon himself to ferry them home in a taxi. He asked me to thank Oscar for him as he would not be able to do so himself."

I was glad Ozzie hadn't arrested the man.

Later that day I went in to the office. I had a vague notion that Mohan would try to contact me. When he did, I would rather that Ma and Oscar were not around. I sat at my desk fiddling with a pile of flight crew reports. I had been there for over three hours and was about to leave when the phone rang.

It was Mohan. "I am glad there was something to take you to the office today. You wouldn't have been able to talk as freely if you had been at home." His voice was jolly. "After some self-searching, I concluded that the arrangements of last night would not deceive the inspector. That being the case, it was possible that your home phone would be tapped. I think I have surmised correctly and I am now what is called 'a fugitive from justice'." He chuckled merrily.

It was difficult to know what to say to a man who had killed his father and sister and still had room in his heart for laughter.

"Where are you, Mohan?"

"I would rather not divulge my whereabouts for that would only tempt you to betray me to the police."

I wanted a chat with the man before the inspector and his crew got hold of him. "I need to talk to you, Mohan. I need to know exactly what has been going on." I needed to reassemble myself, to find all the missing pieces, and this man could help me do so.

"I tried to give you some indication of the way in which my thinking was leading me. I did this on the morning we cast Vani's ashes and on the night we had dinner together. You are the one person who would understand my actions and I too need to speak with you. We must meet and talk soon but you must assure me that, whatever you promised them, you will not betray me to the police."

"How do you know you can trust me?"

"Your word is all the assurance I am asking for, How Kum."

"All right. I promise I won't let on to the inspector or his men." I paused before asking, "Where shall we meet?"

He considered the question for a while. "At the park where you and Vani used to spend your nights."

"At East Coast Park?" I couldn't hide my surprise at his choice of rendezvous.

"Yes. It's as good place as any. And I like open spaces. I can make sure you are alone before I show myself." He laughed. This time, a little unpleasantly. "Just in case you change your mind about telling the police. I don't mean to give offence but a man in my position must take all the precautions he can."

"The park's a big place. Where exactly in it shall we meet?"

"At the spot where you and my sister used to . . . get together."

"Give me a time, Mohan."

"It's about four now. Let's say we meet around six-thirty when it will be cool but still light enough for me to see just how many people I'm meeting."

I spent the next two hours trying to find things to do in the office, debating all the while whether or not I should get in touch with D'Cruz. If I did, the inspector was sure to want to set a trap for Mohan. I didn't really care what happened to the man. What I wanted was a chance to talk to him. I feared that, even if D'Cruz allowed me to speak to Mohan, he would be impatient and the trap would be sprung before I had all my questions answered. Despite this, I felt some kind of obligation to the policeman and I reached for the phone several times. Each time I stopped myself before I dialled the inspector's number.

Mohan had, all along, been straight with me and, though the man was a killer many times over, I felt, perhaps perversely, that I should be likewise with him.

Moreover, if he thought that I was being dishonest, it was unlikely that he would give me the answers to the questions I had. The more I thought about it, the more convinced I became that I had no real interest in seeing Mohan punished. All I really wanted was to find out how it came about that the only woman I had ever loved got herself murdered. I knew that Vanita's ghost would not rest till I had done this. I put down the phone which had, somehow, found itself in my hand. I would go it alone.

The park was beginning to empty when I got there.

Teenagers carrying floats, surf boards and other beach things were walking towards the exits. There was an air of disappointment about the place and, despite their sunburns and the music from their transistors, the weekend had not been as good as it could have been to all the young people who were making their way home.

I remembered how Vanita and I were on Sundays: happy, drained of desire but loving each other and the world. It was with difficulty that I put these thoughts out of my mind. I wished to be as unsentimental as possible when I talked to Mohan. I found our old place easily enough. I expected some sense of attachment to the spot where I had known so much joy, and was disappointed on discovering none. It was just another patch of grass sheltered by a few bushes and not popular with the youngsters because it was situated away from the sea. With Vanita gone, nothing remained.

There were few people around. Some late joggers were doing stretching exercises, an elderly couple walked slowly towards the sea, a vagrant who was leaning idly against a tree shot a glance in my direction.

There was no sign of Mohan.

I walked slowly towards the beach. It was beginning to get dark and the tide was in. It was the first night of the lunar month and no moon accompanied the rising waters. Nevertheless, the flecks of foam on the waves would acquire a ghostly phosphorescence as darkness fell. The water was high, but a Sunday evening tide tempted no swimmers. At the far end of the beach, I watched a lone fisherman cast his line. There was nothing optimistic about his action.

I turned and walked back to where I was to wait for Mohan. It was well after six-thirty. Perhaps he thought it was wiser not to come. I couldn't keep my disappointment from affecting my stride as I began slowly making my way towards the exit. The vagrant who was propping up a tree turned slowly to look more directly at me. Then he raised a hand and began walking in my direction. It wasn't until I got really close that I recognised him.

Mohan was dressed in a loincloth and had tattered chapals on his feet. The ends of the open slippers were turned up from use. His cotton shirt was threadbare in parts and sweat-stained. What struck me most, however, was the change that had come over his complexion. The Mohan I remembered had a skin that was so clean and smooth that it appeared oiled. It fitted his plump, effeminate body well. The man who stood before me had a complexion that was roughened by dirt and the weather like that of an aboriginal tribesman. On his face and arms were a variety of encrustations made up of a mixture of mud and body secretions. Three days' growth of beard dappled his chin and, as he got closer, I realised that he smelled strongly.

"Namaste Iyer," he said, placing palm to palm in traditional Indian greeting. "You are surprised to find me in this condition." I nodded and he explained, "Things have not been going well with me, old friend, and I have had to make changes in my appearance for the sake of my survival."

"You must come home with me, Mohan. Have a bath and a meal."

He looked as though he had not eaten for several days.

"Later. Maybe, later, How Kum. Now let us sit here awhile and let me tell you my story."

We sat on a patch of grass on which his sister and I once made love.

"Yes, Mohan. I must know everything."

"I will start at the beginning. First, I will tell you things you want to know about my sister. With Leela in India and father dead, no one else can." He crossed his legs, then over-crossed them till he was sitting in the lotus position.

"Vani was a sweet child, a warm child, always wanting to show how affectionate she was. Even in her early teens, she began showing her liking for men, first in innocent harmless ways, then in a manner that was less innocent. I took it upon myself to watch over her, to see that no one took advantage of her. I don't know if that is quite the correct term though. For Vani took what she could from people, not the other way round. I don't know who her first man was but whoever it was was guilty of statutory rape, for at fourteen Vani was no longer a virgin. I loved my little sister, and I was disturbed by the kind of things she had to do to make her life complete. I spoke to her, told her it would kill father if he found out. I begged her to stop. She was the apple of my father's eye and, every time she stayed out the night, he aged ten years."

"This has been going on from the time she was fourteen? For the past six years?" No wonder she was surprised at my being a virgin at twenty-seven.

He nodded. "Till she met you. Then I think it almost stopped."

"Almost?"

"I think she did go out once or twice, to meet men, but I think these were purely business transactions."

I remembered Vanita's own admission on the tape and didn't push the line of questioning further. "Your father didn't ask you to stop her . . . doing what she was doing?"

"He said nothing till you turned up."

"But I was serious about your sister. I wanted to marry her."

"That is exactly what bothered him. Our father was sure that whatever Vani did, he could, for a large dowry, get some middle-aged Tamil to marry her. When he found that she was serious about a Chinese called How Kum, he exploded. He shouted at his beloved girl and told her he was going to cut her out of the will in which she was left everything. Vanita said that she wasn't interested in his wealth. If she needed money, she knew how to make it herself."

"He was kind to me . . ."

"Only when he found out from me, after Vani died, that you were not a Chinese at all but technically an Indian, a Malayalee. Then he saved face by thinking of you as the son-in-law that should have been. Our father, you see, was a bigot and a hypocrite. An expert in self deception. A true Hindu does not deceive himself. He has no need to. He sees things as they are and lives for the moment, for the present is the only reality that life offers."

It was dark now. The lights on ships swinging at anchor became twinkling stars. To the west was the glow of the city. Mohan was a shadow beside me.

"And killing, is that all right too?"

I heard the grass rustle as he moved. "We know only one thing in this world, dharma. One moves from moment to moment, acting as one's perception of dharma demands, and it is this kind of action that makes each moment of the present complete."

"So you feel that your sister's murder was justified?"

"You must try to understand, How Kum. I loved Vani as an elder brother should. But it is proper that the boy in the family inherits. It is contrary to dharma that a girl should come into the family's wealth. I know that after meeting you, Vani wanted the money. She pretended that she didn't want anything of the fortune father had amassed, but she began to think about houses and children. She began to do so only after she became serious about you, How Kum.

"I talked to her. I begged her. I told her that the wealth

was mine by right of birth. I explained that she was threatening the ways of a thousand years. I said that I had important things that I needed to do with the money. If I was a wealthy man, even if I looked like becoming a wealthy man, I and our group could change the face of Hinduism. We could make it more like the religion it once was and should be today."

"But your sister didn't want the money. You could have persuaded her, given her more time to think about things."

"As I said, she sometimes pretended that she didn't want father's money. Said that she had good reasons for rejecting it. She also claimed that she had ways of earning money herself. But what she sold would not make her what she wanted quickly enough, and Vani was an impatient girl."

I asked, "Did you feel no pity for this sister that you loved, no remorse, no shame . . .?"

"Pity, shame, guilt, fear . . . , even love, are all terms we use to conceal how attached we are to our personalities. Unless we can get detached from ourselves, we are doomed never to understand why stars move or what initiated the explosion that started the universe. Only the moment exists, the act. The victim is not superior to the murderer."

At last I was able to find out something that had been bothering me for a long time. "Why did you not kill me as well?"

"If you had woken up, I would have had to. But as it was, you were asleep under Vani's body. And I had ensured that both of you slept well. I knew that Vani spiked the semolina with Benedictine. I added several helpings of valium to the Benedictine at home so you could both sleep well. And die without pain." He chuckled.

I thought again of how I saw Vanita and me, of the sky-goddess Nut lying over the body of her lover, the earth-god Geb, remembering as I did Vanita's voice on the tape. "I will protect you with my body, keep it snugly around you, so no one can harm you." I thought again of my shame at not waking to defend my love the way that Lip Bin and Stella had, and felt absolved of guilt. It was valium not indolence that had caused me to sleep.

I would have stayed with my thoughts but Mohan was speaking, leaving me no time for reminiscing. "It was clearly not the moment to kill you."

"And you, of course, live from moment to moment?"

"If you will only admit it, you will see that we all do."

"Killing the other people, the young couple and the two girls, that was all right too?"

"Once one sees the path, one closes one's eyes and follows it, unfettered by sentimental rubbish like the value of life. Life and death are both part of the Universal consciousness and one, therefore, cannot be superior or inferior to the other." He sighed contentedly. "If I was convicted of murder, my sister's death would have been for nothing. It was necessary therefore that the four died to throw suspicion off me."

"But they had nothing to do with your problems. They were innocent, Mohan."

"We are all innocent, just as we are all guilty. We find the road laid out for us and walk along it. The only immorality is to deny the existence of the road."

A plane, its headlights streaking the sky, came in from the west and began its descent. The sea was silent and the hum of jet engines was the only sound in the air.

"Why was it necessary to kill your father?" I added as an afterthought. "You did kill him, didn't you?"

Mohan was silent. He seemed to be listening to the noise of the aircraft. He waited till this had quite faded away before speaking.

"Our father announced, after the so-called raising of Vani's spirit, that, though she was gone, the money would be dedicated to her through the power of Kishore. He was going to put the family fortune in the hands of that crook. I had no choice but to kill him. I had to do this before father had a chance to change the will in Kishore's favour. The existing will left all to Vani but, with her and father dead, I, as the only surviving member of the family, would inherit. Father was talking about going to a lawyer with Kishore on Monday. You know what that would have meant?"

It seemed as good a time as any, and I told Mohan about Vanita's tape diary, and how Kishore had known so much about her personal life, and what her voice was like.

"Thank you, How Kum. I see the whole plan now. What he did not reveal at the first session would be revealed at later seances. And once faith was established, he would simply invent things as he needed to." I was quite sure that Mohan was smiling to himself. "Perhaps I should have killed Kishore instead of father but then the old man would have only replaced him with some other crook, and the whole thing would start all over again." He was silent. "No, How Kum, I did things in the way that my own dharma demanded and I was not wrong to act as I did."

Somewhere in the darkness, a ship began to move, initiating the flurry of waves that crashed on to the beach.

"What made you get in touch with me, Mohan?"

"You were the only one who might understand. I have expounded my views to you and you seemed sympathetic. Even though you were so carnally attracted to my sister, I do not think you are sitting in judgement over me. It is good for a man like you to know the truth."

"But that is not the only reason for your seeing me?"

He breathed deeply before speaking. "No. There is a more practical reason. My father suspected that I had a hand in Vani's death. Last night, he had a long session with Kishore. After it was over, he called me to his room and accused me to my face. He knew I was not at home on the night I had to kill the two girls and, all in all, guessed how I was throwing the police off the scent."

"Did he threaten to expose you to them?"

"Not directly. I knew, however, that I would never be safe as long as father knew and Kishore was around. Last night, father went on and on about killing one's flesh and blood. I tried to explain that it was he, in fact, who was responsible for his beloved daughter's death. If he had not disinherited me, if he had been true to custom, none of this would have happened. But his mind was too poisoned by Kishore's nonsense to understand true causality. Karma eludes those who are tied to the imperatives of this world. As father went on and on about Vani's death, he worked himself into a kind of rage I have never seen him in. Suddenly, a man who had never struck me, even when I was a child, began to scream and slap. I knew than that he was out of his mind and would not be guided by reason. We struggled and, as we did, the lights went out. I was behind him. Both my palms were round his neck. I pushed down a little, not strongly the way I had to do with the girl. I was only trying to frighten him, to show him how strong I was through yoga. Then I heard a crack and he went limp in my hands.

"There was nothing I could do. No one would believe that, though it was necessary for our father to die, I had not intended to kill him then." A cool breeze began blowing in from the sea and I heard Mohan sigh against it.

"Why are you telling me all this? I only wanted to know about Vanita."

"There is something I need to know from you."

"What is it?"

"When I knew that father was dead, I decided to make it look like he hanged himself. I had some difficulty in stringing him from the fan as I had to do this in complete darkness. But I have doubts that the deception was successful." He paused before asking, "The police inspector in charge of this case is in touch with you. Has he said anything about father's death?"

The man was guilty not only of killing Vanita but five other people. All I had to say was that D'Cruz was convinced that Sundram had committed suicide. Mohan would have returned home and justice would have been done.

I said, "No, Mohan. The inspector knows that your father's neck was broken before he was strung up."

"So he must suspect me."

"He knows that you are the murderer. I thought so myself after we had dinner together."

"What shall I do?"

"There is nothing else you can do except give yourself up. Singapore is small and well policed. There is nowhere you can hide."

Far away, I could hear the murmur of traffic and, if I listened very carefully, make out the sound of human voices. Both of us seemed to be listening in case they had something important to say to us.

Finally Mohan spoke. "That would not be in keeping with dharma. I have acted in all propriety and now I will have to live out the consequences of my actions. I will go into hiding or find ways of leaving the country. I cannot let them hang me."

He stood up, lifted his hand in a farewell salute, and began moving off. I did not try to stop him.

TWENTY

I didn't sleep all night and at seven the next morning called Symons. It was Monday and he was in early. I told him that I wanted two weeks off work.

"It's OK with me when you take your vacation, HK. You can fill in the necessary forms later," he said. Then asked, "Are you ill?"

"Not really," I replied. "Just a little depressed."

Depression was something I resorted to when things got difficult. Right now, I felt that I had reason enough to remain locked up in my room. The love of my life was dead. I had let her murderer go free and by doing so had betrayed a policeman who trusted me. D'Cruz phoned in the afternoon. I told Ma to say that I was too ill to answer the phone. He called round in the evening but Ma stopped him at the door and informed him that I wasn't seeing visitors. On Tuesday morning, I felt that I could no longer avoid the inspector and spoke to him on the phone.

"You OK, How Kum?" he asked. He sounded anxious.

"As well as I can be," I replied.

"Finding the body was too much for you, uh?"

"Ozzie, I think I've seen more murders than my system can ever hope to deal with."

"I'm sorry to disturb you," he said. He paused for a while before adding, "I called to say that we have not been able to contact Mohan. I think he realises the game is up and has done a bunk." Another pause. "Has he or any of his friends tried to get in touch?"

I took a while to say no, then added, "I don't think he would contact me and I don't know any of Mohan's friends."

"Well, you did meet a few when he took you to dinner and I thought he opened up a bit then."

"I don't know about opening up. . ."

"Enough for you to realise that he was the killer. Something a trained policeman failed to see."

"That was just gut feeling. . ."

"I teach the young lads on the force that murder is always about money, and I myself screw it up by thinking of racial prejudice as a motive."

I didn't say anything and he went on. "It's never sex or race, you know. It's always cash, big dong. Cash is what makes people kill."

The inspector's intuition had served him well and I wondered how far it had taken him. "Why did he kill his father then?"

"Even if the old man changed the will in his favour, it could be several years before Mohan could get his hands on the dough, assuming father was allowed to die a natural death. Years in which he could give the money to somebody else, somebody like the crook Kishore. That would be reason to snuff the old bugger as fast as possible. Vanita would have inherited but she dies. Father dies soon after so the fortune winds up with Mohan who, in his eyes, should have inherited in the first place."

I was impressed by the way the inspector had put the pieces together but wanted to test him more. "After going to the trouble of committing six murders, why is he not around to collect?"

"This bothers me, How Kum. This really bothers me." He hesitated. "Murderers are usually arrogant. You have

to be to take a life. They believe that all of us are arseholes who they can easily fool. What is more, we are
dispensable and must not be allowed to get in the way of
their grand design. From what you have told me about
this bloke, I would say that he certainly holds all of us
in contempt. Why then has he not believed that the fake
suicide has not fooled the dumb police inspector?"

I seemed to have lost control of my tongue and I heard
myself say, "Perhaps someone warned him."

"No one could have, big dong, because, apart from the
forensic boys, you are the only one who knows that it was
not suicide but murder." He waited for me to speak and,
when I didn't, said, "Therefore, I asked if Mohan had
been in contact. If he had been, you could have said
something that indicated I was on to him."

"Like what?"

"Like forgetting to offer condolences at his father's suicide or even just asking in a too anxious voice why he
had not been in touch."

I was relieved that Ozzie didn't suspect me of treachery.
I feared that if I continued talking, I would give myself
away. "No. He's not tried to contact me."

"Call me at 2227534 as soon as he does. It's a twenty-
four-hour keep-in-touch number. Someone there will
always know exactly where I am."

"I will," I said and hung up quickly.

He phoned several times over the next six days. I didn't
trust myself to take his calls and got Ma to say that I
was asleep or too low to speak to him. I told her to assure
him that Mohan had not been in touch.

After a few days I did, in fact, begin to feel depressed.
I lay in bed all day and stared at the wall or the ceiling.
Vanita's ghost was no longer around and I knew she was
truly gone forever.

Perhaps, I should have been relieved. Now I could

relegate her to the kingdom of the dead and begin building memories of my beloved which I could keep for the
rest of my life; begin to fashion pictures that would make
the world mine again. I wanted very much to do so.
But the ceiling-fan refused to become a merry-go-round
that provided the coolness of movement, the voices I
heard through thin walls were meaningless mumbles
which told me no secrets. I listened to the tape again and
again but my heart remained empty.

I heard Oscar talking to Ma. "It's the realisation that
the girl is really dead, Lili. That has only just hit the
poor boy. Let him alone and he will in slow stages become
himself again. Brandy helps but I don't think he will
use it."

Poor Oscar, I thought, with the part of me that
remained outside my depression. I wondered if he would
still think kindly of me if he knew that I had allowed a
mass murderer go free, and even assisted him by giving
him information which only the police had? And Ma.
What would she feel about her son, her little boy, who
allowed the man who murdered the woman he loved to
go free? She would, I suspect, have thought me as callous
as my father. Perhaps I was like him, with the added
advantage of being literally a bastard.

There was no one I could turn to for I had isolated
myself from the world. A week went by, and the next.
Then on the Sunday, exactly four weeks after Vanita's
death, Jafri phoned. "Ozzie says you've gone into purdah,"
he said, laughing. His voice had its familiar, confident
ring.

"I'm not a Muslim, I'm not a woman, and I don't wear
a veil. I'm just tired and sad, Jafri."

"Too tired and sad to have tea with an old friend."

Suddenly, I was afraid. Perhaps Zainah had told him

what had happened on their living-room couch and Jafri
wanted to have things out with me. "Zainah as well?"

"No. Zainah is having a little stomach trouble. Vomiting
for the slightest thing."

"Oh."

"No need to 'Oh'." He laughed. "She's just slightly
pregnant."

It wasn't just relief that I felt. It was a wild happiness.
The world was coming right again. I could feel my
depression lifting. Vanita had loved me, had taught me
to love, died for it and had done things that only she
could do for love. What were justice and truth beside
this?

I agreed to meet him a little after six that evening at
a restaurant on Mount Faber.

Mount Faber is a low hill which, because of Singapore's
flatness, is looked upon as a mountain. It stands at the
southern tip of the island and overlooks the harbour.
From where we sat, I could see the ships, which came
right up against the land and seemed close enough to
touch. Looking to the east, towards East Coast Park, I
could see dozens more, waiting their turn to dock, and,
behind these, were the Indonesian islands. Further away
was the horizon, the edge of the world from which ships
came and over which they went.

In the west, the sun was beginning to settle, and it was
cool enough for tea to be enjoyable.

"Ozzie is worried about you. Zainah too when she's
not busy vomiting. Ozzie fears you may go into a deep,
irreversible depression."

"I have been depressed, Jafri."

"About Vanita not being around?"

"That and other things."

"I'm a Muslim, How Kum. If nothing else, my religion
teaches me to accept death and incorporate it into the

fabric of life. I know it's no use telling you that you will find someone else . . . and I hope very soon." He looked sideways at me.

"Zainah says you are badly in need of a woman's company." He allowed himself a cryptic smile. "But you say that something else bothers you."

"I've done a terrible thing, Jafri."

"Do you think getting involved with Quincy was something of which I am excessively proud?"

"What I've done is more terrible. Much, much more terrible."

"Tell a battle-scarred lawyer like me. Whatever it is, I'm sure I've seen worse."

"I let Vanita's murderer go free."

"I am already relieved. I wondered what I would say if you told me that you were the murderer." He smiled to let his worry lines relax before asking, "Was the murderer responsible for all the deaths?"

"I'm afraid so."

"I think you should start at the beginning and tell me everything."

I did, with a growing sense of relief. Jafri didn't interrupt to ask questions or obtain details. He merely tilted his head or raised an eyebrow. When I had finished he said, "Well, that makes you a criminal too."

"Only morally."

"I don't know too much about morals. I do know about legality and you are a criminal in the eyes of the law. You are an accessory after the fact."

"Oh God."

He patted my shoulder. "There's no need to think of it as a terrible crime. From what you have told me, Ozzie D'Cruz is, after a fashion, in the same boat as you, though in his case it was fifteen years after the event, whereas in yours," he looked at the date on his watch, "it is exactly four weeks. Nevertheless, the crimes are legally very similar."

"What can I do about it?"

"You could tell D'Cruz." My face fell and he said, "I could tell him, though I suspect that he already knows. Our Oswald is nobody's fool. You can be sure he'll get the murdering swine in the end."

I wasn't sure. Mohan could disappear into the vagrant life and, however well policed Singapore was, it would be difficult to find him. He could also slip out of the island. The inspector had talked about watching the airport and the railway station, but he seemed to have forgotten one thing. Singapore is a diamond, forty-two kilometres wide and twenty-three long. Its area isn't large but it has a coastline of a hundred and forty kilometres, too long to be guarded day and night.

From where I sat, I could see the islands of Indonesia. They were places in which a man could disappear completely and they were only an hour away by motor-launch.

I knew Mohan would get away. "I let a murderer escape, Jafri, a mass murderer. I don't even know why."

"I don't either, but I can guess." I looked puzzled and he continued, "When it comes to a murder trial, we all think of the judge saying, 'you shall be taken to a place of execution and there hanged by the neck till you are dead'. It is a more premeditated, a more cold-blooded killing than any murder that one can imagine."

I let what he said sink in before I remarked. "D'Cruz says that all murders are committed for money. I don't think Mohan was money-minded, do you? He only wanted the money to advance his cause."

Jafri shook his head. "I can't allow you that, How Kum. We all want money to advance our cause, dharma or whatever. It usually transpires that our causes are ourselves. And, whatever your cause, it does not justify killing someone to advance it."

In the west, the sun was slowly falling into the sea. The red ball stained the clouds blue and purple, colouring their edges with a mean yellow tinge. They looked like bruises growing old. As always at sunset, a light breeze begins to blow in from the sea. Breezes carry memories. I thought of my last evening with Vanita and how I woke to find her dead beside me. I remembered what had awakened me.

"You know, Jafri, Mohan maintained that things were only in the present. The evening Vanita died, I was telling her how difficult it was to tell moonrise from sunset just by looking."

"Vanita was a sensible girl and I hope she told you how stupid you are. We identify things not by what they look like but by where they are taking us. There is a world of difference between sunset and moonrise. Sunset leads into the darkness, moonrise into the glorious light of love."

Vanita hadn't taught me that. All she had taught me was that there was love, that it was real. I realised that it could be, again. On the edge of the world, a full moon was beginning to rise.